Johnny, my friend

Peter Pohl

Johnny,
my friend

Translated from the Swedish by
LAURIE THOMPSON

TURTON & CHAMBERS

© Peter Pohl 1985
English translation © Laurie Thompson 1991
First published 1985 in Sweden
under the title *Janne, min vän*
by AWE/Gebers, Stockholm

First published 1991
in England and Australia
by Turton & Chambers Ltd
Station Road, Woodchester
Stroud, Glos GL5 5EQ, England
and 10 Armagh Street
Victoria Park, W. Australia 6100

Typesetting by Avonset, Bath
Printed in England by
Short Run Press, Exeter

Catalogue-in-Publication Data
available from the British Library

ISBN 1 872148 70 0

Johnny, my friend

CHRIS'S AREA OF STOCKHOLM

Key

1 Chris's place
2 South Side Grammar School
3 Medis – the Forsgrenska swimming pool
4 The Kvarngatan steps
5 Bjurholmsplan workshop – Johnny's place
6 The bridge over Södergatan
7 The girls' school (known as the Birdcage)
8 John Pelle's Sports Shop
9 EPA department store
10 South Station
11 The Crown café
12 Beginning of Skanstull Bridge – the way to the south suburbs, South Cemetery, and Flaten
13 Towards Hornstull and Liljeholmsplan

Now then, lads, do you recognize this? says the cop, lifting out Johnny's bicycle.

We flash the whites of our eyes at each other, but nobody feels the urge to volunteer. The cop's mate is still sitting there in the cop car, wittering into his mike. The corner of Swedenborgsgatan and Maria Prästgårdsgata. About ten young lads. I'll get back to you.

The cop's eyes settle on Sten, but Sten's having problems with his shoe laces, enormous problems; Sten's shoelaces are taking up all his attention. There's something wrong with Pecka's belt as well, snarled up all of a sudden, you know how it is. Harold's giving him a hand – good old Harold, being nice to his kid brother.

With little movements, so little they'd be unobtrusive if they weren't so obvious, the lads regroup. Turning this way. Turning that way. Turning the other way. All their little movements leave a stage, and in the middle of the stage is me, with the cop as an audience of one. Everybody else is looking somewhere different. The whole audience wants to know if I – just me – recognize Johnny's bicycle.

Do I recognize Johnny's bicycle!

You got to know Johnny by his bicycle. Half past six on the last day of August in my case, 18.32, 31.08.1954. Summer holidays had just petered out, and school – a new school for me, South Side Grammar – had got going 13.30 that afternoon. An easy-going sort of start with a roll call and a parade in the hall, featuring ancient, mouldy gents with walking sticks and ear trumpets and gravelly coughs and other aches and pains, each with one and a half feet in the grave. Our future teachers.

At half past six you came riding down one street or another, down St Paulsgatan in my case, and it's my case I'm talking about now. Aimed a few quick shots over my shoulder, ducked down to avoid the volleys fired back from the doorways, turned off suddenly just to confuse the car. Which had to ram on its brakes: we young hopefuls, the guardians of Sweden's future, have to survive today's traffic in order to grow up and contribute to tomorrow's.

At 18.32 I was caught up by somebody who came from nowhere, just was there. Shouldered me off, blocked me dead.

What precision! I managed that much in the way of admiration, but I was scared stiff. Though when I saw the rider's fizzog, that grin, my heart fell back into place. It was a girl. Sheer luck it must have been, getting it that good.

Where had I seen her before?

I knew I'd seen her before. Somewhere, somewhere quite different.

Pippi Longstocking, I reckoned. Pippi Longstocking, that was it, suddenly come to life, by magic. Her hair wasn't in plaits, but the colour was right. The grin white and dazzling among a few million freckles, when she made contact on 31.08.54, at 18.32.

Hiya! My name's Johnny. What's yours?

The girl was called Johnny, then, well, yes, OK, and Chris, that was me, and quick as a flash I slammed a gag on the idea that I thought her name was Pippi.

Said nothing, just sized up the way he reared his bicycle while he nattered away. I kept on saying nothing, cos if life has taught me one thing it's that if a boy looks like a girl, he doesn't want to go on about what he looks like. And if he can control a bicycle like Johnny evidently could, there's other things to talk about.

This amazing bicycle was largely constructed by

Johnny himself, it would slowly transpire. What transpired right now were a number of things I noted with due reverence, such as an assembly of grips and levers on the handlebars that would keep an octopus working overtime. And there was a mileometer and a speedometer and a rev counter and goodness knows what else. Shiny bundles of wires heading for front and back wheels. He'd better demonstrate it all one of these days. My own bicycle was hiding in shame behind my back without gears or even handbrakes.

There's no mistaking Johnny's bicycle!

But the cop's not happy with a yes, course I've seen that before. He wants more. So, you've seen it before then. When did you see it last? Whose is it?

He's called Johnny.

Just Johnny?

Johnny! I'm on the spot now. And a cop in earshot, as if sent for. But still! Shall I tell him? Never talk to cops! was your advice. I know what you want, what you wanted. Hasn't that changed now?

The bus, number fifty-two, roars off at just the right moment, giving me breathing space, and when I've finished breathing I know what I want to say and what I don't.

We won't start at the end, Johnny. We'll take it from the beginning. So I'll soft-pedal a bit till I know what the cop's after. OK, Johnny?

I count up all the grips and levers and I see Johnny's fingers playing with them. See his marvellous white grin when he's just blocked somebody. There's half a tooth missing from that grin.

The cop's interested in that front tooth, in that gap. Asking right or left. Notes down right, but changes it to left when I add, From where I am.

Part of the tooth, or all of it?

Half the tooth is missing, as stated above: the lower half to be more precise, in the upper right front molar. From where I am.

11

How did he lose that then?

Johnny's own version is, I bit it off when some old bloke made a grab at my dick.

But I don't try that fairy tale on the cop. Partly cos I never believed it myself, partly cos it would give a false picture of Johnny to kick off by describing him like that.

That was the only time Johnny ever mentioned the word dick, in fact. The gang weren't so particular, and Sten especially had a big store of dick and fanny jokes. The first time Sten tried it on with Johnny, with his, Have you heard the one about the prick?, Johnny thought doublequick and came out with, Five times at least, but let's hear it again if you really have to.

That wasn't the way newcomers generally answered. The tone of voice, and that look! He made it sound as if Sten was a right twit, and Sten dropped the topic.

That was more or less what always happened. Everybody who tried on a smutty joke soon looked foolish and felt like a little kid. Johnny would do his doublequick thinking then give it two out of ten.

It was him who started us off giving marks. Marks out of ten.

When Bert introduced Harold as The biggest of us all!, Johnny eyed him up and down and gave seven out of ten, no more. I've seen bigger.

Harold was chuffed, cos he's bigger than everything and feels really embarrassed about it, but here was this little brat who could get lost in one of Harold's socks, and he didn't seem to think that was anything special.

This giving marks business caught on in the gang, and before long marks were showering down on anybody who did anything special. High marks usually, but sometimes low ones as a real put-down. Dicks and fannies never got more than two out of ten, and before long it was the marks you laughed at, not the joke. Two out of ten was a thumbs-down all right, and that soon put a sock on all the dick talk.

Pecka wanted to get a few marks and turned up all smiles

and showed Johnny his spanking new pocket knife that he'd got as a birthday present. This was early on; Pecka's a bit childish, and Johnny was the leading light, the one to show everything to.

Pecka opened up big first blade, then medium-sized second blade and third little blade and big screwdriver and little screwdriver – Wow! said Johnny – and tin opener and corkscrew and scissors – I don't believe this! said Johnny – and file and awl and little drill – Is there no end to it! said Johnny – and coarse-toothed saw and fine-toothed saw and pincers – Cor! gasped Johnny – and teaspoon and fork – I can't take any more! – and lacing needle and lacing hook and last of all a tape measure which could be extended to thirty-five centimetres. Johnny had never seen anything like it, matterfact.

Five out of ten, six mebbe? asked Pecka modestly.

Johnny put his arm round him and said you just couldn't include a super fantastic thing like that in the marks business, it wasn't fair to . . . He nodded in the direction of us poor swine who were trying to scrape together a few high scores with our bare hands. And nodded meaningfully at Pecka: That knife. Something you can use all your life long, matterfact. For absolutely everything.

A few days later Pecka got a puncture in his back wheel outside the Birdcage in Timmermansgatan. Johnny produced from his tool bag every kind of spanner and screwdriver you can think of and then a few more besides. When the contents of that tool bag came to light, it was obvious to me at least that Pecka's knife must have been a pretty silly little toy in Johnny's eyes. But there was no mention of that now. Johnny had the inner tube out before you could say It, and homed in on the hole straightaway, no messing, and polished and smoothed down and squeezed out solution and slapped on a patch and stuffed the tube back in again and wrenched the tyre back into place without using any tools at all. Just his bare hands.

13

While he was working, a crowd of skirt from the Birdcage, doing overtime in the choir by the look of it, gathered round to gape. It was his topknot that attracted them: one of them slunk up and asked if the thatch was real, but Johnny just told her to go and play hopscotch.

All the birds started chirping at that. It was a nasty moment.

And then the tyre was sitting pretty and duly pumped up, and Pecka could get rolling again. Next time make sure it happens somewhere else, ordered Johnny, glowering in dark green at the bird choir who were having the time of their lives.

Johnny was a wizard at fixing bikes, you see.

It wasn't me who said that, though, cos I have a blank spot, a speech impediment you might say. I can't call a bicycle anything but a bicycle.

Most people call a bicycle a bike, everybody knows that. Wheels was the latest flavour of the month – but I just couldn't say either word, I don't know why. The lads all knew about my weakness, obviously, but it wasn't so awful that we couldn't joke about it.

Cut out the swearing, Chris! said Bert, poker-faced, when I tried to slip a bike in. It's called a bicycle, Christopher. Bicycle.

And when he said bicycle, it sounded just as peculiar as my bike. We could laugh at that no end, when we were in the mood.

Apart from that, I have no problems when it comes to language. Words are my favourite meal. The harangues in RULES AND REGULATIONS CONCERNING ORDER AND GOOD BEHAVIOUR IN STATE GRAMMAR SCHOOLS sent shivers of delight down my spine when I read them on the notice board after roll call.

Paragraph 51 (b): All pupils will attend classes promptly at the preordained time, neatly and respectably dressed, and will bring with them the prescribed text-books, observe the rules governing orderly behaviour, and partake in lessons with due attention. Similarly, all

14

pupils will attend morning assembly at the specified time, and will observe silence and pay pious attention throughout.

That's what I call clear, straightforward language! Prescribed textbooks! Preordained time! I made up my mind there and then to learn the complete regulations off by heart, and then pester everybody within earshot with appropriate quotations whenever the opportunity arose.

And I like numbers! Essential and inessential statistical information, useless figures and numerical data. Exact numbers are magic. I'll see you at 17.04 is a more important meeting than See you at five past five.

Figures are knowledge. When I left South Side Grammar after roll call, I knew my art master was called Brattström. First name Bengt. No one would have been impressed by that bit of knowledge, even though it was correct and exact, and even though I'd never met the man. If I'd said he had 33 hours teaching per week during the autumn term, i.e. 33 h/w, w. 35-50, 1954 (and of course, fewer hours some weeks when there were holidays, such as the half-term holiday in October, week 41, when Thursday, Friday and Saturday were free) my knowledge would have seemed enormous, even though all my 997 fellow-pupils at South Side Grammar could have produced exactly the same facts by reading the timetable in the classroom. If I'd added that his monthly salary was at least 1,329 and at most 1,560 kronor (depending on how long he'd been in service, a fact not revealed by the papers for the first day of term) and that he got his wages during holidays as well as in term-time, all the data would have been fantastically impressive. Even if all the figures are public knowledge, people never fail to be impressed if you know them.

Then combining all the data like this seems to give the figures extra significance. So much so that some people get all upset when anybody comes along and churns out a series of figures available to all and sundry. But it's the new implications that fascinate me, that lure me into reading tables and spreadsheets with more enthusiasm than my mates read the comics. With all due respect to Kilroy, he doesn't carry hidden messages.

My dad, who finds my hobby rather amusing, brings home statistics on all kinds of familiar and unfamiliar phenomena. I study them and try to read between the lines.

The lads used to tease me, in a good-natured way, reckoned I sounded like an encyclopaedia once I got going. But if they wanted to know the world shot-put record – 18.54 metres, O'Brien last spring – or the Swedish record for the men's 1,500 metres free style – 19.07.2, Arne Borg, 1927 – or the winning line on the football pools last week, all they had to do was ask. Sport is more statistics than athletics for me.

Catalogue Chris goes to South Side Grammar now; what's he doing there, do you think? . . . Learning the stock exchange index, of course.

But bike and all its cousins stuck in my throat.

Johnny, naturally, used all the words with gay abandon – bicycle, bike, wheels, pedals, velocipede . . . and a whole load of other nicknames he'd made up for his own.

We all caught on to how handy he was, and so I asked him to help me tighten my back wheel clicker – it kept on going slack, and then it didn't make much of a clatter. He fixed it all right, but aren't you a bit grown-up for one of these?

Asked *he*!

How old was he then, you might well ask. Judging by his height and his weight, he looked about ten or so, when he first joined the gang that is; but going by the way he talked, well, he could be older than I was, or so I reckoned sometimes.

Do you have to have a clicker licence plus special permission once you're over eleven then?

OK, OK, I could have whatever I wanted on my own set of wheels. Johnny had all his little pennants come to that, and they didn't exactly add up to a certificate of maturity.

He tightened the clicker so that it clattered more cheerfully than ever, and it obeyed every little pull I made on the cord. But it seemed to be making mock of me now, and telling me no matter how hard I pulled, it was only a bicycle after all, and I'd never make as much noise as Olle the Wolf, never mind match him for speed: 160. One hundred and sixty! Kilometres per hour!

It was on account of Olle the Wolf Nygren we all had clickers. Now we had Johnny in our gang, though, showing us a bicycle was a bicycle. Anybody who's seen Johnny ride a bicycle doesn't need to dream about Olle the Wolf Nygren any more. A week later, I dismantled the whole clicker business and threw it away. Johnny never referred to it.

Everybody's bicycle was in tiptop shape all that autumn, whether they asked for help or not. The slightest squeaking or scraping or rattling and Johnny would be on to the culprit, tightening screws, adjusting nuts, oiling, testing, muttering magic formulae . . . Noise is for cars and amateurs, see. A bike should w h i z z down the street like a breath of air, matterfact.

Oh, so it wasn't just my age Johnny was getting at when he turned his nose up at my clicker. Eventually, all the bicycles in our gang whizzed down the street like a breath of air. Nobody could hear us coming. The noisiest thing was the flapping of Johnny's pennants. Nobody else put pennants on his bicycle, though; that would have been too obviously copy-cat.

> First he came and blocked my bike,
> Then he fixed it as I like.

That was Pecka's snazzy poem thought up when, at zero cost, Johnny took away his old battered saddle and tattered old saddle-bag, and replaced them with a Vienna-roll saddle like the one Johnny had on his own bicycle.

Yes, this blocking business, to get back to the subject. Johnny blocked all of us, one after another. That's how we all got to know him. On our bicycles. Me first, at 18.32, 31.08.54.

Could be trouble, you might think, when Johnny Nobody turns up and starts playing the smart guy. Even Bert was won over. Despite what he said about Harold, *he* was actually the biggest of us. Not according to size, mind you. Our leading man, perhaps we should say, and our oldest. All of fourteen. Old Bert must have felt a bit put out when he got blocked by a mere kid who looked like Pippi Longstocking. Just for a moment, it looked as if we might see a bunch of fives in action.

That could only have ended with Johnny slumped over the ropes. But Bert always thinks three times before he starts clenching his fist, and in the meantime, Johnny had time to show him that freckled fizzog, and to flash the big white grin of his with the little gap in the top right. From where I am.

You never felt that he was trying to put anybody down. It was just his way of saying hello, that blocking. His speciality. And his entry ticket into the gang, of course. With anybody else but Bert as boss it might have been a ticket to the back door out and home again thank you very much. But Bert gave in with a laugh, and we took Johnny for what he was: on the small side, red-haired, and with a girlish face – *but*: a wizard on a bicycle.

Girlish face? Well, once you got used to it, it wasn't all that girlish. The right description for a façade like that is freckly. Nobody had ever seen so many freckles in such a small space.

It wasn't exactly something he liked to go on about. And after a bit, nobody else even mentioned freckles, not even in passing. Cos Johnny had hard fists. Not that he was all that strong: most of us were probably stronger than he was. But he was so bloody rough when he was angry, and he always did get angry if you went on about his freckles or his red hair. Thump you one quick as a flash, right where it hurt: he knew all about weak points

18

on your body, and he knew a trick or two. Then dodged away before you could give him one back.

How about this:

On Wednesdays, if nothing else cropped up, which meant more or less every other week, we all used to go off to Medis, the indoor pool, for a swim. Gather outside and wait for each other and admire the gravestone in the meantime – the big hoarding in the middle of Medborgarplatsen Square where they used to post up the latest figures for deaths, severe injuries and slight injuries in road accidents so far that year. The score to date was 674 – 2,479 – 7,615. The number of deaths last year had been 872, and they claimed that record would be broken if this year's trend continued.

Before you say tut-tut, though, you should bear in mind that *in fact* the accident rate was more or less constant, despite the steady increase. Due to the number of cars on the road practically doubling between 1950 and 1954: on 31 December 1950, there were 252,503 cars registered, and on 31 July, 1954, there were 514,095 . . .

Thank you, Catalogue Chris!

Don't interrupt! Those figures are for the country as a whole, as are the statistics on the gravestone. You should also remember, lads, that sixteen point seven per cent, or virtually one car in every six, is a Volvo – but no way is there a Volvo in every sixth road accident involving private cars. That position is reversed for Volkswagen beetles though: nine point one per cent, or one in every eleven, is a VW, but they're involved in one accident in every seven, note that, One in Seven. Generally the only car involved. They just get blown off the road, unstable, them beetles. And there's a clear connection with the driver's profession. Of the twenty thousand Volvos sold so far this year, four hundred were bought by doctors, for instance, but three hundred and fifty doctors bought a VW, though only ten thousand of them have been registered . . .

Come on, Chris! For C h r i s t ' s   s a k e !

It's true, you just listen: three and a half per cent

doctor-beetles but only two per cent Volvos. Doctors drive like the very devil when they're on call. There are two thousand five hundred new doctors and vets on the roads day after day now.

Great, great, Catalogue Chris! Tell us more!

In the first six months of this year alone, 59,309 private cars have been registered. Just in six months, mind. Thirteen and three quarters per cent increase on the New Year figures.

Can't somebody sit on the prat? Turn the tap off!

So an increase of thirteen, fourteen per cent on that gravestone is absolutely normal.

I'm not really that daft. But me going on like that stopped George from coming out with his, Christ, lads, you should have seen that crash at Slussen! Four brains sloshing about at my feet like pea soup . . . Or a blow by blow account of how some pregnant woman dived off the Katarina Lift and hit the asphalt with such a thump that she split right down the middle and the kid popped out yelling blue murder . . . As soon as George saw the gravestone, he remembered all those fascinating deaths, traffic accidents or whatever, and the only way I could put him off was by reciting statistics as loud as I knew how, going on about makes of car, occupational groups, you name it. If I paused for breath, I could see him starting to open his mouth, and I didn't want to know about his mashed-up women – I didn't care whether what he said was true or if he made it all up, and it's obvious he was making it up come to that – and so I'd keep going full tilt all the time we were waiting.

And there was bags of time while we were waiting for Harold to turn up. He was always last, never mind how late anybody else was. Sometimes we'd taunt Pecka cos his brother was so slow, but it was a waste of time. Back at home, Pecka would say, Come on, let's go now. And Harold would say, Right, I'm coming. I'm just going to . . . And Pecka would go on ahead, and Harold would eventually roll up last, ages after Pecka, who only knew that Harold would be there any minute, he was just going to.

When Harold eventually did turn up, we'd go in. We could be two to a locker or even three if it was That Nice Lady on the turnstile, and so we could manage the cost of the whole menu: a swim, bath, shower and sauna.

The big game was seeing how long we could sit in the sauna with our swimming trunks on before miserable old Harry the Caretaker came in to tell us off. No swimming trunks, how many times do I have to tell you?

He's a poof! was Sten's explanation. Why else should we be in the raw? Go and let him play with your little goldfish, Pecka!

Then Pecka would turn all sour and Harold would get at Sten and Sten would just guffaw and challenge all comers to a contest for the biggest hard on, but nobody wanted to. Instead Bert suggested Sten should go out and see Harry himself, or else take a cold shower.

That's more or less what happened every time, and I think Johnny knew that, cos whenever we tried to get him to come to Medis with us on a Wednesday, he'd hum and haw and find any old excuse just to get out of it. As if it wouldn't have been enough just to say he didn't want to. Haven't time, Wednesday's my busy day, specially evenings, matterfact, mebbe, mebbe not . . . In other words, no.

If he hadn't been so obviously evasive, we might not have given it a second thought; but as it was, some of us got a bit huffy and wanted to know the real reason.

You can't swim, is that it? wondered Bobby.

Johnny could swim as far as you like, matterfact. But if Bobby really wanted to know, it just wasn't any fun, cos anything you can do in a little bath tub like that isn't exactly what you'd call swimming, not real swimming, like in the sea, for instance.

Which put the kibosh on that discussion, needless to say. Nobody who hadn't even been to try Medis was going to tell Bobby whether it was fun or not. And in any case, just how far is as far as you like?

21

As far as you like, matterfact, what else? Right across the sea, till you hit your head on the horizon. As far as Bobby could walk. But then you don't walk, do you. No, of course not, matterfact. And I'm blowed if I'm going swimming in a b-b-bath-tub, cos all you do is s-st-stop and turn round all the time.

Yeah, it's easy enough to say that, but believing, that's something else that is.

All right, he could believe whatever he wanted. But in that c-c-case, it must mean you can't walk. Not more than twenty-five metres at a time.

Of course Bobby could, and what's more, he could prove it right here in the street.

Johnny didn't need Bobby's proof and he didn't need to prove anything either, cos I kn-kn-know what I can do and I couldn't give a toss what you believe, matterfact.

And Bobby couldn't give a toss toss toss about J-J-Johnny, for Christ's sake.

Oh, v-v-very f-f-funny!

Fun-fun-funny for you, eh! Fan-fan-fanny.

The fact that Johnny started stuttering when he got excited was a godsend for Bobby, and he was going to make the most of it. But Bert cleared his throat just behind him, and Bobby knew what that meant and so he decided to cool it a bit and shrugged his shoulders, and just as Johnny was starting to explain that as far as he was concerned he hadn't asked him to bother about anything at all, Bobby said it was all right cos he wasn't the kind of bloke who'd try and force little kids to go swimming.

Yer what? Would he mind repeating that last bit, right away, matterfact, cos I'm not d-d-dead sure I heard you properly, cos you k-k-keep interrupting me all the time.

Just listen to Johnny! Now he's trying to cover up for the fact that he can't swim!

Cover up? There's nothing to c-c-cover up, matter-fact, cept that y-y-you're a bit stupid, matterfact, cos th-th-that's something you can't c-c-cover up.

Stupid was something Johnny was, come to that, George said.

But he wasn't that at all, in fact, Johnny said, cos he had his f-f-freedom to choose whether to go sw-sw-swimming or not to go sw-sw-swimming, and his stammer got worse the angrier he became, but Bobby just jeered at him and kept on questioning whether or not Johnny could swim.

They're still there, and they'll still be at it for another ten years, and then their kids and their grandkids'll take over, and half the audience think Johnny can but doesn't want to and the other half go along with Bobby, but everybody thinks it's time Bobby dropped it, cos somehow or other they feel sorry for Johnny.

That's why Bert put his oar in, when they'd been at it hammer and tongs for quarter of an hour or a couple of years, and he said we couldn't give a toss which way round it was, but if you change your mind, just turn up.

That was smart of him, cos the argument died down and Johnny came out with his first credible bit of information:

Cos the chlorine makes me feel bad.

I couldn't care less, said Bobby. It'll bleach away those funny things you have all over your fizzog.

A thunderbolt caught Bobby right on the snitch. He staggered back, and looked really ridiculous.

Johnny was dancing up and down just out of reach, shouting that if Bobby had anything sensible to say he'd better hurry up and say it. B-b-but stick to the s-s-subject. Chlorine.

Come a bit closer, you little bastard! said Bobby.

Johnny must have done so, cos Bobby got another one on the hooter. And another, and another, till Bert and Sten grabbed hold of Johnny and dragged him away.

Blood was pouring off Bobby, and he still looked really ridiculous.

He kept on looking like that for some time after. You didn't know what colour his nose was cos there were so many to choose from. For weeks to come, we used to point at him, right in the middle of his fizz, and tell him, but only when Johnny wasn't there: You ought to try bleaching your conk, Bobby.

It was a joke Bobby didn't appreciate at all.

The cop noted down this freckles business as well. Can you describe them in more detail: dense, patchy, just dotted about? Even, uneven? Forehead, nose, chin, neck?

Johnny's girlish face hovered there in front of us: freckles dotted evenly all over it, apart from his chin.

Not his chin? Neck? Forehead?

The cop wanted to know exactly.

It wasn't so easy to comment on his forehead. His red quiff blocked the view.

OK, freckly. And red-haired. No doubt he had green eyes as well, then?

The cop could be damn sure of that: Johnny's lights flashed green!

You soon discovered that, cos Johnny wasn't the type to roll down the blinds and check the paving stones when talking to somebody. Green searchlight straight in the face of whoever he was talking to. His eyes blazed when he was in that mood.

Often when you've met somebody else of the green-eyed variety you're not quite sure afterwards: maybe his eyes were really blue, in fact! Or grey? Or . . . ? Johnny's gooseberries left no room for doubt.

There's plenty to say about Johnny's peepers all right. But let's cut! You can't describe him like that: hair, eyes, skin, and colours. Smile, voice, deportment, gestures. That's just wishy-washy, and Johnny was anything but wishy-washy.

The question was, did Johnny have green eyes as well? The answer is Yes. Certainly.

And that stutter?

He only did it when he was excited. Then we knew, those of us who got to know Johnny and his ways and his signals, that there was danger ahead. As long as he was talking normally, he had the situation and himself under control, and you could be with him without any risks at all.

And so, Johnny blocked and bike-repaired and punched his way into the gang, and when he'd made his mark with everybody in it, it was time for the rest of the world to meet him as well.

There was a gorilla in the fifth form called Greenwood or Greenland or something like that. We first-formers tried to keep out of his way, but unfortunately, he had a habit of making his presence felt. Running off with your ball, knocking down the high-jump bar, jumping the queue in refec, farting in your face, and other subtle methods of introduction. He was backed up by his beefy disciples, and by all the old traditions of South Side Grammar. And the Spirit of course. The Spirit of South Side Grammar from the moment you walked in through the main gate. The proles never had a chance against the gang of prison warders known as prefects, whose job it was to make sure the Spirit lived on. Experienced South Side Grammarians, democratically elected by their fellows, supported by the staff – the old fogeys were just pleased they didn't have to dirty their hands by getting involved.

When I brought the gang into the playground at South Side Grammar after school, though, the balance of power was different. You could put up with the sight of Greenwoodland lolling over the railings without trembling when you knew you had the lads with you, and they were only too keen to bounce a few coconuts off the odd gorilla whenever they had the chance. He sniggered at

26

the sight of Johnny. Are you so short of mates you've got to start playing with kiddywinkies!

We all knew by now, of course, that the centimetres Johnny lacked in height he made up for in some other way. The bulging muscles normally required were replaced by coil springs in Johnny. Whenever he triggered them off, he got the thumbs up. Greenwood didn't know anything about that, though. For him, Johnny was just a novelty, a stupid little red-haired novelty.

As soon as he heard the word Kiddywinkie, Johnny went on red alert. He stopped his bicycle dead, balancing motionless, and stared into the distance as he asked why a bloody big baboon like you don't just leave young lads alone, matterfact.

Needless to say, Greenland suggested Johnny ought to run home to Mummy and go to bye-byes.

But Johnny reared up his bicycle on one wheel and said he'd never had any time for fatties who started going on about bye-byes at six o'clock in the afternoon.

Then they went on for a bit about being short in the leg and thick in the head, while the rest of us started picking teams for a game of football. We let Johnny look after himself, on the principle that we were there if needed. Just how they got round to talking about Johnny's bicycle, nobody knew.

Johnny thought that Greengreen, whose baboon-brain was obviously short-circuited by a banana, shouldn't go on about bikes, cos he just didn't know what he was talking about.

But Green knew all there was to know about velocipedes, specially the ones with engines, and he was going to get one of them soon, so there.

He claimed, and proceeded to go through the whole catalogue in boring detail: Apollo (the pick of the Swedish makes, OK?) and Marathon and Monarped, right, Swedish mopeds, though they'll set you back 800 kronor at least. And the Froggie Velo-Solex, only 675, and a set of cog-wheels instead of a chain, like the

27

Swedish ones. Then the Kraut efforts, dirt cheap: Amo for 440, Fuchs 445, ILO 420, Komet 395, Lohmann 360, Victoria 425. All of 'em push-bikes with an engine tagged on. Then there's the Dutch Berini, cheapest at 325, but a pile of crap. I'm going for a Kreibler – now there's a bike for you: chain drive, 975 smackers.

Johnny wagged his head. Could well be. Even his kid sister, who'd just crawled out of her cradle, could recite that little lot. But she couldn't ride a bike, matterfact. Reckoned Johnny.

That might be true for his little sister, but Greenwoodland had ridden his bike down that set of steps over there, without falling off, before Johnny knew how many wheels there were on a velocipede.

Johnny took a look at the steps: sixty-two steps, a hundred and twenty centimetres wide between the iron rails, divided into five sections with twelve or thirteen steps in each, and a stretch of badly laid paving stones two and a half metres long between each section. Straight down by the side of the school yard, from Kvarngatan at the top to Högbergsgatan at the bottom.

Then he disdainfully regarded Greenfrog's waist measurement and announced that he was talking through the back of his neck, cos you *haven't* ridden your wheels down that lot of steps, come off it, cos it's just not on.

At which Greenfrog laughed condescendingly – the little boy couldn't be expected to know any better. Course it's on, he'd done it himself, and if you'll just shove that pathetic little treadmill over here, I'll do it again, just to show you.

Needless to say, Johnny didn't lend his set of wheels to any old fool, cos a jaunt like that would just turn it into scrap iron, matterfact.

Greenfrog shrugged his shoulders, and reckoned talking was easy.

Exactly, said Johnny. Matterfact.

A pity really, said Greenfrog. He could do this little trick and lots of others that Johnny would never manage.

At that, Johnny drew himself up to his full height and said when it came to riding a bike, I could do things you've never even dreamed of.

Greenfrog's next move was obvious.

He pointed to the sixty-two steps and said quite simply, Ride down that little lot then.

Johnny was cornered, you might say, and weighed up his chances of doing what he himself had just said was impossible, not on, while Greenfrog spelt out the conditions:

No putting your foot down, nor nothing else neither, no falling off, no grabbing the rails – just ride straight down, or else it won't count.

What do you mean, count? asked Johnny. Did he think he was going to risk his bike on a hopeless jaunt for nothing at all?

Yes, yes, OK, what did I tell you? Greenwotsit knew all along Johnny wouldn't dare.

Johnny dared all right, but he reckoned he ought to get something for the effort and the risk.

All right, he could have a bottle of pop. If you do the whole lot, sticking to the rules.

At last they seemed to be talking the same language, kind of.

One bottle of pop?

Two then.

Don't be stupid. He'd be bound to puncture his tyres. That wasn't worth a couple of bottles of pop.

Punctures or not, it'd still count even if he got a puncture. But no putting your foot down, no falling down, no grabbing the handrail.

My God, but you do go on! Johnny couldn't give a toss if he counted it or not. He'd do it for a crate of Tizer though.

A whole crate!

Greenfrog groaned, and forced his monkey-brain to do a spot of adding up and multiplication and got it to eighteen kronor seventy-five, with the crate and all that. But as Johnny wasn't going to do it anyway, the stakes

29

didn't make any difference. So, Greenfroggy agreed to pay him a crate of Tizer if he could pull it off. If he didn't Johnny would have to carry his books to and from school every day for three weeks.

What would Greenfrog want books for? Johnny wondered. And he wanted to know if Froggy had eighteen seventy-five on him. He wasn't exactly credit-worthy, so there.

Somewhat reluctantly, Greenwotsit produced a couple of tenners.

Lambert's Grocery in Kvarngatan was the obvious place, just across the road. But buying could wait until another time, when they were open. Froggy wasn't the type to go and buy a crate of Tizer till he really had to. Anyway, the sight of the tenners was good enough for Johnny. In any case, the presence of such reliable witnesses, and so many of them, more or less guaranteed he would get his winnings if the descent was successful.

Johnny pumped up the front tyre, pumped up the back, listened to the echo from the inner tubes, let out a bit of air, pumped in some more, and checked the tyres. Having completed that little ceremony, he handed over the pump to me. Me!

Then he whipped out his spanners and magical fancy screwdrivers, and turned a bit here and screwed a bit there, in every conceivable and inconceivable place, while Greenfrog sat watching him, rolling the notes between his fingers, and asking whether he was thinking of rebuilding the whole vehicle.

But Johnny: Don't remember anything about not being allowed to set up the old wreck, matterfact. And he went on regardless, calmly chatting away to his friend the Bicycle.

No doubt he'd have given the thing a dose of spit and polish if there'd been more time. As it was, he made do with taking off the lights, the dynamo, all the meters and counters, horns, pennants and the tool box. He tightened the screws on everything else as far as they'd go.

30

He gave everybody in the gang something to look after. I got the pump.

Last of all, he took a strap from his tool box, put his tools away and handed the box to Bert. Then he hoisted up his orange-red track-suit trousers, put the strap round his waist to hold them, tightened it, and ended up looking like a wasp, if there is such a thing as an orange-red wasp, tightened his Adidas and tied the laces with tight, multiple bows.

Greenwotsit sighed loudly and asked if it was all right if he came back after lunch the day after tomorrow, if you'll be ready by then. Or mebbe next week?

In the end, Johnny was standing there in Kvarngatan, looking down over the sixty-two steps in five sections, each of them with twelve or thirteen steps, and assessing the length and breadth of each one, and the distance between them.

He spent a long long time contemplating what he saw. Sten, George and Harold had gone down ahead, and were stationed on landings number two and four respectively as well as at the very bottom, their white faces turned up expectantly towards the top.

We all trusted Johnny. When something earth-shattering is about to happen, you always know if it's going to come off or whether it'll be a disaster. We knew this was going to come off.

Johnny made a move.

What he did was turn towards Greenfrog and make sure the tenners hadn't turned into autumn leaves.

No matter how I do, said Johnny, it's got nothing to do with proving that you've done it. Cos you haven't.

Why don't you take a tablet for your verbal diarrhoea? wondered Froggy.

But by that time, Johnny had already shoved his front wheel over the edge, and put both feet on his pedals.

He proceeded down the steps in the first section at a

steady pace, and we followed on behind, shoving Greenfrog in front of us and holding our breath. Nobody cheered or shouted encouragement, nobody even drew breath for fear of disturbing his progress down the steps. The thud of rubber bounce-bouncing from one step to the next was the only sound effect. So tight was every nut that no hint of a rattle betrayed the presence of the bicycle. Not even the chain made a sound.

When he got to the first landing, the bumpy one between the first and second lot of steps about twenty-five decimetres long, we realized what tactics Johnny was using. In that short distance he accelerated so the bicycle wouldn't drop down at an angle when his front wheel crossed over the next step down. That way, his pedals wouldn't catch the edge of the step. Johnny kept his bicycle more or less horizontal till his back wheel got as far as the edge. He must have jammed on his back brake then, cos the bicycle suddenly tipped down forwards and the front wheel thumped against the step. Then there was a hell of a bang as the front tyre exploded. Johnny had got it wrong! We reckoned he'd had it, but he kept on bouncing down, only the bumps sounded harsher now, and there was a nasty scraping noise from the front wheel.

As he careered down the second section, Johnny pulled over to the left, and only then did we realize, those of us who hadn't looked carefully enough beforehand, that the council gravediggers had been at it, and dug a trench straight across the second landing. Johnny would have to try and go round that, so there was no chance of him repeating the trick he'd used on the one before.

When his front wheel hits this second flat section, he brakes a bit so he can turn his front wheel without capsizing, and he heads the bicycle diagonally to the right over what there is left of the landing. His back wheel doesn't like this one little bit, back there on the second lot of steps. It skids out to the left, more and more sideways on, and you don't get the impression it's all under control any longer, and the shredded front tyre isn't gripping properly, bouncing about on the flags, and the bloody landing is so tiny, so tiny around the grave.

Then we all shudder in sheer delight as the back wheel hits flat ground and Johnny actually REARS UP his bicycle and using the pedals and some scientific braking he coaxes it on one wheel round the trench onto the little strip to the right, then in a new direction, rolling, still on one wheel, skidding and sliding in all the muck, but no foot on the ground nor nothing else, no falling, no grabbing the handrail, just a virtuoso performance as he goes on to the top of the third lot of steps.

He lets the front wheel drop down with a terrific thud, and starts his way down.

But there must be something wrong with the brakes, cos the speed's not good. Too fast, far too fast, he's bouncing around all over the place. The loud clang as his front rim bashes down on the third landing screams out that Johnny's lost control of the fancy bits now, and is riding hell for leather.

Just as his shredded front tyre plonks itself down onto the fourth lot of steps, a doddery old lady wanders round the corner at the bottom and braces herself for the climb up to the top. We can all see her, she's a catastrophe, this old girl, the unexpected, the impossible. Harold holds his hand out across her path, but she brushes it aside. Then she looks up.

Life should teach old ladies to be careful. This specimen looks up and sees a whole gang of us: a bunch of lads on their way down, and a Johnny on a bicycle careering down at full speed. You'd have thought she'd have put two and two together. But no, she stands there gawping and drops a whole mountain of carrier bags in the middle of the path which till then had been a hundred and twenty centimetres across, and she's rooted to the spot as well, leaving just thirty centimetres of path, unfortunately divided into two narrow strips of fifteen centimetres each on either side of the mountain.

Harold! Come on! Do something! Fling the old hag out of the way!

33

Maybe things look different to Harold down there. But from where we are, a bit higher up, we're not breathing any more, we've stopped breathing altogether.

There's none of your fancy tripping down the fourth lot of steps and the back wheel just thumps down on to each one without the front wheel having a chance to start pointing downwards, it seems the brakes aren't working at all now for God's sake, he's just bouncing from one to the next and leaning forward, forward, to try and force the front wheel down and he manages to get it on to the ground just after the last step in the fourth section and it rolls or slides or whatever to one side as it thuds down and goes out of shape and skids on the gravel and the back wheel bounces up so that the whole bicycle rears up behind Johnny and he races across this last landing on his peculiar front wheel right up the edge of the fifth set of steps, with him pressing his whole body backwards, backwards, trying to get this rear wheel down again, it seems to have decided it's going flying, but Johnny gets the better of it and the wheel accepts defeat and drops down again, and I note how Johnny gives it an extra push at the last split second and so the other tyre goes off with a bang so that there's no fatal bounce, if only he weren't going so hellishly fast, no brakes, no tyres as Johnny flies out over section five, the last one, and the old girl has somehow caught on to the importance of staying alive and flung herself to the side so that there's a pass opened up through the mountain of carrier bags for Johnny to fly through, and he touches down on the pavement, on the north side of Högbergsgatan, and now we know the Angel of Death is about to call on us, cos Johnny's bound to dive head first into the asphalt or else get cut into slices by the railings along the edge of the pavement, but we've overlooked the fact that Johnny wants to collect his case of Tizer before he signs off, and as his bike crashes into the railings Johnny's already airborne on his own, and instead of flopping down onto the road and breaking into thousands of pieces, Johnny becomes an orange-red ball that just rolls over and over and over, and all credit to the

34

driver of the number thirty-six trolley-bus who values Johnny more highly than all his passengers and slams his dirty great boot on the brake pedal so that the enormous black tyres dig long, shrieking ditches down the middle of the street and the bus makes a bow and lets Johnny go by.

After the shortest of silences, during which the trolley poles on the roof of the bus are waving around in confusion in all directions and everybody is wondering what on earth is going on, the driver leaps out of his cab and dashes over to the orange-red ball. When it starts moving and stretching out its arms and legs, the driver gives vent to such a storm of abuse that you can bet your life Johnny'd have been most put out if he'd heard it. But Johnny has only one thought in his head and that's his beloved bicycle, he just sits there staring at it, examining it, and gauging its chances of a life after this.

By the time the driver has come out with his full range of rude words and actually given Johnny a box on the ears without Johnny realizing it, the conductor has managed to get the trolley poles back in place so the gentlemen can get back into their bus and return to their timetable, and allow all the other traffic that has piled up in the meantime to get going again, as the number fifty-two coming from the other direction has also stopped, purely out of sympathy, nothing dramatic. The two drivers squeeze their giant charges past each other, shaking their heads in disgust by way of greeting. They normally greet each other by waggling their right paws in the air.

Then at last Johnny turns his freckled face towards us as we stand there waiting patiently at the foot of the conquered steps. His green eyes are gleaming brightly as he homes in on Greenfrog's face, which is displaying genuine admiration by the way. Two tenners change owners. Keep the change.

Good for Froggy, coughing up an extra one krona twenty-five.

That was that then, apart from Johnny asking, Do you

still reckon you've ever done that yourself?

Say what you like about that gorilla called Greenland or whatever, but in these circumstances he owned up and admitted how things really were. But it didn't matter either way, cos we'd all worked out for ourselves how things stood.

And so, twenty smackers better off, Johnny gathered together his belongings, nodded to us all, and set his freckles moving towards Götgatan. A performance like that doesn't come to an end just cos it's finished, though, and so we tagged on and went with him. We could tell there was something not quite right, however. He kept looking round, and after a bit he slowed right down, then he stopped altogether and flung down his bicycle and asked what we wanted, matterfact.

We didn't want anything, in fact, but Bert asked if he wanted us to help him home with the wreckage. Johnny's green eyes came over all shifty, there was obviously something wrong, like running round the corner in a corridor at school and finding somebody with his hand in somebody else's pocket in the cloakroom.

Did he hellas need any help, he said. We could tell he was asking us to clear off. We didn't really think it was right, though, cos it was all Greenfrog's fault, if it was anybody's.

But still, OK, especially as Johnny's eyes were going so funny, OK, OK, we'll leave it at that then, see yer, bloody great that was, ten out of ten, cheers then.

And Johnny looked normal again, 'cept that tonight he was walking away from us with his bicycle over his shoulder, instead of whizzing away, riding on it.

When he'd turned the corner into Götgatan, Bert asked me to go with him and follow Johnny. Only us, insisted Bert when the whole gang showed signs of coming along as well.

We hung back some way behind Johnny, who was easy to pick out as he made his way southwards down

Götgatan. Bert claimed we were doing the right thing cos for all we knew Johnny wasn't feeling too good, and he might need a bit of help all of a sudden. I agreed with him, but I didn't really believe it. And I don't think Bert really believed it either.

It wasn't very exciting, cos Johnny never turned round even once. I didn't really think anything at all, but I thought he was trusting us more than we were worth. Why were we spying on him and trying to find out where he lived if he didn't want to tell us himself?

When friend Johnny just kept on walking and walking, we started to get worried in case he lived out in the suburbs. That would have been hard to take, so we agreed that if he went any further than Skanstull Bridge we'd forget it and let him go. Forget it and say nothing at all to the lads. But then he turned off into Ölandsgatan, just before we got to the bridge. We breathed a sigh of relief. At least Johnny wasn't a suburbanite.

We were now moving into uncharted territory, and it was just a question of hanging on. Ask me anything you like about the area north and west of the railway line, and I'll have no problems. But east of Götgatan and, worse still, south of Folkungagatan, that's uncharted land where I'm completely lost.

When Johnny turned into an entrance at the end of Ölandsgatan, we raced after him, a bit more boldly than we need have, but we didn't want to lose him. According to the signs, the street where the entrance was is called Östgötagatan.

There was a passage going straight through to the other side, and Johnny turned left as he came out. We raced after him again, slammed the brakes on and peered cautiously round the corner. There was Johnny a short way down the street, trying a door and looking in through a shop window. It was locked, of course, but Johnny whipped out his magic screwdrivers and took the wheels off his bicycle, then took them in with him through a side door next to the shop.

We changed position sharpish. Crept up behind a

green Studebaker, a marvellous job, fifty-three model, the nice, low-slung one. It must have got lost, turning up in a place like this. The Popular Car of the Year was more at home round here, a Citroën 2CV, like the one just behind it, looking ashamed of itself. That nasty little car sold, and sold well, as a result of its advertising slogan: Made to work, not to admire! No sign of Art there. Popular car! I'd much rather rest my eyes by looking at a Studebaker, fifty-three model, green!

Actually, I wasn't really resting my eyes on the flashy car all that much just now; we were too busy looking around. So this was where Johnny was at home.

Bjurholmsplan.

High blocks of flats, five storeys at least. I live on the top floor of a two-storey block, and I felt a bit small round here. A kid's playground in the middle, a square retreat with lawn and shrubbery. Shops: Fruit and Veg, P. Frommes German Bakery . . .

Why on earth did he come all the way to us to join our gang of gladiators when he had a territory like this of his own?

Check! whispered Bert.

The door of the shop, which wasn't really a shop in fact but a bicycle repair place, was opened by Johnny from the inside. He carried in the remains of his machine and shut the door behind him. After that, nothing more happened to give any hint about his circumstances. We wondered if we dared risk checking out the list of tenants in the entrance hall, to see if we could guess at Johnny's surname or something like that, but we decided not to. The idea that we might bump into Johnny here put us off.

We left the Studebaker behind and went back to Östgötagatan through the passage. Where the passage opened out into a yard, a sort of oasis between the buildings fronting onto the two streets, we stopped to think about what we were going to report, and agreed to say we'd lost Johnny not long after Medis.

The headmaster went on about it at morning assembly the very next day.

While we're at it, morning assembly used to be called morning prayers till this academic year. Or morning service, as it says in the school regulations. Then some bright spark, a sixth-former called Per Ahlmark*, managed to put a spanner in the whole works by bringing up the business of conscience, since you were forced to turn up to morning service observing silence and paying pious attention throughout, unless you lived as far away as Huddinge or Mälarhöjden or somewhere like that, *or* could produce papers to prove your conscience was troubled by the Christian message. You could get papers if you were a Jew or a Mormon or some such, but Ahlmark went on about how there were conscientious objections you couldn't get documents to prove, and why should religion be the only thing requiring an assembly and silent, attentive meditation?

This Ahlmark bloke was the chosen and crowned champion of the school when it came to yapping. One of the type who actually enter competitions and *talk*. About anything you like, just for the pleasure of formulating things neatly. He won prizes, so he must have been good. Anyway, what he did counts as a great deed in the history of this school, where everything is usually stopped dead

* Per Ahlmark became the leader of the Swedish Liberal party during the 1970s.

by stamping it with a seal marked WE MUST UP-
HOLD OUR TRADITIONS.

Traditions which seem to have been invented. They
claim for instance that Bellman went to South Side
Grammar because he went to a school called Maria
Foundation School a couple of hundred years ago, and
then they call the Maria Foundation School a forerunner
of South Side Grammar.

When I went to Maria Elementary School, we were
given the impression that Maria Foundation School was
a forerunner of Maria Elementary School. But now they
tell us it's South Side Grammar that has the honour.

The old fogeys brought all this stuff up at morning
assemblies in connection with the three-hundred-year
jubilee of South Side Grammar. They managed to get it
to three hundred by including the Södermalm Pedagogia
in the seventeenth century, and then the Maria
Foundation School.

South Side Grammar itself, the present school, celebrated its fiftieth anniversary in 1929, so it should really
have been having its seventy-fifth birthday now. But
three hundredth sounds better. A Big Ball in the City
Hall, where the opera singer and Former South Side
Grammarian Sigurd Björling will challenge current
South Side Grammarian Thomas Fridén, the ace treble
of the Third Form, to a duet. And Former South Side
Grammarians Stolpe, Järrel, and God knows how many
more famous nobs will do their bit. They're all in
training, of course, after all the parties to celebrate
Stockholm's seven hundredth birthday last year.

After three hundred (or seventy-five) years, then,
thanks to this Ahlmark character, the morning gathering
could be devoted to something other than prayer, and the
Head went on about a recent event and disruption and
dangers to traffic. The school's pupils, his audience,
stared round the hall, wondering what he meant.

So it was the Head who started the rumours off, and
before long, everybody who was interested knew that I,
Christopher Nordberg, of class 1C, had a red-headed

40

mate from somewhere or other, nothing to do with the school, who was hot stuff at stepracing. Johnny's feat grew in significance as the rumour spread: before long, they had him standing on his Vienna-roll saddle gulping down a bottle of Tizer as the bicycle careered down the steps. Some of the glow overflowed onto me. It was pleasantly warming.

Only two nights later Johnny's bicycle, none other than Johnny's notorious bicycle, complete with two round wheels, was leaning against the wall of Lambert's Grocery when we arrived to invade the schoolyard.

How can this stupido copper doubt that anyone could be anything but certain that this was Johnny's bicycle? This bicycle *is* Johnny's bicycle, and that's all there is to it. Explain instead why Johnny's bicycle has got into these cophands.

Anyway, there it was. Not long after, Johnny the one and only kicked open the door and emerged from Lambert's with a crate of Tizer. We gave him the three cheers a ten-out-of-ten deserves, and then helped Johnny and his burden as far as the bust of Carl von Friesen, raised by J. Börjeson in the schoolyard of South Side Grammar in 1907 in memory of the greatest of all South Side Grammar's great headmasters, who held the post 1884-1902, after having been a teacher at the school since 1879. Now deceased.

We all got our bottle of Tizer to enjoy on the spot, apart from Bobby, who declined cos he was allergic in some way. Or it might have been cos his conk was still looking a bit peculiar, and he hadn't yet got round to forgiving and forgetting.

Then we sat around belching with pleasure, remembering the marvellous cause of this party, and Johnny told us a bit about how it felt when his brakes went, and when the chain bade farewell, and all the other things that had happened and we had no idea about. As for the old girl with the carrier bags, Johnny hadn't even seen her!

Harold asked how he had managed to get the bike looking OK again so quickly but Johnny just shrugged his shoulders. If you can't keep your treadmill in order, you should only take it out on Sundays.

The chat died away, and I broke the silence that followed by coming out with a thought that had been nagging at me ever since we'd sat down, though it had nothing at all to do with what we were talking about: Do you realize we're sitting on the perpendicular bisector of South Side Grammar?

The lads gave three cheers for the perpendicular bisector, and Bert clapped me on the back and asked me to tell them a bit more about the perpendicular bisector. Then they all sat around tutting and muttering perpendicular bisector, and I wondered why I couldn't keep my mouth shut when obsessions like that came into my head.

My coming to South Side Grammar had created a bit of a gulf between me and the lads, and when I came out with things like this, it just widened the gulf even more. In a way, they thought I was all right to have around, cos the caretaker recognized me and so let the gang hang about in the South Side Grammar yard. Otherwise, though, I often felt things were not what they used to be. The school yard, yes, OK, but the streets weren't mine any more.

Then here I come with this perpendicular bisector business. It was all the fault of the maths master, Strand, a leftover from the days before Carl von Friesen held sway. He used geometrical terms as if they were invocations, magic formulae. He'd swing his walking stick at the inattentive to impress his invocations into them. At the time when he was still open to impression, the cane was still allowed in schools, no doubt.

This old relic, whose first names were Einar Theodor, made us write out our sums in ink. Blue ink, not black, not green, not red, especially not red as he used to correct everything in red ink, and would show us pieces of blotting paper covered in red after every test he'd marked, and he'd bring out to the front our worst performer: Pettersson, come out here! Bend over.

And Pettersson would get a stroke or two across the backside. Pettersson used to show us his red-striped rear end in PE afterwards. Those beatings were no joke. All the same, they had no effect. Pettersson continued to be bottom of the class.

Strand would make us observe rituals, such as exactly where on the blackboard we should start writing out a sum, how to break a piece of chalk, which direction we should move the board cleaner, and at what speed. Mathematics demanded the highest level of accuracy, even in its peripheral manifestations. I was brainwashed already. What would it be like by the time I got into the fifth form, not to mention another three or so maybe in the sixth form! Later on in life, if I ever come across any lecturer who starts writing on the board in a particular place in the top left-hand corner, and rubs things out in that special way, I'll know I've come across another one of Einar Theodor's robotic ex-pupils.

Everybody found him insufferable with his starched collars and his musty-smelling black suit and his meticulous instructions in that hoarse, old-mannish southern accent of his. Even so, he infected me with his invocations. There was Something about mathematics, much more than mere numbers. I found that out thanks to Einar Theodor.

Johnny yawned and said it had been a hard day, and he was going to go and hit the sack. He looked worried as he contemplated the case of Tizer with its eleven unopened bottles snuggling alongside the empties.

Is there anybody who could keep these at home for me? Cos it's too much of an effort to cart them home without a carrier on my bike.

Number 2, Fredmansgatan! Lucky old me, having parents with the sense to pitch tent only a stone's throw away from Carl von Friesen's bust. I praised their good taste even when I used to go to Maria Elementary School and only needed to walk across the road. I never had to worry about putting a scarf on or doing up my jacket when I left home, or to undo it in the crush before lessons started. And it wasn't much further down the street to South Side Grammar. Nice, very, but it meant no chance of getting out of morning assembly, not living where I did. And now that convenient location was bringing me another unexpected bonus. The lads were a bit jealous, but I'd obviously won hands down.

We balanced the crate on his Vienna roll, and wheeled the bicycle home. The lads came with us when we left the school yard, cos when I'd gone, it was usually only a couple of minutes before Karlsson, the caretaker, came out and yelled at them from the base of the perpendicular bisector to clear off. And they would all feel like very small boys, cos Karlsson's voice was really ginormous.

Thanks for the drink, from all sides, tara then, see yer.

I hadn't said anything at home yet about Johnny, and so Mum, my mum, Mrs Nordberg, greeted us in the hall, and asked with great delight, What's all this then? Who's the young lady?

I thought I'd die.

Johnny slammed the crate down with a bang and I thought, Now for it, he's going to kill my mum and I'll have to choose: Mum or Johnny! Where's Dad? I'll be an orphan!

But Johnny stuck his right paw out, curtsied slightly and said, This young lady's called Johnny. Not too easy to explain, but you get used to it.

Then they both roared their heads off, and Mum said she was sorry.

Dad, my dad, chief clerk, Mr Nordberg, came creeping out of his den and wondered what was going on. He eyed all the Tizer bottles and put on his Christopher - have - you - been - robbing - the - corner - shop look, but Johnny and I explained what it was all about, more or less, a bit out of step.

44

Dad had heard about somebody riding a bike down the Kvarngatan steps. So, it was you, was it! He clapped Johnny on the back and said it was lucky Johnny wasn't one of his kids, or he'd have had something to say about it. Johnny didn't look specially worried.

I began to breathe a bit more easily, as it was obvious Johnny had given Mum and Dad the thumbs up, and they approved of him. Not that there's generally any problems between my old folks and my friends. But the thing from my point of view is that everybody else's dad was a welder or a glazier or a bricklayer, apart from Bert's who was a wino. But mine was a chief clerk.

Everybody knows what a bricklayer does, and how things are with winos is also clear, ever since Bert used to come occasionally and hide. He was little then. But I've never sorted out what a chief clerk in the civil service actually does. When I was little, I thought it was something pretty special, cos I'd once heard him chuckling over the newspaper, saying, That Labour crowd think it's them who run the country, but we're the ones with the real power, the ones who actually do the administration. But that business of claiming they're the ones with the real power and making the real decisions, there are others who say that as well. So I still don't know what a chief clerk actually does.

I'd no idea what Johnny's dad was. Bicycle mechanic maybe?

Anyway, Johnny and Dad were nattering away twenty to the dozen, so I felt a bit out of it. Then Johnny suddenly caught sight of Millie, and he forgot all about Dad and everything else. He drooped over the cage sighing and clucking.

What's its name, he wanted to know.

Millie, I said, it's a boy though, and like everybody, he wanted to know how come, and I had to explain *again* about making a mistake when we first got him.

Can I lift him up? he asked then. And he lifted Millie up and stared into his eyes and blew into his fur and held the poor thing up against his cheek, and looked as though he was in seventh heaven.

It must be great, having a pet! he whispered, and then he asked what this kind was called.

Dad laughed and said, It's a dog, but Johnny wasn't having any of that. It's a guinea pig, said Dad then.

Johnny looked at me to check, and when I nodded, he looked at Millie and repeated, Guinea pig. Guinea pig? What the hell's a guinea pig when it's at home?

But Millie didn't answer, just wanted to get back into his cage, and Johnny understood that even though he'd obviously never studied the magical sign language of guinea pigs.

We put the crate of Tizer on the pantry floor, and then Johnny was going to go. Mum, who'd been out doing things in the kitchen, said, Aren't you going to have a sandwich with Christopher before you go home?

Johnny said he didn't mind if he did, thank you.

I signalled, What? What? to Mum, cos we never used to eat at that time in our house. But she just gave me a blank look and was such a friendly mum, laying the table, Would you like milk, chocolate, tea . . . ?

Johnny said that if he could really choose, then he'd like to round things off with a cup of chocolate please, that would be something to remember for the rest of his life. But he didn't really mind, he'd have what the rest of us usually had, that would be fine.

That was lovely, Mum thought, since chocolate was what we usually had in the evening, all of us, always.

There we sat, all four of us, sipping hot chocolate, something we'd never had in that house in the evenings for as long as I'd been around, cos Mum and Dad always say you should give your stomach a bit of a rest at night.

The sandwich became several, for Johnny at least. He kept gobbling them up and Mum produced more and Dad nattered away and Mum gave Johnny a refill and Johnny laughed and nattered on and stuffed himself full. I just sat gaping, wondering what the hell was going on, cos this just couldn't be real.

When the party was at its height, Sis came in from her

secret mission, saw the merry goings-on and joined in. Round about Johnny's fourth cup − I'd lost count of the sandwiches − Sis stretched out her dreamy hand and stroked Johnny's red hair: What fantastic thatch!

She herself had a few pitiful, mousy strands on top that she used to try and spruce up on Saturdays.

Johnny stopped short and glared at her. She was in the fortunate position of being a girl, my sister of course, but a girl even so, and girls are not liable to be felled by a gentleman. Sis didn't seem to notice Johnny's glare, but just went on and on, What fantastic thatch! If only I had something like that.

She sat there dreaming away with her hand buried in Johnny's thatch, and the red colour spread and blotted out his freckles and in the end the poor lad was red all over. So I yelled, For God's sake, Suzie, get a grip on yourself!

Even Dad realized where his duty lay and he took Sis's hand away from Johnny's hair, but she was in a trance, I swear it.

And that was how Sis spoiled our perfect evening, cos when his blood had sunk again Johnny said thank you for the sandwich but he'd have to be going now. I went with him to his bicycle and tried to explain that Sis wasn't quite right in the head.

But Johnny just shrugged and said, Girls!

So everything was all right really.

He fiddled with the lock. It seemed to me it was taking him a lot longer than usual. Then he looked up, and I could see his eyes looked a bit funny before he flung himself onto his bicycle and whispered into my ear:

God, Chris, you're a lucky blighter!

Then he was gone.

That's why, if I've managed to explain the background, that's why the lads give me a stage and leave me all alone on it, all alone with the cop. That Johnny floored me recently isn't why. If so, Bobby or George or somebody might just as well tell the story. No, it's up to me, but it's hellish unpleasant to nod and say, Yes, of course, I recognize it. Johnny's bicycle, no doubt about it.

The cop knows the art of interrogation all right, so now the art of answering is being tested. Not to say too much. I've got away with a few things thanks to the number fifty-two starting up and clattering past every few minutes, and just in time, just in time.

But now we're in trouble. The cop has produced Johnny's Tangerinos, and he's asking me if I know anything about them.

Course I do. Question is, just what does he want to know?

One of the first things Johnny taught us was when Harold passed comment on his flashy tracksuit bottoms.

They weren't flashy tracksuit bottoms, those were Johnny's Tangerinos if you don't mind.

Tangerinos?

Tangerinos. What we were looking at were Tangerinos, matterfact, on Johnny, from his waist down to be more precise. They got their name from the colour. The colour was actually called tangerine. And tangerine was the colour we were looking at, on Johnny.

We'd thought the name was straightforward, like orange-red or something of that kind, same colour as

Johnny's hair in fact, nearly.

Just leave my thatch out of this, and when it comes to colours, you're boss-eyed anyway. My Tangerinos are tangerine-coloured. And my shirt's called Crimsonita. Cos it's crimson, see. And it's made of flannel, so now you know.

OK, we'd been instructed on the science of colours, and it wasn't every day you got away as lightly as that after making some comment about Johnny's thatch. The last word in fashion just then was to have your bonce shaved for the summer, and most lads still looked peeled when they went back to school in the autumn. So a blazing inferno on the topknot was bound to be noticed, and attract comment. Still, Johnny managed to fend off cracks about his red hair just as effectively as he did any mention of his freckles.

So, he was red, from top to toe, in fact. His toes were stuck in purple Adidas. Only they weren't purple, of course, they're wine-red, God but you lot are ignorant about colours.

Moreover – as our Swedish teacher keeps on saying – moreover, even if a pair of wine-red Adidas are right at the bottom, naturally enough, they were the dot over the the i. The dot under the exclamation mark if you prefer. Cos everybody knows Adidas make the dearest sports shoes you can buy. Kangaroo hide, a cushion of air round your feet, light as a feather. We've all sidled into the sports shops in Götgatan, pretending to be a millionaire, and tried a pair on. But to o w n a pair! Anybody who could persuade his old man to invest in a pair of Adidas was blessed by the gods.

He was always dressed the same, every time we saw him. And so he always stood out from the grey-blue-green-brown crowd. Plus fours or awkward long flannels. Greeny-grey jackets when it got colder, edged, if you were lucky, with artificial fur round your collar. Johnny didn't change his clothes in step with the seasons. All that happened when it was coldest, in February, was that he turned up in a top to match his tangerine bottoms. It was blue, in fact. You can bet your life there's a special name for that shade as well. Still, I call it blue, and Johnny's never corrected me. Blue with a tangerine hoop.

When we practised high-jumping in the back yard at South Side Grammar, we all wore gym shorts. But not Johnny. We got the impression he never took off his Tangerinos. We used to make fun of it a bit. Not when Johnny was listening, though.

He'd come storming up on his bike at about six o'clock, sounding both his horns to let us know he was there.

Benke Nilsson's new European record of two eleven had gone to all our heads. Just one miserable little centimetre short of the world record! But by six o'clock, our bar hadn't got any higher than one twenty. Johnny screeched to a halt, leapt off his bicycle and fairly flew at the bar, hurling himself over in perfect Benke Nilsson style.

As we all knew that was going to happen every time, we used to stand to one side as soon as we heard him sound his horn by the gate. Once we raised the bar to one eighty. He came haring round the corner of the gym, screeched to a halt, jumped off and started his run-up before he realized what the problem was. He gave it all he'd got even so. By that stage I wouldn't have been surprised if he'd cleared one eighty thanks to his speed alone but he didn't in fact.

We clapped even so, for trying hard, as it were, and gave him two out of ten.

They were great times, in the rear yard. It was just as closely guarded as the front yard, only it was Ekholm, Hugo, the caretaker in charge of the gym. Like Karlsson, he used to let the lads play there as long as he saw me. So when he came towards us, threatening murder, a bit heavy-footed he was, the lads used to shove me forward: Catalogue Chris, the bloke with a right to be here, and to collect the high-jump bar from the store under the great hall. Ekholm didn't usually seem to like people, but he liked me, God knows why. He changed his tune, and pretended not to understand the others had no right to be there.

This caretaker business is one big mystery, and I intend to solve it one of these days. But first I'll have to work out just what it is. Part of it is that the school caretakers have always existed. Say you meet an old bloke in the street. He catches on that you go to South Side Grammar. He starts going on about his own lost youth at that very same South Side Grammar. Could well be, when you think the school's been there for three hundred years. Or seventy-five. But then, going all emotional, he starts digging up memories about Martin and Hugo, the same Martin and Hugo as nowadays look after the front and back yards respectively. The first part of the mystery, therefore, has to do with why caretakers of all people can live for ever, just like the Phantom. Nobody's ever said anything about Karlsson's or Ekholm's grandsons taking over.

The second part of the mystery concerns why these complaining, argumentative caretakers can be so much liked. When Karlsson yells at you in his megatonne roar, the whole school shudders. But everybody likes Karlsson. More or less the same goes for Ekholm.

There must be a caretaker mystery, then.

Why do these stern gentlemen pretend to believe the lads are all schoolmates of mine? I know, everybody knows, that within a couple of weeks of a new term starting the caretakers have learned the names of every new pupil at South Side Grammar.

We were so well in with Ekholm that he even came over and told off sixth-formers and others who sometimes tried to stop us using the jumping pit. The only one of us the sixth-formers could accept was George, who actually cleared one sixty when he'd gone over to Benke Nilsson's Western Roll style. He could give them a run for their money, and so they didn't lose respect for the gang as a whole. But he was in a class of his own, and having matches with that lot wasn't much fun for the rest of us.

That particular night, when Johnny failed at one thirty for the second time, Sten muttered something about being able to clear it with no trouble at all if he'd only take off his Tangerinos and his Crimsonita.

Johnny reckoned his underpants weren't exactly presentable for public viewing, but everybody scoffed, cos that was no excuse. None of us was prudish enough to be worried about a pair of boggy underpants.

But Johnny insisted he just couldn't bear to be parted from his beloved Tangerinos. They'd get all miserable and fall out with him, even for the briefest of separations. In any case, he'd welded them in place, and promised not to take them off till his fiftieth birthday.

George was standing just behind him, the only begotten son of Mr Berggren the welder. The gang's expert in both the high jump and welding, in other words. When he heard that, he grabbed hold of Johnny's Tangerinos and whipped them down in a flash. Not much of a welding job, eh?

Nobody had time to note anything scandalous about Johnny's underpants before he'd pulled up his trousers again, spun round, and butted George in the stomach. George doubled up, only to get an uppercut from the back of Johnny's head, and then a left hook to the chin which adjusted his bearing by ninety degrees. I, Einar Theodor's devoted disciple, noted that he no longer emulated the perpendicular coordinate.

Johnny and his bicycle were out of the yard and away down the street in a flash of tangerine before George even hit the ground.

The only begotten son of the welder turned out to be still alive, and when he surfaced again Bert announced that he had a bit of advice for him. And for anybody else who was interested.

Of course we were interested. It wasn't every day Bert gave a speech.

The complete text of the speech was: Don't pull down Johnny's Tangerinos without good cause.

George was most grateful for the advice.

Eventually, Benke Nilsson failed us, along with his big-mouthed defenders in the world of Sport. It would be nice to sacrifice yourself for Sweden, but the lads turned their backs on Benke Nilsson and his injections and his excuses.

His roll was pretty good, though.

And now the cop is standing here with Johnny's Tangerinos, and Johnny obviously isn't inside them, though there's a long long way to go before his fiftieth birthday.

Now that we know what his trousers are called, and his shirt, it would be nice to know what Johnny himself is called. Apart from Johnny, that is.

Reckoned Mum. I was embarrassed. Don't be so nosy, for God's sake!

But Johnny didn't react, just sat there miles away, playing with Millie, letting him creep down his Crimsonita, giggling when it tickled, letting him out again and rolling him around.

When Dad turned up, I asked him if he knew what colour tangerine was, and he knew all right. He pointed straight at Johnny's track suit bottoms. Johnny was drooling over Millie's cage, and didn't see that Dad was also pointing at his hair, which was probably just as well.

Millie sneezed and wanted to go back into his cage, and so Johnny let him be in the end.

Then it was the same as last time: Johnny took the bottle of Tizer he'd come to collect and was about to leave when Mum produced a pile of sandwiches and buckets of hot chocolate, and Johnny stayed on and seemed to be enjoying himself no end. He had a marvellous time with the tube of cheese spread. He had lots of extra sandwiches just so he could have the pleasure of squeezing the cheese out in pretty patterns.

What a smashing flat you've got, he said, looking round at nothing more than the ordinary bits and pieces of what we call home. Dad agreed that the old place had a certain charm, but it wouldn't be there for much longer. We've tried to have it classified as a listed monument, but it's not quite charming enough for that. You're not supposed to have an outside loo and a wood-burning stove to cook on any more, not even if they're part of the cultural heritage. And it'd be too expensive to do it up. So they're planning to pull the whole thing down, and replace it with something better. Bigger. Higher.

We contemplated this bleak future, and I announced once again that I had no intention of moving out to some suburb or other when the time came. We'd talked about this before, of course, and it seemed they just allocated you to some place at random. And hardly anybody ever goes back to the new building they put up on the old site. Dad used to say we'd be happy enough with what we got when the time came.

When Suzie came home from her secret mission and started eyeing Johnny's fantastic thatch again, he weighed anchor before she had a chance to start pawing him. He managed without his bottle of Tizer. Just put it back, and ran for it.

Fancy having a sis like that! When I got back upstairs after waving goodbye to Johnny, she was just standing there, staring at the door. In a trance! Dad gave her a little dig and warned her to go easy on little boys. That made her dead annoyed.

Mum was in the kitchen clearing away after the party, looking really odd. Poor kid! she said. Poor kid! once again.

I felt twisted into a question mark. Was it Johnny she was on about? The Johnny who'd thumped his way into our gang? Nice little John sometimes, with a white grin, with half a tooth missing, on the right, from where I am. Completely wild at times, with his thump 'em first and ask questions later. Or don't ask at all. Was he the poor kid she was on about?

But Mum didn't reply.

I tried to put myself in her place, and see Johnny from

her point of view, but I couldn't. Poor kid? That was the last thing I'd think of in connection with Johnny. And Mum still didn't explain.

The cop wonders if there's any Tizer left, but I tell him I don't know. What's that got to do with it anyway? In fact, there is something funny about Johnny's Tizer, so odd I couldn't explain it to the cop, but still. Johnny came round now and then to fetch a bottle of his Tizer. It's not that I counted them, but there were eleven unopened bottles to start with, so eleven minus a few leaves five, maybe. Four eventually. But there are still nine unopened bottles of Tizer in the crate on the pantry floor, and there's never been less than eight.

When I first noticed this phenomenon, I kept my eyes skinned. It was Dad who kept replacing the bottles.

I haven't let on that I know about it. I don't want to force Dad into telling a lie. Reckon some explanation will emerge all by itself one of these days.

Johnny's never said if he's noticed anything. Dad's never explained. So what is there for me to say to the cop?

And what does the cop need to know anyway? That Johnny rode his bicycle down the steps, OK, that was something he could hear about. That the prize was a case of Tizer, OK. That fame ensued?

It was some time before Johnny's stepracing faded away sufficiently for us to go back to the South Side Grammar yard again. But eventually we were all there anyway, in the front yard, playing ball again, without crowds flocking round to gape.

Johnny's not much good with a ball. You throw like a tart, Pecka happened to say when we were slinging a ball around not long ago. He regretted it, cos Johnny turned dead sour and left.

I felt sorry for Pecka. He'd done all he could to get noticed by Johnny, then Johnny goes and picks me as his mate. All I did was swot all the time and had nothing interesting about me, from Pecka's point of view. Harold tried to explain to his kid brother that he was too little for a big shot like Johnny even to notice that he was there, but that wasn't an explanation to make Pecka feel any better. And then he goes and says something awful, and true come to that, about Johnny throwing a ball like a tart!

Well, at least he didn't thump me, was Pecka's comment. But then he went after Johnny. Not that Johnny came back that night, but all was well even so, cos Pecka seemed cheerful afterwards, more cheerful than he'd been for ages.

But Johnny wasn't much good with a ball, true enough, and so he preferred to ride around on his bicycle when we didn't need him. The caretakers used to let us ride bicycles in the yard in the evenings. The perfect racing track went alongside the fence behind the flower beds, with little detours around the flagpole and Carl von Friesen.

Some late fourth-formers appeared round the pitch. We thought they were some more of Johnny's admirers, but when they pinched our ball and started slinging it around over our heads, we realized our mistake.

We hadn't a chance when that lot came, in fact. The best part of the handball team were in the fourth form, and those wizards used to win every game all over the town that year, the previous year, the following year and every other year, so what could we do? If you chased around and jumped after the ball, they thought it was great fun. Just pretending nothing had happened was no good either. They'd start their own game in that case, and make sure we didn't get near the ball again. Or, if they hadn't time, simply boot the ball away. Once you saw it bouncing down into the ravine that was Södergatan, you'd had it. Either it disappeared for good, or you'd find it miles away, guarded by some old bloke whose car had been dented and had a word or two to say. And the prats who'd booted it away would only roar with laughter if you complained. So you didn't complain.

As soon as he saw what was going on, Johnny put his

bicycle down and came over to help. He was so tiny, though, the prats thought that was especially funny. Which made Johnny raving mad, of course: he can't stand remarks about his appearance. And nobody likes being laughed at. Before we knew where we were, he'd whipped out an enormous spanner from one of the secret pockets in his Tangerinos.

Steady on, Johnny, hold on, said Bert, cos this was no good. There were limits, even when people were playing dirty.

But Johnny took no notice, he just marched up and rapped the nearest of them on the back of the knee with his spanner. He was no innocent bystander, I can assure you of that, he was a tall bloke, one of those who were always, always there when the balls were pinched. He doubled up, yelling and screaming, and was obviously having trouble with his leg.

When Johnny turned to the next one, the game came to a halt. The next one was the fat monster who played in goal for the team, a very safe pair of hands, but my God, what a type! He asked if Johnny was completely crackers.

Johnny didn't pause to consider the question, but kept on advancing towards his victim and believe it or not, the man-mountain started backing away. Backing away from the murderous gleam in Johnny's green lights, backing away from the weapon in his hand. But as I said, he was a solid type who'd probably seen dangerous things coming towards him many times before, and so he got a grip on himself and stopped and tutted and told Johnny to calm down for Chrissake, can't you take a joke, there are limits you know.

His voice got quicker and jerkier the closer Johnny came to him, and when Johnny lashed out, he flung himself sideways, but just caught a glancing blow from the spanner. A goalkeeper is more used to facing up than jumping out of the way.

But Johnny kept on after him, and had evidently decided he was going to kill this particular human. And this particular human had no fellow human to help him just now, cos they were all standing there gaping, waiting for blood and brain fluid.

They lost control of the situation to such an extent that the ball came down to our level. Harold just grabbed it and shouted that he'd got it back.

This acted as a kind of signal. The enemy came to life, and were obviously going to set on Johnny from behind. Mind your back, Johnny, look out!

He turned round in a flash and said with steel in his voice that if you come any closer, somebody's going to get their sk-sk-skull bashed in, I'm warning you.

He was serious, everybody could see that.

The ball didn't matter any more, really, the whole universe was circling round the spanner in Johnny's right hand.

He didn't bother moving at all. He just kept his eye on their movements and intentions, the spanner heavy in his hand. But nobody budged, not towards Johnny at least.

The goalkeeper kept on backing away, and when he reckoned he was far enough off, which happened to be just in front of me, he said he thought Johnny was a hell of a coward.

Johnny glared at him and asked who was a coward, matterfact, j-j-just think about it: who's a c-c-coward, matterfact?

But the goalie wasn't in the mood for thinking. He sniggered, Carrot-headed bastard!, and turned to go away.

I don't know what he meant to do next. If it hadn't been for the carrot-headed bastard bit, he might have been allowed to depart in peace, cos Johnny had won now, that much was clear. But Johnny gave a yell and came racing at him, and the goalie just managed to catch on as he was turning round, and reacted with a lightning leap to one side.

But I was in the way, and on top of me comes this 130, 190, maybe 380 kgs worth of muscle. I collapsed, of course, what else. And Johnny pounced on top of us.

I saw the spanner coming, and Johnny's terrifying

murderous eyes and I thought this is it, I'm going to die! But in the midst of his fury Johnny realized it was me.

I saw how he woke out of his trance and his eyes changed altogether. I'll never forget those eyes! I'll never forget them!

Crashing into me saved the goalkeeper's life, if I understood the situation rightly. That was the end of it all, in fact, cos all of a sudden the caretaker was in among us, and he wasn't impressed by the spanner nor by the goalkeeper's prowess.

After four years at Maria Elementary School, using the South Side Grammar yard at break time, and a year at the grammar school itself, I've realized that the windows from the headmaster's study, the staff room and the caretaker's room that look out onto the front yard, are the life insurance for the underdogs round here. We shared the yard with the upper school, and survived because when things hotted up, there was always Somebody there. Just before the fatal blow was adminstered. In the back yard, we came up against more devious methods, inaudible and barely visible: the sixth-formers were deeply into the Spirit and Traditions of South Side Grammar. The school regulations stipulate that: Pupils will work together in a spirit of tolerance and harmony; all violent or offensive behaviour on the part of pupils is forbidden. Nevertheless, intolerance and offensive behaviour were a fact of everyday life. No benevolent windows looked down on the rear yard.

Well, this life insurance policy was of only limited relevance. By this time of day, vigilance was relaxed. If all this had happened during school, Karlsson would have appeared the moment Johnny took out his spanner. As it was, he was really too late.

But I'm not blaming our guardian angel – if Karlsson, the tough caretaker at South Side Grammar, will excuse this tender epithet. I'm not blaming him on this occasion. Outside working hours, we were dicing with death without any life insurance.

I felt all a-quiver while the memory of Johnny's eyes

sank slowly down through my whole body.

When Johnny came home with me afterwards, one spanner the poorer, he gave me rather an odd look and asked if I'd been frightened. I don't know what I said in reply, cos I still hadn't calmed down, but Johnny held out his hand, his spanner hand, and said he was sorry.

I don't quite know what I said then either, but it eventually occurred to me to ask if he'd really intended to bury his spanner in his enemy's skull.

A silly question, in fact. I'd seen Johnny's eyes.

The cop wanted to know as well: Had Johnny, on the occasion in question, intended to kill, or not? Was my question a silly one, or was it not? My view? On Johnny's intention. What did Johnny have to say about it?

Johnny thought it over for ages, or at least, I thought he was thinking. In any case, he didn't say anything for quite a while, and then he said he didn't know, matterfact. Or rather, he didn't really remember, matterfact.

And when I asked, What?, he corrected himself to, Well, matterfact, he didn't really remember.

I thought that sounded very interesting, so I asked him what was the last thing he could remember clearly.

All of a sudden, Johnny couldn't remember that either.

And then it was Millie and Mum and sandwiches and drinking chocolate and Dad and nattering and Sis back home from her secret mission with that dreamy look of hers.

Till Johnny was standing at the front door again, playing with the delicate little girl's hand that forms the knocker on the entrance to Number 2 Fredmansgatan, a remnant from the days when Fredmansgatan used to be called Parisgränd and crossed over Maria Quarngränd, and travellers came to this crossroads and banged away at this knocker, shaking hands with the house, till a sleepy caretaker opened up. According to our neighbour,

Werner, an old-age pensioner who's been writing away at *The History of Quarnberget* ever since he was a young man.

Then Johnny said, You've always got to prove it . . .

Unlocked his bicycle. Nodded goodbye. Rode away.

Johnny just had to prove it – that he could do a tightrope walk along the handrail of the viaduct over Södergatan. It was the same old story: Johnny's girlish face meant that nobody outside the gang took him seriously. And now he had to prove it to some stuck-up types who had laughed at him once too often, who had shrugged their shoulders once too often, who had raised doubts once too often. All at Johnny's expense.

I hated him, cos if his stepracing had been a terrific ten-out-of-tenner, this balancing act was deadly dangerous and sheer madness. Johnny was now much more than just one of the lads. By this stage, I was so fond of Johnny he'd become part of me. He was my friend, my mate, my bosom pal, till death us do part. I didn't want to see him crash down from St Paulsgatan to Södergatan just for the sake of some stuck-up types who didn't matter.

I wished Johnny would break his arm, or his leg, or would get concussion, or what the hell you like as long as it hurt a lot, and he survived and learnt the lesson that he had to take things a bit easier. But he was so blasted brilliant, he never broke his arm or his leg, and never hurt his head.

OK, now he just had to prove it . . .

This time the price on his life was only ten kronor.

It all started with: If he was such a wizard on wheels, he could ride his bike along that handrail over there, then.

That showed they didn't know what they were talking

about, matterfact, cos that's just impossible, less than impossible, it's minuspossible, matterfact, cos there are such things as laws of nature. And these were top grade principles from the science of gravitation and centrifugal force, till calculations were whizzing back and forth round Johnny's carrot-bonce and everybody could see Johnny knew what he was on about.

But that handrail's six centimetres wide. – Fifty-nine millimetres. I put him right. – That's wide enough for a bike, for Christ's sake!

But didn't they get what Johnny had just spelt out in words of one syllable! Every little kid knew that the principle of balancing on a bike depended on the thing being propelled forward in big circles. Thing is here, with fifty-nine millimetres to play with, then you've got to be going, let's see, at least thirty-five kph, if you're going to have a theoretical chance even. The quicker the speed, the wider the circle, see. But OK, build up a starting ramp to give me that speed, preferably a bit more, and I'll show you.

Well, some of us could see that Johnny was trying to get out of it. There were loads of people cycling around and keeping their balance without being engineers, so it couldn't be quite as bad as Johnny was making out. But if it really was that peculiar he could have a go without the bike, that would do. Or does the rail have to be circular?

There we had it! And while I could still bear to listen, before all their gabbling on became deadly serious, it occurred to me that Johnny had an inborn bargaining technique. I recognized every move from the exchange with Greenland.

To start with, he called this little task absolutely impossible as well: only fifty-nine mill wide, side winds, traffic, everything shaking – hard, nightmarish hard. Then he pushed it till he was more or less bound to go ahead, demanded payment, but was offered only a few miserly öre for doing it. Then, in view of all the risks, he upped the price something awful, and they were as much caught in the trap as he was. The only difference being he wouldn't have to pay if he didn't bring it off.

When he set off along this strip of iron fifty-nine millimetres wide, I stayed where I was on our side of the viaduct, hating him and bashing my head against this blasted rail, closing my eyes and stealing a look in turn, and I could see one Adidas after another balancing quite securely, and the lads hanging back so as not to distract him.

They were walking along the ordinary everyday pavements of St Paulsgatan, keeping behind Johnny but watching him all the time, Johnny on the fifty-nine millimetre rail, watching the bloke destined to become The Hero. Cos when he falls they'll all rush up to the rail and gaze twenty metres down the Södergatan ravine and see his deformed remains, and it'll be The Hero who had fallen like a hero and The Hero who had died a hero's death, and for ever and a day, whenever any of the lads happen to meet, old gents occupying their allotted slots in the caring society, the conversation will suddenly turn to, Do you remember when Johnny did a tightrope walk over the rail . . ., and they'll all recall the tangerine figure's last shaky steps, the gasp as he fell and the sight down there in the ravine, and, after a few moments' silence, He was a hell of a tough guy, that Johnny!

But I won't be there in that future, cos when Johnny falls, I fall as well.

It doesn't take much!

And then there was George's ruddy daft comment that the rail will hold, I can promise you that, cos my dad was one of them as put it up. His clever dad had no doubt made the rail only fifty-nine millimetres wide so that George, or any other kid even dafter than him, would never think of going for a walk along it.

Down in Södergatan all the cars were stopping and folks were staring up. More and more came to gape. The cocoa advert on the gable wall over in Hornsgatan was staring as well, that one with the big eyes on the packet.

Drink cocoa morning, noon and night. With a good-night sandwich all day long, Johnny, as long as you pack this up!

An old bloke yelled at Johnny to get down at once, just like I wanted to. Jump, Johnny! But the right way, for God's sake!

But Johnny took no notice of what old blokes shouted, nor old ladies, and he ignored my invisible shouts altogether. So everybody soon caught on that they'd better shut up and leave the idiot on the rail alone. Shut up and not be the reason for the fall, the fatal twenty-metre fall into the ravine.

I felt sick, and embarrassed to find I was crying. Cos I knew Johnny was going to fall, and he couldn't survive a fall like that, and I didn't want to lose him.

But he made it, of course. All the way. And so he became The Hero instead, and I hated him for that as well. It looked as if he was ready to come back again the same way, but oddly enough, nobody suggested it.

When nothing else happened, people moved off, traffic started going again, the eyes on the cocoa tin winked ever so quickly then went back to normal again, I was the only one who noticed that. The old bloke resumed his evening stroll, muttering away at Johnny, and by God I'd have gone and joined him and worked out a view of life same as his if Johnny hadn't chosen that moment to come back to me. Me.

I reckon he could see I'd been crying. He put his arm round me and walked a bit in front of the others and asked whether it was OK now, matterfact, now that he'd made it. Cos you know, don't you, I'd never have tried it if I didn't know I'd make it?

But I couldn't raise an answer, cos it wasn't OK at all.

What about this then, Chris?

Johnny waved a whole fortune in front of my face, four tenners.

They cocked it up! Thought we'd agreed on a tenner apiece!

But I said nothing, cos it didn't change anything.

Johnny fixed me with his green, piercing eyes. None out of ten then?

Why did he have to ask? I hadn't accused him of anything after all, hadn't even said anything, come to that. Just stayed where I was, on our side of Södergatan. Kept an eye on things from a distance, you could say, so what was he on about? I tried to say something like that, but what actually came out was, None out of ten. Piss-awful.

At the street leading up to South Grammar, Johnny held his hand out and said, Sorry, Chris!

By God, he's incredible, my friend John! I've never managed to say sorry for anything without feeling a right twit. But Johnny said he was sorry, head held high, and you knew he meant what he said.

So I said, OK, nothing to do with me really.

Oh yes, he knew exactly what I meant, he said, and he'd pull his socks up from now on. From today onwards, it'd be different.

We shook on it again, but God knows if I knew what he was on about, or what it was he thought he understood. But obviously, I shook with Johnny when he offered me his mitt, whether we were on the same wavelength or all to cock.

A shake's a shake. Specially when it's Johnny's hand.

That promise about turning over a new leaf wasn't just talk: there were no more dangerous escapades for a while. It could be Johnny was now so well known, he didn't need to prove himself any more. Everybody knew now he wasn't girlish, despite what his face suggested; everybody knew you couldn't just brush him aside, even though he was small; everybody knew he wasn't a cissy, even though he might be thin, and so on. Promises or some other reason, you no longer felt Death was staring him in the face every night of the week. This meant he could reveal other sides to his character instead. They might not make him a Hero, but they earned him a few plus-points even so.

The ostrich, for example! How about this:

We were playing soccer when The Bottle came past. If you can imagine a bottle with a round top and glasses and a hand to carry a violin case in. Something like that was in the upper sixth and used to come past us on certain nights when he'd evidently been having a nice quiet violin class with old man Wiebe up in the music room.

We called him The Bottle, everybody called him The Bottle, cos of his wondrous body. He was a completely harmless type, and used to smile at us: Let the little boys play away! or something like that, or maybe he was wishing he was a kid again, so he could play as well. Actually, I don't think he saw us at all, he was too wrapped up in his own little world.

If the lads called me Catalogue Chris, then this bloke must have been Lexicon Les. In fifty volumes, leather bound, up on the shelf. Whenever I read in some book or other that somebody is a swot, I see The Bottle before my very eyes. The archetype, he is: The Bibliophile Bottle.

So, this bibliophile bottle used to wend his way past us, smiling his stupid smile. And then, for once, he paused to study our game. What I mean is he directed his gaze in the direction of where we were playing. He put us right off after a while, and we just gaped back at him. Then he opened his mouth and, in just the kind of squeaky voice you'd expect of a bibliophile bottle, he said,

Well done, boys! Exercise! Organs not stimulated will wither away. Compare the wings of an ostrich.

We all stared at him, struck dumb by his words of wisdom. Then we all burst out laughing.

In the Donald Duck cartoons, Huey, Dewey and Louie sometimes writhe about on the floor, pointing and guffawing till the tears pour down their cheeks and they have to hold on to their tummies. That's just what we all did for a few minutes on end, a real Disney haha. In the dim distance we could see The Bottle, standing there, smiling.

Johnny was so carried away, he leapt at him like a monkey, flung his arms round his neck, and planted a real plonker of a kiss right on his cheek, singing, Ostrich, you're an Ostrich! in between his giggles.

The Bottle, now rechristened Ostrich, was bowled over backwards, but all he could think of was his violin, and he made sure that wasn't damaged. Johnny sat there in his lap, singing,

> Ostrich, you're an Ostrich,
> Ostrich, Ostrich is your name . . .

We all roared our approval. The Ostrich looked priceless, sitting there with a bewildered smile on his face and a singing tangerine baby on his knee.

Johnny calmed down eventually, got off, and helped The Ostrich to his feet. Dusted him down a bit, all friendly like, handed him his school cap which had dropped off when he fell of course, and danced around him as he strutted away from the school yard. The Ostrich was a much better name for that phenomenon, in fact.

He was a bit odd after all, not just a swot. We thought it was the highlight of the week and gave Johnny eight out of ten for his plonker of a kiss; but The Ostrich just seemed bewildered at first, then he strutted off as if he hadn't noticed anything unusual at all. Perhaps he felt honoured because we'd paid so much attention to him.

So he was called The Ostrich from then on, and it stuck. And nothing against us. He'd pass by now and again, smiling his ostrich smile, just as he used to do. There was always somebody who announced, We're stimulating our organs, Ostrich!

He would smile a bit more broadly, showing approval, and strut on his way.

Did he really kiss the sixth-former? The cop notes it all down. I get the feeling he hasn't given it eight out of ten.

Well, kiss might not be the right word. Besides, we were laughing so much we didn't really see exactly what happened. But the lads all nodded, what I said was right. If the cop doesn't believe us he can always bring in The Ostrich. Although the bloke seems a bit out of this world, he might remember how he got to know Johnny. From then on, his smiles and nods seemed to be directed specially at Johnny. A sign of recognition, don't you think? You can teach ostriches things all right. In spite of their withered wings.

It might not be all that relevant here, but I'd like to mention another time we were competing for points, without risking life and limb.

We were sitting round in a circle, taking it in turns. You had to be as flesh-creeping as possible.

George: You're riding round this corner on your bike, see, and you get in this monster skid and come off in a heap and one leg gets coated in gravel and sand as your skin's peeled off in strips, and your other leg gets caught in the chain so that your toes snap off and get sliced up like bacon by the spokes in your back wheel, and your elbows and your chest are all peppered with gravel and sand, and just then a car comes round the corner and, crunch, it steamrollers right over you and the bloke inside says, I say, was there something there? and so he backs and steamrollers over you again, but he can't see anything so he drives off and steamrollers you for the third time, and you just lie there like a lump of sausage meat, and nothing moves except your heart beating slowly, slowly, till it stops altogether.

That was great, everybody thought so. Eight out of ten. Nine maybe. Eight. The car was a bit much, really. That was a different flesh-creeper. Gravel all over, under your skin: that would have been enough. Everybody could feel the gravel prickling under their own skin. But nobody had been mashed up to make sausage meat. And the end bit with the heart was a typical minus detail.

Pecka: You're carving a stick, right. You're making something, a . . . well, dun't matter what really. And there's this stick, right, about this thick. You know that if you really press hard you can cut it off in one cut, right, just like that. So you really try, right. But you don't notice you've turned the knife over, right, so it folds over and snips your thumb off, right, just one cut, here, right across.

Pecka showed us his scar, and got seven out of ten. No more, cos it was hardly the first time we'd heard his story. Harold was very patient and explained that you should have said right at the start it was a claspknife.

Pecka is so childish that we'd all love to sock him one when he gets going. But Harold a l w a y s stands up for his kid brother. And Harold the giant is incredibly nice. To everybody, but especially his kid brother. It was Harold's turn now:

You're on the ten-metre diving board at Medis, and you sort of wonder why there's so few people around. Only Harry, and you take no notice of him, though he's yelling his head off and pointing. And you launch out into a swallow dive . . .

And? We all wonder during the long pause. Belly flop? From ten metres?

Harold made his mind up: No, they're cleaning the pool. So the water is ninety-five degrees. That's what Harry was on about.

That was very nearly nine out of ten. But I reckoned it just couldn't happen like that. The stories we told had to be possible; they could be flesh-creeping, creepier, creepiest, but they had to be possible, we'd agreed on that from the start. Harold got six out of ten, and Pecka looked pleased with himself, and so it was my turn:

You're walking along in the dark, the usual way, you know it off by heart. But they've dug a trench right across the pavement for new drains, and they've put down some pipes and a big cement tube going straight down into the underworld. You step right into it, you've no idea, and over you go, bashing against the edge of the concrete and splitting your forehead open, and you bounce back and smash your fizz against the other edge and your teeth fly out in all directions, and you slide down and get caught upside down and you hang there in this drum with all the sewage floating past your nose. You just hang there.

The lads checked with their tongues to see their teeth were still there, and gave it seven out of ten. You could have put your hands up, reckoned Bobby, and broken your fall. If I'd thought of getting my hands tied up somehow I'd have got a higher score.

Bobby: You're standing there carving with your sheath knife. Not a claspknife, note, unlike a previous speaker this evening. It's top-grade birch wood you're carving, you're making a boat. Lovely big splinters you're cutting off. Then ouch! As you pull your hand back one of these splinters goes right into your thumb. Swinish bad luck. It goes in just here, sharp as a darning needle, and it's even worse cos you're holding the knife so hard. Goes right through your thumb, bounces off the bone and comes out against your nail. But your nail stops

71

it and the point of the splinter breaks and bends over to one side, and it comes out just here underneath your nail. And it all happens before you can say bottle – sorry, I mean ostrich – and you can't push the splinter through and you can't pull it back either cos the break holds it back in both directions.

We sat there gripping our thumbs and grimacing, and Bobby got nine out of ten. There was a bit of lack of emotion in the telling, that little bit extra that would have really gripped you and turned your stomach over.

Hey, come on! Bobby was the only one who'd have thought of complaining about the agreed judgement. That's exactly what happened. I was there.

That's fair enough in itself. Course you should be involved, said Johnny. In one way or another anyway. Yourself. Or seen it. Somehow or other.

It was Johnny's turn now. Johnny sought and found inspiration from somewhere in the far distance. All the time he was telling his story, he was staring into the far distance.

You're standing on your mark, your line four metres away from the tree, this big tree, a tree as thick as this.

Johnny indicated a girth nearly twice his own.

You've drawn a circle on the trunk, this high, and you're aiming at the circle with your knife. Lots of knives today. It's going in smashing. You're pretty good at that. The knife goes in dead straight and sticks there trembling in the tree. Mebbe not right in the ring every time. You're not quite as good at aiming. But it's going in terrific. As I say.

Four metres, did I say that? The knife loops the loop three times in four metres, when you throw it like this. Good knife. Heavy. Sticks in terrific and shivers in the trunk.

You throw and then you walk the four metres and you fetch your knife. You pull it out. It sticks in smashing. You walk back your four metres. One step, two, three . . . You're looking at your mark. Get your foot just right, then you whip round and throw straight away without aiming. Oh my God! In front of the tree! Your brother! Your kid brother! Where the hell did he come from?

Johnny goes all quiet.

We look at each other, all worried. Harold puts his arm round Pecka. Nobody even mentions a score. One after another, we mumble our excuses, get up and go home.

When I go, Johnny's left sitting there all on his own, gazing at something in the far distance, something I can't see, towards the Skanstull Bridge maybe. I can't bring myself to ask him if he wants to come home with me.

All that year, I was the rope in the tug-of-war between the gang and school. That was the big conflict, if I can use such a high-flown word for what was going on inside me, pulling and pushing.

It was so great, so fantastic to get to South Side Grammar, the Upper Secondary School for Boys at Södermalm. But you soon came down to earth. Cos what did you do all day long, in fact?

We had a horrible man as our class-teacher and English master. Mr G.G. was the codename he'd hit upon for himself, and wanted us to use. We hardly knew any other, forgot his real name.

That was the man we could look forward to seven or eight years with, if the worst came to the worst. It dampened our enthusiasm for school work.

And my new classmates? After only a couple of weeks, we split up into two roughly equal camps. One half used the long dinner break, free periods, and even occasionally the shorter breaks to nip down Götgatan to the EPA department store. They picked up all sorts of things there, the boys from the Grammar School.

They worked as a team. It went very well. They were proud of themselves, and used to show us what they'd taken. The rest of us ought to get in on it. Join in, for Chrissake!

It was OK for a while, but then the staff no doubt started putting two and two together, and sure enough, in November, they caught five of them.

Then they squeezed the truth out of those five till they

had fifteen names, which was a bit much for a first-year class of thirty-five.

Our worthy class teacher, Mr G.G. that is, probed and probed; there were interrogations and little talks every day. You might have thought it'd be in his interest to play the whole thing down, but not at all. Oh no, boys. I'm a bit too long in the tooth for that. And he muttered away about such things as My class and My boys and Betrayed my trust.

Trust? The last thing in the world that man could be said to have shown us was trust. Now his big task was to sort this one out, sort it out to the bitter end.

We started to notice the whole staff were looking askance at our class, at the ones who'd been caught, the ones who'd admitted it, at the ones who hadn't admitted anything, especially those who hadn't admitted anything. Those of us who hadn't been caught were naturally the brains behind the whole operation, since we'd managed to slip through the net. No doubt we were torturing our unfortunate fellows to make sure they wouldn't dare give us away.

Those of us who knew could console ourselves with the fact that we knew, of course, and that a conduct mark couldn't be based on mere suspicion. All the same, it didn't feel too good to be suspected like that, specially when we managed to withstand the enormous pressure put on us to join in with the rest. Resisting like that hadn't been a big decision, in case anybody should think it was. Not that we had a sensitive conscience inscribed with Thou Shalt Not Steal. The plain fact was, we knew you were bound to get caught doing that sort of thing sooner or later, no matter how much fun it was just now. And I was scared stiff of *that*. Of getting caught.

But we were scared even so. There was a risk that somebody who'd been caught might take it into his head to put the finger on somebody who was innocent, just to get his own back. As I say, the whole complicated affair had divided the class into two more or less equal groups, and feelings between the two camps were not all that warm. There were already plenty of old scores to settle. But nobody made any false accusations as it happens. Which meant, therefore, that those of us who didn't get caught were the real villains, the gang of crooks who worked in secret.

And Mr G.G. kept probing away.

He was one of those bloodhounds who ought to be taken on in hopeless murder hunts or tax evasion cases. As a teacher, he was a pain in the neck with his petty pedantry.

Some thought that if you compared the school business with the gang of women the papers were writing about just then, who'd been caught after robbing department stores for three years, the school thing was less than nothing. Mr G.G. knew all about starting on the slippery slope, look at the gang of women, shoplifting, petty thieving, more serious thieving, millions, etc., QED.

There are lots of ways of looking at it all. Personally, I think it was odd that these blokes should want to pinch so much stuff, cos I reckon none of them needed it. Their dads are architects and dentists and professors, and so posh they'd have had heart failure if their son came home and referred to them as the old man. These are lads with pocket money so they can go and buy the necessities of life from Lambert's grocery if they don't fancy the school lunch. Or even go to the café if they don't fancy what Lambert's have to offer either. And still they've got to pinch masses of stuff from EPA.

Maybe you shouldn't do this, but as I'd only just started at South Side Grammar and could feel that just by going there a gap had opened up between me and my friends, I sometimes compared my classmates with the lads in the gang. The lads hardly know what money looks like, and have even less idea of what it's like to go into a café. But they've never talked about pinching anything. Maybe a hub cap, if it looks attractive enough, but that's sort of different, I reckon. Not quite legal, but different.

There's a sort of built-in honesty in the gang, but even so there's a constant guilty conscience which is just as

76

much built-in. When the cops come, it's serious.

Never talk to a cop! That's what you always said, Johnny. Never, not to a cop, I'm just telling you.

Maybe I should do as you said and not say so much. But that wasn't all you said, all you did. You also floored me, Johnny. That changed things a lot.

And so this cop, who just keeps on asking and asking about Johnny, is frightening. You never heard anything about the architect's son or the solicitor's son being scared when the sheriff popped out from behind a curtain at EPA. Embarrassing, maybe, but not dangerous. As far as the gang's concerned, cops are dangerous.

In fact, so-called honesty might be just cowardice really. The inbuilt honesty in the rest of the lads might really just be fear of getting caught, as it was in my case. I don't know for sure, but if you are going to talk about honesty among the lads, inbuilt honesty in the gang, then it's only right to point out it was Bert who built it in. And as far as he's concerned, honesty is not the same as being frightened at all.

It's possible – how do I know if it's true when it's never been tried? – but it's possible that if Bert left the gang, we'd soon go to pieces. But for the moment anyway, if anybody wasn't sure about what was right or wrong, you went to Bert and asked him. He'd show you the straight and narrow, and I don't know of him ever being wrong.

It's characters like Mr G.G. who make you think, Well, if that's the way it is . . . , and go and rob a bank. But when Bert had his eye on you, none of the lads would ever go into EPA and nick so much as a jelly baby. Bert would have been so disappointed when it all came out in the end. Everything always comes out in the end. It's doubtful if you'd have been able to stay in the gang afterwards.

I just get confused when I compare my different worlds like this. They're two different worlds, but the dividing line is as thin as a line can be according to Einar Theodor

Strand's pronouncements on the concept: a line has length but no breadth. Without taking area into account, it divides a plane into two portions. Two worlds with no common ground. On one side of the line, kids have got into South Side Grammar, and on the other side they haven't, haven't even tried. The difference is a matter of how you think, how you look at things, what you see from where you are. From one side of the line life looks one way, from the other it looks completely different.

I've got one foot in both camps. One of these days I'll have to make up my mind where I stand. That's why I'm going on about conflicts and tugs of war.

In one of those worlds, we're called Chris and Bert and Harold. In the other it's Nordberg and Nyborg and Jernström. Anybody who insists on using first names at South Side Grammar will never get as far as the sixth form. It's a sure sign.

At the beginning of this year Stockholm had 776,947 inhabitants. Two of them were Johnny and me. He didn't need to put the blame on Tizer, he could come round anyway.

He got more and more well in with Millie, who started going crazy as soon as he heard Johnny's voice in the hall and ran round and round in little circles in the cage till Johnny picked him up, stroked him, blew at him, muttered strange things at him and slid him inside his Crimsonita where he was in his element sniffing and poking around.

First stop, then: The Johnny and Millie session by the cage and Millie was in no hurry for it to end. Nor was Johnny, come to that. A pet of his own, that'd be great, but borrowing someone else's guinea pig like this, well, that would do.

Then he'd come in to me. Nattered a bit if I wasn't too busy with my homework. The first time he came to the room I share with Sis, I more or less had to drag him in. He evidently regarded it as an enormous intrusion into my private territory. He stood in the doorway, checking

78

the place out, and his freckled face betrayed his awe. He can't have had much trouble seeing which part of the room was mine, and which was Sis's. We've got different tastes, you might say.

For some time now the smart marketing boys at Kellogg's had been putting face masks on the back of their cornflake packets depicting animals, characters from fairytales, well-known people, various jobs, and so on. I'd given Mum clear instructions to make sure she got a new mask whenever she went out to buy cornflakes. In this way, bit by bit, I got a full set of the face masks. Mum's task was made easier by my sticking the masks up on the wall, carefully cut out from the packet. I also helped to gobble up the cornflakes, it seemed only right.

It was the never-ending row of masks that grabbed Johnny's attention and drew him into the room. He stopped under the series of Famous Clowns, and just stood there gaping and mumbling Charlie Rivel, August Miehe, Willi Pauli, Toto Brasso . . . and laughing contentedly. All the names I'd learnt from the Kellogg's packet he knew straight off. He knew their best tricks, and he could tell me all about them, chuckling and imitating them for me. Or maybe for himself; I don't know if he was aware of me at all, or where he really was. In any case, his little show was so effective that Mum and Dad, who'd turned up in the doorway without Johnny seeing them, joined me in enthusiastic applause. Johnny wasn't the least embarrassed, as I'd have been, but just gave a fancy little bow to thank his audience. Then they could go. It didn't make any difference to Johnny.

He went through all the clowns. What's all this then? he wondered when he saw Little Red Riding Hood, Snow White, Happy and Dopey and various other Famous Fairytale Characters.

I explained, but he wasn't interested. He went back to the clowns.

Whenever he came into my room after that, he always made a beeline for the clowns. Had there been any new ones? Had I moved Charlie Chaplin? He ought to be in among the film stars, he's nothing to do with circuses.

When I did have homework to do, Johnny would lie on my bed reading quietly. I've got all the Donald Duck comics from the very first issue in September '48 to the latest. The speed Johnny read, he had enough Ducks to keep him going all winter. He'd laugh himself hoarse at some of the best issues, read them over and over again, and find them just as incredibly funny every time. When I glanced at the cover, I generally used to know exactly what he was laughing at. I knew them more or less off by heart, but I'd never found them *quite* so funny as Johnny did.

I was practically brought up on Donald Duck. Dad used to buy them and read them aloud for me before I could read myself. Now it's up to me to read them and buy them as well. They used to cost sixty öre in those days, and they're seventy-five now. It's worth it. Even if they go up to a krona, Donald Duck & Co. are worth it.

Donald Duck et Consortes, was how Dad always used to start off in the days when he read them to me. It was a magic formula, before the new Tobacconist-and-Newsagent-smelling Donald Duck was opened. Here's Donald Duck, all the rest of them are & Co., et Consortes, are you awake, Chris?

That's why the first letter I ever learnt to recognize was that ridiculous twiddly &. When all the other twiddly things came to me, I used to go round town spelling out the names on the signs: Silver Et Gold, Fish Et Game, Borg Et Sons. It was only in the spring term of the second year that Et cropped up in our reader, but then it was called And. Donald Duck and Company. I never accepted that.

There was one issue missing, the one I'd lent to Sten, and his gormless sister chewed it up. It was the August issue for 1952, with the cover where Donald Duck is carrying the triplets in a golf bag so that he doesn't have to pay their fare. But I found a copy in the second-hand bookshop in Högbergsgatan just opposite EPA, and it was only ten öre. So the collection is complete again now. It used to be a good second-hand bookshop, but when the lady running it, Britta, snuffed it, it went downhill, and I don't go there nowadays.

I've got all the Superman and Batman comics as well, but Johnny wasn't specially keen on them. Reckoned they were unrealistic. It's all very well for someone who's the Phantom himself to say that kind of thing, but I like every single one of them, like the contents, unrealistic or not, like sorting them, like reading them when my books get a bit hard going.

When Johnny didn't fancy reading Superman, I suggested he ought to go through the pile in Sis's corner. He had a look. The covers meant nothing to him, which made me think he didn't have a sister himself. But when he thumbed through them and realized what a lot of old crap they were, with page after page of slush and sloppy love stories, he thought the joke I'd played on him was in such poor taste that he flew at me, and we rolled over and over and bashed against the furniture.

It was great, wrestling with Johnny, when it was just for fun. When he didn't come it with any of his dirty tricks, like he did when he was in a temper, you realized he wasn't really all that strong. He noticed that himself as well, but as long as it was in secret, just between the two of us, he didn't mind being the underdog. When he was hopelessly beaten, he'd give up by tickling me till I had to let him go.

The hardest thing was not making too much row, cos then Mum would look in and remind me about my homework and the delicate furniture. So we used to lie there fighting on the floor, choking our laughter in each other's stomachs. Johnny, or maybe it was just his clothes, smelt of asphalt and resin, tar and pine needles. We used to press up hard against each other so that we didn't kick the furniture and we suffocated and choked so that we wouldn't be heard, but Mum obviously heard us even so.

She used to break up our fights with hot chocolate and sandwiches.

As Johnny was coming round so often, I got hot chocolate and sandwiches in the blood that winter. It wasn't a bad thing, and Johnny never spoilt it all by saying no thank you. Once or twice at the beginning, he said he really ought to go cos he couldn't very well come round here gobbling every single night, matterfact.

But then Mum would come out with some reason or other why he really had to stay. She'd put his Adidas out to dry, so he'd have to wait another hour anyway. Or we won't be able to eat all these sandwiches ourselves.

And so Johnny would stay, and he liked it.

Mum had left a few slices of bread in reserve, and Johnny could spread them himself with cheese from the tube: a hobby he picked up at our place, and he was happy as a sandboy doing it.

The first time Johnny saw my card index, he thumbed through it a bit, but he soon gave up, bowled over by all the numbers, and he asked what it was supposed to be.

It's a card index.

A card index?

That's what it's supposed to be.

He went through it all again, and after a while it came out that he was looking for the picture postcards. He tried to hide his embarrassment when I explained what a card index was. But when I told him, not quite honestly, that I'd only just found the term in a dictionary the week before and thought it sounded rather good, and till then it was called a file, his face lit up and he agreed with me that it sounded rather good, yep, just right for this little lot. But for God's sake, what on earth are all these num–beridoodahs?

He kept on going through, and I let him. My secret box is hidden away under lock and key. Nobody can see that without use of force, not even Johnny.

Pretty boring way to live, was Johnny's comment on my precious card index.

I said nothing to that. I was resigned to the fact that I was misunderstood. Somebody's bound to understand me one of these days.

Just as I thought, said Johnny.

What?

No indick about colours.

Colours?

You know nothing at all about colours. Not even that there are such things.

Red, I suggested. Blue.

I was just going to mention the fancy colour tangerine when Johnny came out with, Exactly, red and blue. No subtleties, no shades, no depth, no taste. The lads are all just the same. What a world you lot live in. No colour. No smell. No taste. Swot up your colours a bit, you'll see. You'll need another indickybox.

Why couldn't Johnny teach me then, if he was such a wizard at colours and smells and tastes? But Johnny wasn't interested in teaching. Catalogue Chris would have to swot it all up on his own. Look it up in your books.

He used my Catalogue name in a way which was marvellously different from the rest of the lads. It was like an honorary form of address the way he said it. Nice and gentle, with smiling little quotation marks all round it.

I told him I'd looked up tangerine, but couldn't find it. Have you made it up yourself?

Hell no! Get yourself some bigger books, Chris old lad!

One day he happened to drift into the drawing room and catch sight of the tiled stove, and he was a goner.

Jimminy Cricket, one of them! he said, gaping. And for Chrissake, the tears started rolling down his cheeks. Johnny!

I hadn't a clue what was going on, but I flung some wood in and set fire to it. Johnny sat all huddled up in front of the grate, while Mum and Dad padded around as if it was Christmas Eve. Sandwiches were served up in front of the stove.

Johnny eventually let on he hadn't seen one of them things since he was a kid.

I almost expected him to start off on his memoirs at last, featuring open fires and loads more poetic scenes from the idyllic past. But if that was about to happen, he was put off by Mum roaring with laughter and giving him a big hug and saying excuse me but really, you really are still a kid. So not all chances are lost yet.

The odds are that Mum made Johnny really embarrassed by hugging him like that. But he let her, didn't get really mad as you might have expected when you think of how he used to wallop anybody who dared to tell him he looked little. He let himself be hugged, in the warmth of the tiled stove. I looked the other way, like a true gentleman.

From then on he had another excuse for coming round, as well as the Tizer and Millie. A tiled stove. But he didn't cry any more when he saw it, thank God. It was harder to cope with Johnny's tears than with my own.

Johnny evidently couldn't care less about getting home by a particular time. He never seemed to care about what his folks might think. I've never been able to feel indifferent like that. Not cos I'd get walloped if I came home at some impossible time now and then, but you get used to the law and order routine: back home by dark o'clock, or not much later at any rate, otherwise we want to know where you are, Chris, because you never know what might happen if you're just wandering about the town.

When Sis came back from her secret mission, Johnny generally went more or less straight away, cos she could never get used to his fantastic thatch, nor to his fabulous eyes. All of smashing Johnny set Sis a-quiver. So when she came home and he was there, she'd start to m a k e a d v a n c e s. It was worst of all when he was in our room, cos then she could block his exit, as it were. Dad was frightened she'd gobble Johnny up one of these days.

84

Johnny never said anything, maybe he thought I'd be offended; a sis is a sis, blood bond and all that. But good God: there are limits, even for a sister, so I told him to dot her one if she got too much of a pain in the neck, it was OK by me, just in case he wanted to know. But he could never do that, he reckoned. A girl!

In any case, he usually thought it was about time he was leaving just as Suzie turned up. And as she turned up later and later as winter drew on, Johnny left to go home later and later. But he never stayed the night. That would have caused a few problems, cos where could he have slept? Next to my bed? Sis would have had heart failure over in her corner. Or come creeping up to finger his thatch.

That's how it started and that's how it developed and that's how it went on. It isn't just cos Johnny had floored me recently that the lads leave it to me to speak about Johnny when the cop starts asking questions. We were a pair. Everybody knew that as soon as it started.

The more the cop asks, the more obvious it is the others haven't a clue about Johnny. If the stage around me could be any emptier than it is now, it would be as soon as the cop starts asking about Johnny's thoughts, and what he said. I know a bit, but maybe not enough. And what I do know might not be suitable for cop's ears.

It's only afterwards, when you've been through all that happened like this, that you realize how blind you were then, when it was all going on. It never occurred to me there was anything odd about Johnny and his Secret Home. Not even on the ninth of December, it was a Thursday, when he said, just before he went home that night, that he was going on holiday tomorrow, so I won't be seeing you for a month.

I was a bit taken aback. Holiday?

Hesitant, errr, well, you see . . . hum, it's like this . . . and mumble mumble about some uncle or other in mumbletown.

And that's how it was. He was away for a month.

Turned up again on the tenth of January, the Monday our term started.

I reckoned it was dead boring when he was away. Christmas Eve, Christmas Day, New Year, Twelfth Night, it could all have been great fun if only Johnny'd been there. But it never occurred to me then that, well it was dead boring all right, but not that it was odd as well. And he didn't say a word about his so-called holiday when he got back. But *that* was nothing special, that was Johnny's style.

You so rarely opened up the tiniest little door to your life out there at Bjurholmsplan. I waited and waited and asked you practically nothing at all, because curiosity is a deadly sin on a par with cowardice. All doors are closed when Curiosity comes along. Of course, I reaped my reward, or however one should put it, when you finally opened up. I got to know without asking. But I didn't catch on. And now the cop's here, Johnny, and I'd love to know how much I ought to tell him.

Winter helped to widen the gap between me and the rest of the lads. In the autumn there was still nothing to stop me going out, after gulping down my dinner, and chasing up the gang. Then came winter, and the pile of homework got higher as the nights got darker. If you were at South Side Grammar, there was nothing odd about you disappearing from view for weeks on end. If I missed the swimming session one Wednesday it could be four whole weeks. If it hadn't been for Johnny, I'd have been a forgotten man, snowed over by silence. As it was, I did exist: Chris? Oh, do you mean Catalogue Chris, that egghead Johnny likes?

Or whatever it was they said when I wasn't around to hear. I wasn't cast out, just buried in a grave of homework. Nobody would ever have asked where I was if it hadn't been for Johnny.

Sometimes I asked myself, dared to ask, why Johnny had picked on me, and why he clung on to me. I didn't have an answer, of course. A bottomless crate of Tizer, a nightly pile of sandwiches, a tiled stove and a guinea pig. Was that the complete answer? I liked to think that I myself meant something to him. Johnny meant an awful lot to me, but don't ask me what.

Winter played havoc with Johnny's Adidas: by the end of February, when it was freezing cold, those proud kangaroo-skin shoes were in tatters. Mum kept sighing more and more heavily, dried them and looked after them every night, but they became a right mess even so.

One evening there was an awful stink in the flat. It was the smell of burnt Adidas coming from the oven.

Dad told Mum off for ruining those lovely shoes, then disappeared. Johnny sat fiddling with what was left of them and tried to force his face into an itdoesn'tmatter expression, but he couldn't quite manage it, cos his beloved Adidas were no use at all except as charcoal sticks.

On top of that there was Mum going round tutting, and insisting it did matter, it was awful, how could she . . .

When the mourning was at its height, Sis came home from her secret mission. Her supersensitive nasal organ quivered and shrunk, and she started flinging open all the windows and moaning about the pong, what on earth was it that stank so horrible? Were we out of our minds!

Mum slammed all the windows shut again, cos we didn't want to freeze to death, and Sis flung them all open again, and for once she didn't even look at Johnny. He was just sitting there roaring with laughter at the pandemonium all around him when Dad came back in and threw him a parcel. Containing a brand new pair of wine-red Adidas.

The Sports Shop in Götgatan had them in, he said. Make sure you keep them well away from Mother!

Johnny eased his feet into the new arrivals, and they stuck fast straight away. He handed the bits of cinder to Suzie: You can have these.

Ingratitude is typical of my sister.

Dad's way with the truth is masterly. It's true that the Sports Shop had Johnny's Adidas in, and that's exactly what Dad said. But that shop closes at 18.00 and doesn't open again until about nine the next morning, not even if Mr Chief Clerk Nordberg knocks at the door and asks to buy a pair of the most expensive footwear on the market. My father was remarkably unaffected after having run the distance to the shop there and back, up and down the hill, and he'd clocked up an amazing world record time for the distance as well. Gunder Hägg took two minutes longer. Wearing spikes, on a cinder track.

These Adidas?

The cop takes Johnny's shoes out of the car.

No doubt about it.

As no doubt as you can be, about a pair of wine-red Adidas with no Johnny in them.

Here we are with Johnny's bicycle, Johnny's Tangerinos, Johnny's Adidas.

All stuff Johnny would never let out of his sight.

I made a point of inviting Johnny to my birthday party on the fourth of March, to make sure he didn't miss the one day when the whole gang would be round, for a change.

Twelve is the magical dividing line, we all know that. I don't care what grown-ups say, but that's when your childhood comes to an end. The only person I knew who could keep going after his twelfth birthday, and even his thirteenth, was Bert. He was fourteen now. He was a wise man all right, but he used to bring his talk down to our level, and he was brilliant at holding the gang together. He was a terrific yakker, was Bert: talk it over first, then thump 'em, but only if you have to. When Bert had finished talking, you rarely had to thump 'em.

Anyway, Johnny, it's my birthday on Friday. Easy to remember: born 4.3.43. Everybody's coming. You as well.

But no, no, he wasn't.

Why not?

No. Johnny didn't celebrate birthdays.

He didn't need to come and celebrate, he could just come round as usual.

No, cos now you'd gone and said it was your birthday, and Johnny didn't celebrate birthdays. Like I said.

Why not, when you've been invited?

No, cos I refuse to accept age.

Eh?

Johnny said it again.

Refuse to accept?? Me, I'm only too glad to be getting

older. Every year, on the fourth of March: one step nearer human dignity. One step nearer the day when not every grown-up can grab you and go on about how they think somebody like me ought to behave.

Johnny looked dubiously at me and repeated, Glad? with lots of question marks after.

How old was he, then? Wasn't it nice not to be eight, for instance?

I don't have an age, matterfact, said Johnny, and I never will, matterfact. Cos I've no intention of ever celebrating a birthday, matterfact.

I let him go at that point, didn't ask him any more, didn't discuss it any further. He'd opened a door just a little bit, but I didn't understand what I saw inside. But don't ask questions! The door might close again then. Wait instead!

. Maybe he wasn't all that odd, in fact. I thought of Pippi Longstocking, as she sits making up rhymes:

> Lovely sweeties in my cup,
> I don't want to be growed-up.

Pippi was a fairytale character though, put in her own house with no parents, more or less, and outside all rules and reality. When grown-ups tried anything, she could make it rebound on them. An ordinary little kid has to be pleased he can grow up till he's old enough to look after himself. Then he's grown-up as well, and there's no point to it any more.

I don't want to be growed-up, I muttered, and then asked Johnny if he'd read *Pippi Longstocking*. Cos him and her were two of a kind, and they'd probably get on well together – though I was careful not to say *that*.

No, Johnny hadn't, never heard of Pippi Long-chicken, though God knows how he'd managed that.

When I took the book off the shelf, he glowered at the red-haired freckly picture I'd always thought was terrific. Johnny had no desire to read that thing.

I promised him he'd like the book, once he started he

wouldn't be able to put it down, she's so strong she can lift a horse, she lives all on her own with a chest of gold sovereigns in Villekulla Cottage, a fantastic place . . .

Johnny wasn't a professor, matterfact, so he wasn't going to start swotting up on all that stuff. Do you know you're pretty weird, Chris, you really are!

I've never thought of myself that way. How do you mean?

Well, you're so stuffed up with weird facts and deep thoughts, and an ordinary bloke hasn't a clue what you're on about half the time, matterfact. You've got card indicks and dreams of being growed-up dropping out of your ears. And then you start drooling on about a k i d ' s b o o k! Some made-up rubbish! Have you a screw loose or something? I reckon so, if you ask me, matterfact.

I objected, of course. I was just keeping in touch. You've got to keep a bit of the kid inside you, even though you're growing up. Eleven now, knocking twelve. If you've ever been eleven – twelve even – you'll know what I mean!

Johnny just roared with laughter, the dark green glint disappeared from his eye and he thumped me gently in the chest. No! That's just it, see: I've never been eleven or twelve. Never will be neither, so I'll never get what you're on about.

So I didn't think my twelfth birthday came up to scratch when Johnny wasn't around on that day of all days last winter. But it got even worse, cos the days went by and there was no sign of Johnny. Had I said something stupid after all?

On the fourteenth of March I went past Bjur-holmsplan, but saw no trace of him. On the twentieth of March I went past that same Bjurholmsplan again, same result. I pretended to be examining the green Studebaker and stood close behind it for several hours, rode around the block a few times, came back but the place was still Johnnyless.

91

At least I got to know a bit about the geography of the district.

You didn't happen to notice the registration number of that Studebaker, I suppose?

Happen! When you see a luxury liner like that, of course you write down the number automatically. I thumb through my diary, but it's the wrong year. I'd noted the number when Bert and I followed Johnny home that day. The right year was in my archive drawer.

But it has a Stockholm number, started with 3, I remember that, and ended with a 6. Or was it a 9?

The information is passed on to the cop's mate, who starts wittering into his mike again.

All this time the weather was very cavalier, in a nasty sort of way, with snow one day and spring sunshine the next. Weather like that hurts when you're feeling lonely.

On the twenty-fifth, I went round again, but I wasn't slinking this time. I went close, right up to the cycle repair shop and tried to see if I could make out anything through the window, but it was like looking through plywood. Layers of mud and muck from all the seven hundred years since Stockholm was founded got in the way. It must be eternal night in there.

I tried turning the door handle. No problem, but the door was locked, of course.

I tried to read the sign over the door, but it was in the same state as the windows. Seven hundred years, and caked on thick. The first letter could easily have been C and the last one S, and the word was just about long enough for it to have been CYCLES.

The sixth of April, a Wednesday, the last day at school before the Easter holidays, I was marching along to school good and early for once. I generally observe the rule which says the nearer you live, the harder it is to get there on time.

A couple of old dears were standing outside

92

Lambert's, keeping one eye on the school yard through the snowflakes.

But just fancy, it's on the front page! I heard one of them say.

Way off among the snow flurries, the caretaker was just coming back from the flagpole.

Never! croaked old dear number two. Surely they're not putting the flag up just for a boy, I can't believe that.

The flag was trying to fly valiantly in among the snowflakes, yes, very true. But only halfway up.

Half mast!?

Do you know, every single paper's writing about it.

But not just for a boy, surely not!

I leapt on the old girl, slit her throat and kicked her down the nearest drain. No! There was no time to assassinate old dears. I was already flying up the stairs, on my way into the kitchen, without taking my shoes off. When that old girl snuffs it, they'll be flying the flag in triumph. She knows that. That's why she's so jealous.

A boy?

I grabbed the newspaper. But, my dear brother . . .

Shut up, Sis, shut up! And I read, read, read.

FATHER AND SON DIE
IN BLAZE AT BROMMA

(picture of a burnt-out chalet)

The homicide squad was summoned to the Kortenslund holiday chalets near Bromma airport on Tuesday afternoon. Karl Hildur Andersson, a cobbler of 57 Södermannagatan in Stockholm and his thirteen-year-old son Per Anders had been found dead after a fire in the family chalet. The son had head injuries which led the police to suspect violence. The father was an invalid and walked with the aid of crutches . . .

Do you mind, give me that newspaper back! Sis grabbed it, but I grabbed it back again.

93

The tragedy appears to have happened in mysterious circumstances. Relatives of the deceased had no idea the father and son were intending to go to the chalet. When the fire brigade arrived at the scene, they found the door locked from the inside and the key in the lock. The father was lying dead on a bed. The son was on the floor just inside the door. He may have been trying to escape, but been prevented. Homicide will continue their investigation on Wednesday. Police inquiries have so far established that after leaving school at about three o'clock, Per Anders went to his father's shoe repair shop at Bjurholmsplan, and that the pair of them then went to the chalet. They may have driven there by car, or could have taken a bus. The father is known to have been very depressed recently.

Poor little kid, said Mum over my shoulder.

I yelled like a madman, frothing at the mouth, you say that about everybody, don't you! Slammed the door and brought the ceiling down, raced down the stairs, Kvarngatan, school yard, and the caretaker closed the door just a little bit more slowly, just a tiny bit, so that Christopher Nordberg managed to squeeze through (Nordberg's come, so everybody must be here. My daily greeting from the caretaker) and get to his place in the hall, right at the front, on the outside, where 1C were supposed to be.

It said Per Anders, right? It said Per Anders. Twice.

I spent twenty minutes muttering my own morning prayers. The worst thing was, the pic of the burnt-out chalet had an insert with a blurred picture of the dead thirteen-year-old, and I couldn't make out if the blur hid his real appearance, or if it emphasized his features, no idea, but it could be Johnny, it looked like Johnny, it mustn't be Johnny, it was Johnny I saw in the newspaper on Wednesday morning, but surely it couldn't be Johnny, what had Johnny got to do with Per Anders . . .

The Headmaster started rambling on and – My God!

What a relief! – asked for a minute's silence for our schoolmate who had passed on in such tragic circumstances, Per Anders Andersson, from 2C.

I was on the point of yelling out and hugging Nyborg, who was sitting next to me, but I realized at the last moment what decency required of me. We stood up, and the silence to end all silences built up layer by layer in the hall. No superficial sounds of gaiety penetrated the room from outside, a prefect was posted at each of the exits, keeping watch on every one of the hundred or so boys in his sector who had been excluded from morning assembly because of late arrival or concessions due to travelling distance, and not yet allowed into the corridors for registration. Karlsson, at the front, had the drooping flag at half mast to help him dampen down the playfulness of the lower school. Ekholm, at the back, raised his hand and pointed over the heads of the sixth-formers at no one knew what, but they took off their caps and silence reigned. The prefects at all the doors stood to attention.

That's how an ancient school pays tribute to one of its pupils who has died, died in tragic circumstances.

For the rest of the day, every kid in 2C had a group round him asking questions, but nobody knew more than was in the newspapers.

I tried to remember what this Andersson looked like, wondering if I knew him at all.

He was our goalkeeper, said one of the 2C boys wistfully. We haven't got one now.

Then I remembered who he was. Not much like Johnny in fact. Quite small, but a wizard in goal! You could never forget him once you'd seen him diving after the ball, completely ignoring his own safety.

I took the incident as an excuse for another excursion to Bjurholmsplan. I was evidently not the only one. Bjurholmsplan had become a place of pilgrimage that Wednesday evening, and a constant stream of curious folk filed past the cobbler's workshop, paused, but could no doubt see nothing interesting, cos the window was caked up with seven hundred years' mud and muck.

Exactly. Thunder rumbled and shattered my skull. I'd got over the shock of that morning. Now here came the next bomb. I counted the doors and pinched myself on the arm and changed my standpoint, but no matter what I did, what I saw clashed with my memory of what I'd seen before, most recently last Friday, and the Friday before that, the twenty-fifth, that is, and so on.

I looked and looked, but there was no getting away from it. The sign was grotty and cracked and had been there since time began. You could just about manage to make out that the word began with a C, and could maybe end with an R, and was just long enough for the word COBBLER. If I'd a ladder in my pocket, I swear I'd have climbed up and had a really good look.

That was when I realized the price for having a twenty-minute prayer answered, a prayer that went, Dear God, don't let, don't let . . . , was that a cycle repair shop had changed into a cobbler's.

I cycled home very slowly, but turned off towards Bert's place. Rang the bell and, surprise, surprise, he was in and welcomed me with a delighted grin: Chris, a voice from the past! Are you still alive?

What a sight he looked! Problems with spots and pimples? Try our new wonder cure, Prittiface . . .

I shouldn't make fun of an invalid. These spots are called chicken-pox. The little kids caught it and brought it home, and since then it's spread like the Black Death. Itches more than the Black Death. So make it quick, chicken-pox gives you a pretty short fuse.

I knocked on the door of his memory. Could he remember last autumn? Could he remember Johnny's stepracing? . . . Bert sighed with pleasure . . . Did he remember our little detective trip?

Bert could remember we'd agreed to forget it.

But now you've got to remember again, Bert! Let's

have a demonstration of your famous photographic super-memory: What kind of a shop was it that Johnny took his cycle into, over there at Bjurholmsplan?

What shop?

Come on, Bert the Memory Man, don't disappoint me. Don't you remember he carried his cycle into a shop?

You're rambling, Chris! Are you sure it isn't you who's got the fever, eh?

Stop mucking me about, Bert. You know I haven't got much of a sense of humour. What did Johnny do at Bjurholmsplan? Didn't he carry his cycle in? What did he carry his cycle into?

Bert raised himself up to his full height and pronounced into the void, Johnny dismantled his bike into three parts: two wheels and the rest. He took the wheels in through the entrance door. The rest through the next door down.

There you are, Bert! Would he mind coming round now to what kind of a shop it was, attached to the next door down. It's important this is, Bert, my whole sanity rests on your reply.

Hell, but you're still rambling, Chris. Don't come blaming me cos your mind's gone.

Oh, for hell's sake, Bert! You're contradicting yourself. First you say he carried the remains of the cycle into the shop, then you say he didn't carry it in. It must be a terrible thing, chicken-pox.

It's you who don't understand, Catalogue Chris. I've been working hard every day to try and forget everything, cos that's what we agreed to do. But blow me if I don't remember there wasn't any shop there at all.

I started to get really worried, cos Bert looked as if he meant what he said. I'd had enough shocks for one day. And now to be told I'd remembered the entire thing quite wrongly set the whole earth rocking.

In the end Bert couldn't keep his face straight any longer, grinned, and poked me in the stomach with a, Ssss, it wasn't a shop, see! It was a workshop, dammit!

God, how pedantic you are today, Bert. You nearly frightened the life out of me.

But Bert raised his hand to prevent me going any further. I couldn't possibly say *that*. Anyone else, OK; but I mustn't complain about Bert being exact. It's very important, L a n g u a g e is, Christopher. There's a right word for everything. How many times have you said that yourself? And then you have the cheek to say I'm being pedantic. You make me weep, Chris, weep.

Come on, Bert, get a grip. What kind of workshop? That's what I want to know. Can't you be a tiny bit helpful?

At least Bert had had his little joke now, cos his constant dream and hobby was to catch me out on my own *idées fixes*, and he reckoned he scored a real bull's eye this time, and was pleased with himself.

Bert was extremely careful when it came to committing himself, when he was supposed to have been a witness. He couldn't say exactly what kind of a workshop it was. If Johnny took his bike into it, no doubt they sorted out bikes in there. Why have you started stirring all this up?

I told him why. Bert thought it was rotten for the kid, Per Anders Andersson, but he couldn't throw any light on how the workshop had changed. Course, they'd drawn certain conclusions when Johnny heaved his bike in, but they had no proof. Don't jump to conclusions, Chris!

Anyway, it's not all that odd, come to that. They might have changed everything behind that door hundreds of times since we were there. Haven't you got any statistics about guest rooms in that card index of yours? Yesterday a dump for mending bikes, today a cobbler's, tomorrow they'll be churning out nuts and bolts. We've been through all that hundreds of times, Chris.

What do you mean?

That when you close your eyes, everything disappears, and when you open them to check, everything comes back again. Things do get a bit chaotic now and then, you can see that.

That was last year, Bert. We were kids then. Haven't you got over that stage yet? Does chicken-pox set you back a few years?

Why do you think it's called a children's disease? Childish? Is that all the thanks I get for helping you out with your daft theories?

In *Amazed*, the popular new magazine with nothing but science fiction, they've gone in for stories based on the idea that we live in a world with parallel alternatives. The theory Bert was referring to was another deep affair we'd rejected now. It maintained the world only existed in so far as I experience it. It didn't hold water, though; we'd blown it by taking it in turns to close our eyes. It only took us a couple of hours to explode that theory of the world.

It's much harder to prove the alternative world theory is wrong, and even more difficult to prove it's right. These worlds exist within and alongside each other with no distance between them, but various gaps in our senses mean we can only experience our own world. Just occasionally, when there's a catastrophe, or an explosion, or you're in some special state of mind, depending on who wrote the story, you can get a glimpse into one of these parallel worlds. In some of the stories this puts you in a state of bliss, in others, you feel lousy. Course, the worst is when you go astray and can't get back into your own world again.

When I got home, I noted down on a card:

```
FIRST PROOF:
     Depressed cobbler (KHA)
     broke through the fifth dimension.
     C-workshop (see Bjurholmsplan)
     changed to shoe - ditto.
     Energy for this break-through
     taken from his son (PAA).
     Two lives needed.
     Hol. chalets at Kortenslund.
     Södermannagatan 57.
```

I waved the card about to dry the ink. You don't blot secret cards. Nobody can tell who might come looking for what, and you can read what it says on blotting paper through a mirror. The enemy is good at codes. The enemy might bribe Sis to rummage round in my secret hiding places. Or she might do it herself out of curiosity. Just as bad. We share a room, but my life is my own. I don't go through her drawers.

I put the card behind Johnny's, Johnny's card, where it just said:

```
JOHNNY.
     Bicycle.
     Tangerine.
     Bjurholmsplan.



```

That's all I knew about him. But FIRST PROOF had to do with Johnny.

I won't pretend I believed that stuff I wrote about the

fifth dimension. As long as you're on the right side of the loony bin door, and that's the outside as far as I'm concerned, you can distinguish between the world represented by *Amazed*, and actual reality. But what *should* I believe?

The enemy is good at codes, that's the top and bottom of it. I reckon the kind of enemy who reads my secret cards just out of curiosity will get fed up if I change all my really important thoughts into childish rubbish. A code so perfect that nobody realizes it is a code. Everybody just shrugs: couldn't care less, Chris is still messing around with toys. I'm the only one who knows what it's really all about.

Thursday. It said:

> All the evidence suggests the drama that took place on Tuesday at the Kortenslund chalets near Bromma airport involved a murder and a suicide. The police have established that the son, who was found lying on the floor, had severe head injuries and cuts on his throat and on one of his wrists. The father, who was lying in a lower bunk, had cuts on one wrist. Among the burnt-out ruins investigators found a small axe and a sheath knife. There was a distinct smell of paraffin in the debris around the boy's body.
>
> The motive for the incident seems to have been Mr Andersson's personal worries and the depression these led to. Andersson was very fond of his son, and it seems he wished to have his company in death.

Are you very fond of me? I asked Dad.

Yes, but I'm not depressed. Why are you studying that so carefully? Dad wasn't used to seeing me poring over any pages apart from the sports results and the cartoons. I explained I was interested because Per Anders Andersson had gone to South Side Grammar.

Oh!

What does depressed mean?

Dad pointed at the dictionary. When you're at home, with books in easy reach, you can never get him to answer a question. It's supposed to be more useful for you to look it up for yourself.

> **depress** [f.Latin DE + primere] to press down;
> to dispirit, cast a gloom over, make miserable.
> **depression** a mental disorder characterized by
> reduction in vigour, vitality or spirits;
> a reduced condition of trade and prosperity.

Ah, miserable.

Extremely miserable, added Dad.

I tried in vain to find some criterion, something to help me understand this miserability, a misery so deep you want to take somebody you're fond of into death with you. Although I didn't feel like that myself, I could understand you might want to follow somebody you were fond of into death. But this?

A black hole for others to live next to. With crumbling edges, yawning black, with no protective fence.

Per Anders flings his thirteen-year-old body after the ball, and keeps a clean sheet. 2-0 to 2C, 3-0, 4-0. He always kept a clean sheet. And then his dad turns to him after locking the door on the inside and exchanging one of his crutches for a little axe and a sheath knife. Per Anders dives for his life between the walls of the family holiday chalet at Kortenslund near Bromma airport. He's little and fast and his dad's an invalid, so Per Anders' chances are good, but he keeps trying the door and it's always locked; his only chance is to dive straight out of the window, what do a few scars matter compared to life, but deep down he just can't believe his dad is really trying to kill him, that Mr Andersson is so fond of his son he wants to have his company in death, and a goalkeeper is more used to facing up to what comes than getting out of the way, and so all of a sudden . . .

It's ages since Johnny was here. Dad's voice. But what on *earth*'s the matter, Chris!

Cos I'd jumped up, and my reason had flown out somewhere into the fifth dimension, and been replaced by a devilish fury. I yelled at Dad to leave me alone, stop interfering in everything all the time. Johnny's not your pal after all. He doesn't live here either, does he, eh . . .

Mum dashed in and stared at me and Dad. When he shook his head slightly, maybe it was meant to be invisible, she went back to whatever she was doing.

I don't know what came over me.

And so it was Easter, the coldest Easter for seventy-two years. So they said, I didn't bother to check. Statistics for Easter are meaningless, I reckon, cos Easter moves around all the time. Still, it was cold, though.

Or so they said. I had to stay in with chicken-pox, which broke out the moment I'd finished yelling at Dad. He nearly died laughing and said some people are punished by the gods, express delivery. It was after Easter Eve before I could see the funny side of it all. Before that, I felt far too prickly.

After that, I didn't feel too bad. Sis had to run for it. She's scared stiff of bacilli, apart from everything else. Especially the kind that could produce spots on her pretty face. And so I was left in peace from Maundy Thursday to Easter Monday, and then another week on top of that, just to be on the safe side. She just disappeared into thin air, don't ask me where, and I had some smashing days with bags of time to catch up on my card index system.

I'd been really idle all winter and just let the statistics pile up, but now I caught up again. Records tumble, sales increase, people die and emigrate, and I have to keep abreast of it all. I was four months behind with the lottery results, and that was something that had never happened before. And car numbers!

I have a fountain pen with an extra-fine nib. That way you can get as much as you like on a single card. I wasn't allowed to use that pen for Einar Theodor's maths tests, of course. For them you needed the horrible nibs on sale in the caretaker's office. You had to fit them onto the clumsy holders the caretaker also sold, and dip them in the useless ink provided by the school. And God help anybody who makes a blot on his sums. Course, there were blots on the sums in these circumstances. Come out here! What's the meaning of this? Bend over! Swish, or tap, with the cane. Swish and a red stripe on your backside for Petterson & Co., who needed a firm hand to keep them in order. Playful little taps for me and those of my fortunate friends who had shown themselves to be quite clever actually, so that those annoying blots were just minor blemishes, aesthetic beauty-spots adorning the calculations.

My own posh pen didn't make blots, even though it was a bit shaky in bed as I brought my archives up to date. Sorting things out and putting them in order kept me so busy I forgot to feel worried about Johnny not being around. Maybe the simple explanation was that he'd just had chicken-pox, and then something else similar. I pretended. But another part of me counted up all the days in March and the ever-increasing number in April, and said there was no known illness that lasted that long. And nobody had ever heard of Johnny being ill. As far as I know, there were no bacilli that bit Johnny. It was something else.

And so I lived through an April that broke all low temperature records. The old country folk reckoned there was bound to be a hot summer as a result.

On the fifteenth of April Mum reported that the school flag was flying at half mast again. By the afternoon it had been raised to the top. I insisted on knowing why. It was Per Anders Andersson's funeral.

Funeral?

I looked up the encyclopaedia and studied the rituals with which we mark the end of our lives. Then wrote a card for Per Anders Andersson, what little I knew: date of death and funeral. If Johnny didn't turn up soon, I'd insist on them opening up the grave and checking it out.

The last snow of the season fell on Thursday, 21st April.

104

That was also the last day I was allowed to stay at home. Fit again, peace and quiet at an end. But my card index was up to date.

Various schoolmates had taken it in turns to come round and pass on the homework, so I wasn't worried about going back on the Friday and coming up against Anteater in the first lesson. That's what he's called, our Swedish master. Or what we call him, to be more precise. His real name's Syrius. I don't think his conk's all that remarkable, really. His paws are much more impressive: great big dinner plates with loads of strength, and he used them to bash us on the bonce and sweep the floor with us. But he got his nickname ages ago, and he's stuck with it.

Arthur Syrius came down like a wolf on the fold,
His sharp fangs were flashing in silver and gold;
The glint in his eye made us shake at the knee
As he launched his attack on my classmates and me . . .

And so on; I forget what comes next. It's not just the prefects and the hoariest of the ancient teachers who carry on the school tradition. Everybody enjoys passing on the lampoons and nicknames.

Now Anteater was marching up and down the rows making chalk crosses on the desks next to the inkwells if anybody managed to parse correctly the weird and wonderful sentences he gave us.

The first-form classrooms are in a row on the ground floor in the west wing of South Side Grammar, and 1C is last in line, next to the glass doors leading to the sixth-form annexe and above all, Refec. The best place in the whole lower school when the lunch bell goes and you're racing to get first in the queue. In the past, several heroes from 1C were shoved through the glass by third-formers racing up, and so they've put reinforced panes in the doors. They don't break any more now, and we don't have to get minced up.

But it's not lunchtime now, it's the first lesson, and Swedish, the language of honour and heroes, and the view I have through the window overlooks our front door, and I could spend the whole day keeping an eye on the comings and goings of Mum and all the ladies in the neighbouring flats, if I wanted to.

And so, just after Mum's disappeared in the direction of Maria Prästgårdsgata, I can see straight away the familiar tangerine figure riding up and leaning his bicycle outside the front door.

He goes in. After the time it takes to go upstairs and belt on the door, wait in vain for somebody to open, and come down again, he comes back into view.

He stands there looking round, then pulls at the hand, the knocker, that is. I can't do anything to contact him. On the contrary: Anteater's standing over me, inviting me in a loud voice to point out the adverbial phrase, adverb of place, in the sentence: I am sitting dreaming and wishing I were out there through the window.

When I fail to answer, he drops one of his dinner plates on my head. First he twists my head round towards the rest of the class, and then he presses with his thumb on the right-hand side so that my head is forced down on to the desk. He holds me there for a while, and is trying to push me right through the desk-top; but I'm not there. I can't hear his voice, can't feel his touch, can't see any of the leering faces of my classmates. Johnny has turned up again, and he wants me for something; but I can't reach him.

There's no chalk for my bench. Anteater lets me go, hammers his gaze onto mine and shouts something which I think is, In this case the adverb governs a preposition phrase. So?

But I haven't a clue what he's on about. All around me my so-called friends are giggling: they're outside the danger zone at the moment, but their turn will come, don't worry. Cos Anteater's way has nothing to do with disliking me, not that I know of. That's just the way he is. Great for those who love the bloke, maybe, if there are any such creatures; I doubt it.

I try to get away with it by answering: I didn't hear the question.

Nordberg is sitting dreaming and wishing he were somewhere outside, Anteater announces in a loud voice. Then he whips round in a flash and yells, Adverb, Bergman!

I take the opportunity of checking Johnny's still there, twisting my head round despite the pain. He seems to be standing still in the doorway, holding onto the door knob, hesitating whether to go or to stay. Stay where you are, Johnny! Stay where you are!

At long last, the bell goes. Say what you like about Anteater, but he never keeps us behind a single second after the bell goes. I fling the window wide open and shout to Johnny, who just has time to register what's going on before a dinner plate heaves me back into the classroom and an angry voice shouts, Now look here, young man! I'm grasped by the scruff of my neck. I'll wipe the floor with you, Nordberg, if you don't learn how to parse, and to behave yourself. A good shaking. Then: At South Side Grammar, when the bell rings we go out through the d o o r .

And with that he flings me out to where I'm aching to be: in the corridor. No need to ask me twice to run away. But of course, one is not allowed to run in the corridors of South Side Grammar. P.G. Reinhard M.A., schoolmaster and librarian, emerges from his sojourn with 1A and raises his briefcase in order to put a stop to the criminal exceeding the speed limit. As I slam on the brakes, brake even more, screech to a halt, he raises his ironical eyebrows, smiles his ironical smile, wags his ironical index finger, his left hand, and declaims a few well-chosen ironical words, which thank goodness are lost in the general row. It's OK to make a row at playtime provided there are lots of us. He lowers his stop sign, and I'm free to go. I said, Walk!

I reckoned that by now I had done enough to observe the fifteenth paragraph, part two, of the school rules regarding good behaviour: Pupils will acknowledge and obey the authority of their teachers, and comply with their instructions, reprimands and punishments.

The next aged prat to try his instructions, reprimands

and punishments on me could reckon with a kick on the shins. Remarkably enough, there were no more candidates.

Johnny had seen me all right, and was waiting patiently. But what a sight he was!

His face and neck were covered in horrible bruises, and I hardly dared think what he looked like lower down. He wasn't just leaning on the door, he was holding himself up by the door knocker. The delicate little girl's hand with the long history had the honour of holding Johnny upright.

C-c-can I b-b-borrow your p-p-pit and l-l-lie down for a bit? he asked the moment I came. Never heard him sound so miserable, never seen him so shattered.

I nodded, and wheeled his bicycle into the hallway for him, and locked it. He didn't even ask for the key, but staggered upstairs in front of me. I let him in, and Millie started scampering around in circles, but Johnny made a bee-line for my bed and slumped down. I reckon he was asleep even before I took his Adidas off. When I tried to loosen his tangerino top, he started squirming, so I just flung a blanket over him and had a good look at his face. It really hurt; just looking at him hurt something awful. What could make such long, red, gashes? Had he been w h i p p e d across his face?

I stood his shoes in the middle of the floor in front of the hall door so that Mum could see something was up when she came back.

All I could do then was dash back to school. It was English now, and: Look here, this won't do. This won't do, Nordberg. We have a ten-minute break, not thirteen minutes, Mr G.G. thought we'd settled that little matter last autumn, and not to put too fine a point on it, haven't we had about enough of these little excursions, Nordberg?

And Mr G.G. made a note in his register and demanded to know where I'd been for the whole of the long break plus three extra minutes, because this won't do, you know.

I said I'd just nipped home, but I could see from his sinking eyebrows that this wouldn't do either, I'd given him the wrong answer. Practically any other answer would have been better; wrong perhaps, but better: you don't just nip home when an English lesson is looming. In any case, that couldn't be true, because Mr G.G. knew I was lying, he'd known for a long time that everything I'd said was lies, lies, and now I was telling another obvious lie.

I was one of the terror gang, of course. And now he'd caught me, more or less in the act.

Mr G.G. kept pressing for more information, so that ten more valuable lesson minutes went to waste, but even so, I couldn't hit on any better explanation for why I'd been late. Telling him why I'd really gone home would have been a complete waste of time.

For just one marvellous moment, I toyed with the idea of spinning some yarn about how two of the prefects had stopped me and wouldn't let me go till I was hopelessly late. That kind of thing did happen now and again in fact, too often. The lads who suffered from such treatment and came racing in after the lesson had started got a black mark for being late, didn't dare tell tales, of course. The prefects were highly regarded. Such things just didn't happen. And anybody who squealed was in for big trouble later.

My idea was a crafty counter-attack. The point was, there'd be a complaint against the prefects without any incident having taken place. So, they wouldn't know who'd shopped them. Me, I'd run away and hide, swearing blind I didn't dare come out and name the two prefects involved, cos if I did, they'd mark me for life. No doubt they would as well, if I just picked on two of them at random.

No matter what happened next, there was a pretty good chance something or other would come out to cause trouble for the prefects.

I dropped the idea before it had gone too far. There were risks. You couldn't trust Mr G.G. He might get to grips with the story and, in order to throw light on the matter, line up the prefects with me marching up and down in front of the swine to pick out two of them.

And my face would be imprinted on the memory of each and every one of the swine, and they'd all know the tale had been made up by this particular little lad, and this little lad might well know that the little tale had been true over and over again in the past, but wasn't true on this particular occasion, and so this little lad could count on big big problems in the future.

Not just a thorough roughing up to warn him never to do it again, but also! Also! How would Christopher Nordberg ever manage to get past a prefect and into Refec? How would Christopher Nordberg ever manage to get out into the yard for breaks quick enough, and back in again? How would Christopher Nordberg cope with all the black marks he would accumulate?

The South Side Grammar system of self-discipline, so-called self-discipline, gave the prefects enormous power. The system was based on the staff having full confidence in the people who presided over and enforced the system of self-discipline, and that they responded to this trust. Which is where the snag was. Self-discipline at South Side Grammar is a penal system. Several of the teachers must be aware of that, cos some of the stories have been just *too* peculiar to be true. But they turn a blind eye. Easier that way.

Mr G.G. couldn't be trusted, and anyway he knew I was lying. This was the starting point as far as he was concerned. If two prefects had in fact detained me, unlikely though it might be, that'd be because I'd done something shocking.

So I stuck to the truth. But that didn't help either. Mr G.G.'s eyes had dropped to zero level, now, to a physically impossible minus level, and he made secret entries in his Black Book. If anybody reported criminal activities at Lambert's or EPA or NK or Gothenburg or anywhere else in the world at large, I'd be the obvious culprit. Sit down, Nordberg, and let's hear what you've made of the homework.

There was an unwritten rule that anybody who'd been off ill for some time shouldn't be put on the spot with homework on his first day back. I'd reckoned on cashing in on that rule on Friday and Saturday as well, even though I'd done what I had to do conscientiously enough, to be on the safe side. But when I referred to my lengthy and serious illness with big temperatures and sweaty sheets, Mr G.G. said without further ado it was a bit late to come out with that when I'd already been asked.

He was within his rights, Mr G.G., who knew the rule-book inside out. Anybody who'd not done his home-work, forgotten his books, or had any other excuse, was supposed to announce that right at the start, before the lesson got under way. And there was no rule which said our grossly overworked teachers had to remember every pupil who'd been ill.

My sympathetic classmates mumbled away about me not having come till I'd come, so I couldn't very well have announced anything at all before the lesson started. I didn't bother to bring that up myself, cos I knew Mr G.G. He'd make short shrift of that excuse unless he wanted to lose his reputation as a right swine.

Where would he be then? If you hadn't done your homework, you'd make sure you turned up late so that you couldn't register that fact before the lesson started. Come off it, boys. I'm too long in the tooth for that one. That's not the way it goes when the flak starts flying. Well, Nordberg. Let's hear what you made of the homework.

I'd have done OK on the homework if only Johnny's battered face hadn't kept getting in the way. But now, it sounded as if I hadn't even looked at my English, which was a personal insult to Mr G.G. who devoted all his life and his time to the details designed to make his lessons meaningful and turn me into an able English-speaker from South Side Grammar and a competent Swedish citizen.

And so Mr G.G. made another note in his Black Book, and there was no secret about it, a nice round zero went down against my name in his Black Book. It gave him great pleasure, that swine Mr G.G., cos this marks system was his pride and joy. It was accurate down to the last millimetre, and marks given were honourably exact, in direct proportion to the answers given. Cos that meant the examinee with his justly awarded mark had the option of objecting to the awarded mark, if the examinee with his justly awarded mark dared to question its justice. And it was just and more honourable than we could grasp, ungrateful as we were, since by glancing down his column of marks Mr G.G. could make sure the questions were spread equally among the thirty-five of us, and towards the end of term he could give all of those with many zeros a just and honourable extra chance. A chance to raise their grade, by answering a few extra questions exemplary in their justice and honourable nature.

The marks could vary between zero and two, the twos being for an outstanding performance. It was just and honourable that marks should be given for all answers, cos then any accidental variations in Mr G.G.'s mood and our own day-by-day form would be evened out in the long run. That was just and honourable, cos Mr G.G. was capable of distinguishing between a difficult question and an easy one. That's why the comprehensive answer I might give to an easy question was justly awarded a lower mark than the almost incorrect answer given by Björnson to a difficult question. Cos Björnson was clever, Björnson was, but I couldn't be trusted. Björnson was the only one who got a three in the Black Book every time he opened his mouth and held forth a bit longer than average.

The zero I got now was just and honourable, cos it was my first zero, and zeros were what I was really worth. The ones and twos I'd had so far were awarded out of necessity: the whole class studies the movement of his pen, and the movements required to make a zero are easy to distinguish from those for a one or a two. And so the check we had, plus the quality of my answers, had thus far forced him to give me ones or twos, but he knew I was cheating somehow or other. He'd catch me out one of these fine days.

No doubt there were reasons for Mr G.G.'s suspicions regarding me and everything I did. Suspicion was built into his nature, but he directed more of that commodity towards me than I could understand. I once asked him which aspect of the simple text we had for homework was more important, the vocabulary or the contents. It was about How English People Live, with guff about the weather and drinking tea and coal fires. That might have been when Mr G.G. decided I was a scoundrel and therefore should be kept in check by means of his honourable system of justice.

When I complained at home last autumn, Mum coached me in English pronunciation and tested me on a few words and facts. Dad said I should play it cool, but say if it got too nasty, cos Mr G.G. couldn't operate all on his own, and you could always talk it over with him. If that didn't do any good, there was a headmaster to discuss it with, and if that was no good either, there were always other schools around. So hang on a bit, Chris, and we'll see how it goes, and say if it gets any worse.

That shows how it can be a good thing to have a dad who's a chief clerk. Who knows the right way to talk in the headmaster's office. The rules of the game up there put a master bricklayer at a disadvantage. Not to mention a wino.

When we'd been exposed to Mr G.G. and his just and honourable marking system for a term and had chance to study it, a few of us started making notes about the way in which marks were awarded.

That's why I knew that at that very moment Nilsson or Öström or maybe both of them were noting down that I'd been given my zero after first being interrogated for ten minutes about why I was three minutes late, for which I'd already got a black mark in the register and a cross in Mr G.G.'s Black Book.

The normal rule is three crosses make a black mark;

it's an unwritten rule, but one the staff seem to follow. There mustn't be any inflation as far as black marks are concerned. You don't need many to have your conduct mark reduced.

We eventually intended going to see the Headmaster about our notes. We reckoned we'd established ages ago that the whole system was riddled with injustice. But Nyborg, who had a brother in the sixth form, advised us to lie low till we really had masses of evidence, including a few blatantly obvious cases.

We shouldn't count too much on the Headmaster either, Nyborg warned. His brother's class had boobed on a similar mission when everything had been swept under the carpet at the last minute.

Nyborg's brother, Nyborg the Elder, also tipped us off that we should never have with us at school any more notes than we needed for that particular day. We should save all our material at home, and give copies to each other.

He was very suspicious, Nyborg the Elder was. He reckoned he'd had his fingers burnt, and he knew the methods used at South Side Grammar to make men out of boys. And he didn't trust anybody. He himself used to make notes about everything you could think of, and when anybody asked he'd tell them he was going to have them published in book form when he left school. That book'll set a few heads rolling, he used to claim. Notes from the inside, smuggled out over eight years. Not a load of old rubbish written ten years later, when everybody can claim you've remembered wrongly.

And why not? That's what I say. Make notes so you'll remember and be all the more sure people will believe you. Just now I can't imagine I'll ever forget how crappy it was to be eleven or twelve at this horrible school. I don't w a n t to forget, never, and so a few relevant notes might help. Cos you most probably do forget normally.

I've been looking at those pictures that appeared when they were celebrating the three-hundredth anniversary, but now and then you can see them at other times as well, pictures of blokes grinning and going on about being old South Side Grammarians, that they're proud, that they're happy, that life has treated them well thanks to the Education they received at our school, and they remember that education with pleasure and gratitude. When I was at Maria Elementary School, pictures like that used to make me long to be a pupil at the big school next door. Now I know their prattle just shows they don't remember how it was.

Cos that's the way it's always been. The kids themselves get pounded to pieces for seven or eight years, so as far as they're concerned, they're all for a change in the Spirit and the Traditions. But there are old fogies on the staff who were around when it was the Maria Foundation School and they make jolly sure the correct Traditions are kept alive.

I reckoned Stig Järrel was on the same wavelength as me when he played Caligula in *Frenzy*. Everybody knows he went to South Side Grammar. Everybody knows who his model was. That's why the film has an X certificate, but it's also why they let under-age South Side Grammar pupils in when *Frenzy*'s on at the local flick.

That bit of acting by Stig Järrel ought to have been a real time bomb. The bomb which blew the Spirit and Traditions all the way to Hell. Stig Järrel can't have forgotten. But he won't explode anything. He's sold himself on the cheap for minor comedy roles, and people generally laugh at him. Anybody who appears in tenth-rate sitcoms can't be taken seriously.

When I eventually got home, Johnny was still asleep, and Millie was snuggling up to him. Worst of all: Sis was sitting guard on the edge of the bed, contemplating his face under that fantastic thatch with a worried expression on her face, hushing me, and wondering who on earth could have done anything like this to Johnny.

I'd no idea about that, but what the hell was she doing there?

My beloved sister reminded me she had at least as much right to this room as I had, and that I should keep quiet and be pleased she allowed me to live in her room rather than packing me off to Mum and Dad. Strictly speaking, she was at an age when a girl doesn't have to agree to share a room with her kid brother.

Well, you couldn't really start a brawl with somebody trying to sleep right at your elbow, but I whispered that she really didn't have to sit by the side of my bed in any case.

But she would sit wherever she liked in her own room, and little brother could sit at his desk and get on with his homework.

And then she started smoothing down Johnny's hair!

For God's sake, leave him alone!

But after her little explosion, which was the nearest thing to life I've seen in Sis for some years now, she relapsed into her nurse's trance and didn't hear a word I said. And Johnny was so fast asleep, he no doubt couldn't care less whether she adjusted his fantastic thatch every third minute. She didn't do more than that.

At about five o'clock, it was time for her secret mission, and she relinquished her seat at last.

Johnny slept and slept. I overheard Mum and Dad talking about him. They were on about child abuse and contacting the police and all that, but they obviously got no further than talking about it. In the end, I folded the carpet to make a mattress, and made up a bed on the floor and fell asleep there.

In the middle of the night I was woken up by Johnny waking up. I put the light on and saw him sitting up and looking round in an odd sort of way, but as soon as he could see me and the room, he came to his senses. He asked what time it was, half past two, and started muttering about going home, but I said he might just as well stay now till it got light, seeing as there were only a couple of hours left.

Good thinking, reckoned Johnny, but he desperately needed to go to the loo. I went with him, cos I reckoned nobody knew how shaky he was on his feet, he might need a bit of help.

His Adidas had disappeared. Mum must have hidden them so he couldn't run away; they couldn't have melted into thin air like that otherwise . . . I lent him Sis's mules – anything, quick, before I piss meself – and so we slipped out to the outside loo in the courtyard.

Out there in the dark I asked him a bit hesitantly what on earth had happened to him, but Johnny parried with a What yer mean? Nothing had happened to him, matterfact. Oh, you mean the bruises, the scratches, the swellings? That was nothing. He'd come up against a wino in Götgatan, that's all.

That didn't sound true at all, but I bit my lip and held back the words that wanted to gush out and tell him to come off it, Johnny! I bit my lip so as not to show how hurt I was that he was lying. If it'd been light, he'd have seen what I was going through, but it was dark, and he didn't hear anything either. But he was telling lies all right, and the only thing that could make it hurt a bit less would be if he had very good cause to lie.

It's all very well standing out there in the dark next to the loo and trying to convince yourself that must be the case, but you can't hold back the voice that keeps thrusting itself forward and shouting out questions, shouting, Why on earth?!

Silence also speaks volumes, in its own way. Johnny noticed I wasn't saying anything, cos he asked me if I didn't believe him.

I couldn't very well say, Of course I believe you, Johnny, why shouldn't I believe you, we're big pals, aren't we, so everything's always OK as far as we're concerned. But I was in agonies inside, and a voice was shouting about how that's just what it ought to be like, everything should always be OK between big pals. Yelling so loud I thought I could hear the reproaches echoing all round the courtyard. The more determined I was to keep quiet, the more agony I was going through deep down inside. In my chest, in my throat. What is there that hurts so much there?

Johnny came out of the loo, and suddenly I could feel his hands touching my face. For Chrissake, Chris, you're blubbing!

Can't a bloke be left alone, even in the middle of the night? I screeched, flinging his hands aside. What I really wanted was quite different.

Johnny mumbled something like, OK, OK, and we plodded back upstairs. He didn't turn round to check my face in the light of the hall, thank God. Then he wanted to kip on the floor so that I could have my bed back, but I wouldn't let him.

Johnny lay there twisting and turning in an attempt to find a good sleeping position. I wasn't especially tired just now, but I kept still cos that's the best thing to do when you're on a hard surface.

You'll hear the whole story one of these days. Johnny's voice in the darkness.

I said nothing.

Chris.

I reckoned that if I'm going to hear all about it one of

these days, OK. If not, then at least Johnny won't have made a promise he can't keep. So I didn't hear a word of it. At least he's admitted now that he was lying down there.

I promise. You'll hear absolutely everything one of these days.

I didn't hear that either.

Now I wonder if the time has come when I'm going to find out. Is it the cop who's going to give me the explanations Johnny had promised? Or will the cop go on asking question after question, and then disappear? Johnny all beaten up interests the cop no end. He makes loads of notes. Mutters, The twenty-second of April, that fits.

What's he mean, that fits?

On Saturdays we only went to school in the morning. Johnny was still asleep when I left, but he was up when I got back. Mum had fed him up a bit, so he didn't seem to be quite as deadly tired as he had been. But his face was a real mess.

There was a smell of questions and answers all over the flat. Maybe I shouldn't have left Johnny on his own with my nosey mum after all. I know the signs and I can deal with Mum quite easily. But once she's got going, she could squeeze the truth out of a tin of sardines before it knew what had hit it.

The lads weren't prepared and were quite shocked when I came out with this new version of Johnny. Lots of questions were asked, unusually many, to tell the truth. But Johnny just smiled, a bit artificially, cos his lips wouldn't quite play along, and he came out with the bit about the wino in Götgatan again. That was the story he was sticking with.

He stood there fiddling with his bicycle, as if there were lots of places he'd rather be, somewhere where nobody kept asking him questions. When the biggest downpour the world has ever seen suddenly took pity on him, he seized his chance and cleared off.

Will you be coming round later? I yelled after him.

Shouldn't think so. Then he was gone.

Bert reckoned he knew what was going on. They're beating him up at home.

He didn't need to remind us what he used to look like at times, when he came round wanting somewhere to hide, before he was big enough to look after himself, quicker and more wary. We all remembered that. When his dad was drunk and set on him, he used to look more or less like Johnny did now.

The big difference was that Bert could talk about it: what had happened, and what it felt like. We all knew about it, and we were all willing to let him in when his dad was on the warpath.

But Johnny just kept quiet. Told lies even.

As if Johnny couldn't have sorted out a whole crowd of winos in Götgatan!

Johnny turned up at our place again on Monday night. He wanted a bit of a natter with Millie, he said. It seemed as if Millie was the only one he wanted to natter to, cos he seemed pretty miserable when anyone else tried to natter to him. But as Millie was thrilled to bits when his best friend started poking around in his cage, Johnny started to thaw out a bit as well. When Dad announced the fire was blazing away and suggested that when it settled down we should all grill our own sausages in the tiled stove, Johnny looked inquiringly at me. I nodded of course, didn't even get why he was hesitating. And so Johnny ensconced himself on his cushion in front of the fire and warmed up his battered face in its glow.

We took a look at the papers I'd brought home from school, advertising South Side Grammar's Summer Camp in their place on Värmdö Island. Johnny didn't go on summer camps, no fear, hell no, and he kept on like that. He could read between the lines of everything I mentioned: an opportunity to read up on things during the holidays – Swotting, huh – everybody can go sailing

– Shut up in a dinghy with some yachting freak, oh yeah
– that classes will be available in life-saving, diving,
competitive swimming, etc. – Everybody has to take
part in all that crap – and all bathing is properly
supervised – Oh yes, that's great that is. No matter how
awful the weather is, everybody has to start swimming at
dead on something o'clock and no other time, cos the rest
of the time the gormless teachers are lounging about and
drinking coffee.

He was very suspicious of the phrase: simple but
nourishing plain food – plain food, what's that when it's
at home? – scoffed at all the sports available, and
moaned non-stop when I read that: Leave of absence will
be granted after an express request has been received in
writing or by telephone from a parent or guardian.

When I got to the bit at the end about: You will be a
respected member of a youthful society at our Summer
Camp where, in a spirit of play and enjoyment, we
attempt to reproduce an environment that will confront
you in all seriousness in your future life, Johnny groaned
and let off a resounding fart which echoed all round our
drawing room. Mum was annoyed and said he'd better
go down to the yard and do his business.

Johnny apologized, but the comment was aimed at
whoever had written that load of rubbish, sorry. And
Mum gradually cooled down again.

A young bloke, a teacher at the camp, had been to tell
our class all about South Side Grammar's own place
where they put on these summer camps. There was a
glass case at school with pictures and models and stuff
like that describing it all. Loads of the kids right up to the
fifth form, and evidently even the sixth form, had been
there out on the island, and now they were all going
round doing their PR job, cos they all thought it was
great. Last autumn, and at half term and Easter, exciting
notes kept appearing on the notice boards telling
members of the Banger-eaters' Club and the Indoor-
skiing Society and the Easter Bunnies and so on to meet
outside the school gates at such-and-such a time for the

121

transport to the SSG Camp.

But no fear, hell no, no summer camps. Piss buckets at night, clean-hand checks at meal times, and timetables all summer long. Just read that bit about accommodation again, will you?

I did as I was told and read it out once more:

> Accommodation is provided in purpose-built dormitories with eight beds in each. Stuffed mattresses, pillows and a blanket are supplied on camping beds. Participants bring their own sheets and an extra blanket if required.

Exactly! Purpose-built dormitories! Can't you just imagine what that means! They lock you in and there's a pee-bucket in the middle of the floor and it smells like a gorilla's armpit and every morning they cane anybody who's pissed the bed.

I thought Johnny would have reacted quite differently, in fact. That's why I'd been to the teacher in charge of it all and asked whether anybody who wasn't a pupil at South Side Grammar could go to the camp. Maybe, he said, maybe, in certain exceptional circumstances.

Exceptional circumstances, that sounded just like Johnny; but now Johnny didn't want to know, even though everybody said this camp wasn't one of those places with pee-buckets and clean-hand checks, but it was all go from morning to night, and sometimes all night as well.

Exactly, Johnny reckoned: regimentation all summer. No fear, summer camps are not for me, I want to be a free man. Read that bit! Down at the bottom.

> Care and maintenance at an establishment the size of the Summer Camp naturally involves a lot of work, and all participants join in to help under the direction of the work leaders. Every participant is thus given tasks associated with the care of gardens and woods, repairs and building works, etc.

122

Dead crafty, eh? Not a word about wages. You can bet your life everybody's booted into repairing all the broken-down shacks for nothing, and digging cesspits, and emptying the shit-buckets! No fear! Can't you see what it means? It's a lot of old codswallop, for crying out loud!

We grilled our sausages, and I changed my mind and decided to drop all my plans for going to the South Side Grammar Summer Camp. I was a free man as well. A summer at the camp *with* Johnny could be great. Without him, it would be a load of crap.

When I said that, Dad muttered, Hello! and Mum came out with, But Christopher!

What they meant was that they'd been counting on my being away all summer, cos Dad had some big job on and wouldn't be able to have any holiday till the autumn. So send Junior off to the summer camp, that's soon solved. And that means Junior can't start changing plans. The alternative to the camp would be staying in town, you see. But staying in town has its attractions; better to be in town with Johnny than at the camp without him.

Dad tried coaxing Johnny and asked him if he realized what he was turning his nose up at. The South Side Grammar Summer Camp was supposed to be great fun, and you only ever heard good things about it.

Johnny was turning up his nose at this summer camp cos I turn my nose up at all summer camps, matterfact. He'd been to summer camps before, he knew what was what.

Never again, no fear, that was the sum total of Johnny's experience at summer camps, and the South Side Grammar Summer Camp sounded worse than any of 'em.

That's as far as we got, cos Sis came home from her secret mission just then, and Johnny ran for it. But if I knew Johnny, nothing would make him change his mind. So I took it up with Mum and Dad, and told them wild horses wouldn't drag me out to Värmdö, so there. It was a bit dodgy for a while, the conversation that

Monday night, but then my clever parents realized that if anybody was going to suffer as a result of that decision it was me. So they let it go at that.

Just before May Day, Mum came up with a smashing idea: Would Johnny like to have dinner with us? And then go out and see the bonfires and then stay the night and then breakfast and then Skansen and then dinner?

Johnny grinned a bit sheepishly and said yes, he'd love to be in on the programme for the Eve, but, well, thanks all the same but not staying the night and all that cos mumble, mumble. Mum nodded, yes, mumble, mumble, of course!

On Saturday she laid the table for a banquet and I begged and pleaded, I got down on my bare knees and pleaded with her not to make everything so incredibly posh so she didn't scare Johnny away before he'd even come in through the door. She knew as well as I did he wasn't going to turn up in a dinner jacket.

But dear old Mum told me to clean my fingernails before dinner and leave her to get on with her own business if I didn't mind, and I didn't need to worry on Johnny's account cos he's your friend and I'm not going to take him away from you.

Johnny came. He hesitated a little bit when he saw the table all set, but the smell from the kitchen seemed promising and so he didn't run away after all. I didn't need to be ashamed of him during dinner either: it turned out he knew how to handle a knife and fork, and he used his serviette just about often enough.

Oh yes, Johnny behaved himself all right. And Sis behaved herself; she was miles away, even though Johnny was there. Mum and Dad behaved themselves;

they didn't give each other meaningful looks every time
something went slightly wrong. I always behave myself.
It was quite nice, in fact, and a bit on the lively side.
Johnny laughed at every little joke Dad made, thought
everything Mum said was wise and right, looked as if he
thought what Suzie said was worth listening to, and
didn't have time or space to say very much himself. As
usual, he had the honour of squeezing the cheese spread
out of the tube every time anybody wanted a bit. And
everybody made sure they wanted a bit, cos Johnny was
still as happy as a sandboy when he could do that.

Eventually it was all over, thank you very much, it was
smashing, right down to the last crumb, I'm full up to
here.

Johnny and I were half-lying on my bed, letting the
meal settle, and he took the opportunity, when nobody
was listening, he thought mebbe, praps he could ask me
what all that was about. He nodded in the direction of the
devastated table.

The meat balls, you mean?

Indicky card idiot! That other business. What your
Dad said.

I thought hard, but I didn't catch on, Dad's always
nattering away.

Right at the start, matterfact. When we sat down.

Did Johnny mean grace?

> In Jesu's name we take our seat.
> May God bless all the food we eat.
> Amen.

That's it!

What that was, you mean? Grace.

Grace? He went all quiet. A minute I reckon it was
before he spoke again, and I didn't know what to do to fill
in the time. Then he asked if they came out with one of
them in all the posh places.

I should think so, I didn't know really, but I expect
they did, but what was he getting at, had Johnny never

heard Grace being said before?

Never, matterfact. What's it getting at?

Eh? Getting at? It isn't really getting at anything special. It's just . . . well . . . sort of . . .

There was no rush, and this time Johnny really wanted to know, cos it couldn't just have been something just, well, sort of when everybody sat there nailed to their chairs for several seconds while it was going on, no, it must have been something special.

I still hadn't worked out what he was getting at, so I went through the Grace quite slowly and carefully from start, In Jesu's name, to finish, Amen. What about it? What did he want to know?

The whole lot! In Jesu's name? God bless? Amen?

I started from the beginning again: In Jesu's name, that meant that Jesus was protecting us, sort of, when we took our seat at the meal table, cos Jesus, as it were, through his name, when we pronounced it, we were protected, like.

But Johnny was none the wiser. Jesus? Protected by his name? What was I on about?

I suddenly started to get the feeling you get when you're being cross-examined on your homework in history or biology: I've got all this and grasped it and mastered it and thought about it and it was all obvious until the teacher comes and asks you questions from another angle and you don't know where you are. Here was Johnny lifting up this familiar, straightforward sentence, In Jesu's name we take our seat, and holding it up to the light till every word loses its meaning, and I realized I didn't know myself what it meant and I couldn't explain it and it was really weird to go to the dining table in Jesu's name, or anybody else's name come to that.

It was a bit easier when we got to the next sentence: May God bless all the food we eat. That just meant God should make sure the grub was OK.

That sounded a bit less weird, Johnny nodded, yes, but then we were in trouble again, cos what do you

127

mean? The grub was exactly as your mum made it. And it was bang on.

What was I to think? Johnny didn't look as if he was having me on, but there again . . . Maybe he'd caught the bug from Bert and was pinning me down to the exact meaning of every word. In that case, he was doing pretty well at keeping a straight face. It was just one big question mark.

Amen, though? Who's he when he's at home?

That was when he went over the top and spoilt it all. I was just wondering if I ought to dream up some fantastic blarney about the holy monk Amen or just plonk him one on the snifter when Dad piped up from the doorway, It means the end, finished. More or less.

Well, I decided to keep quiet and looked up at Dad, who now challenged me to tell Johnny the whole story. As I still hadn't a clue what was going on, he started me off: Jesus was the name of a man who was born 1,955 years ago. He has had enormous influence on western culture and still has even today. Right, Chris! It's your turn now! Don't tell me you've forgotten your homework. You went over all that at school not long ago.

Yes, er, well, er, I pulled myself together. It was Jesus who, er . . .

Dad disappeared again, and Johnny looked at me as I took a deep breath and dragged up all I could remember about the Bible. Odds and ends from Scripture at Maria Elementary School, bits and pieces from assemblies at South Side Grammar, when they were going on about religion that is, a few scraps from when I was a kid and Suzie read me to sleep, and that Christmas Eve when he was born and Good Friday when he died, and so on: the star, the stable, the crib, the cross, baptism, the lot.

Johnny listened and listened, and it was all new to him. Everything was new!

And what about that other one then?

Ah, that other one. That other one. Seeing as I'd already fallen flat on the floor ten times, I couldn't do it any more, I was down in the basement already, but I fell flat even so, I was bowled over, but I fought it, fought it, had to fight it, and I had to keep a straight face and this was perfectly straightforward, get that Chris, perfectly straightforward: Johnny had never heard of God either!

He wasn't pulling my leg. Whatever sense of humour you've got, you wouldn't keep it up for such a long time, not even the best of jokes. No, that's the way it was. Johnny knew absolutely nothing about all this.

I did my best. Dad invited us to sit round the fire, and I went on about the Creation, Paradise, Noah and all that, while the rest of the family kept me at arm's length. I gave up in the end. Time, our valuable time, was slipping away, and this story was very long and rather complicated, and it got weirder and weirder the more I tried to explain things I didn't really understand. But Johnny was catching on now, more or less, but he must have been just saying that, being polite, or maybe it was getting late, cos nobody starting from scratch could possibly have got anything out of what I had to say.

Is this yarn a sort of family thing, or what?

Not really, I said. Cool as a cucumber. We were way over the top now, and I could keep going no matter what. No, that thing is pretty widespread, in fact.

I refrained from mentioning that until that day, the day before May Day, I'd been quite certain everybody had heard the story of Jesus et Consortes. And Johnny nodded and reckoned that if Christmas and Easter and all that were celebrated because of this Jesus bloke, then it was pretty obvious it couldn't just be some private story I'd made up myself.

It took quite a time to go through it all, and I just don't understand what Mum and Dad and Big Sister were up to in the meantime, or where they were doing it in their invisible, inaudible ways; but anyway, now it was time for the next item on the programme. Which meant going down to catch a seventy-nine bus.

Everybody except Sis wanted to go to the stop in Södergatan, but that would mean going down the steps and she'd get all dizzy. Said she. Those wooden steps were temporary yet permanent, and she could see the abyss between each and every one of them. She managed to make us agree to go to the stop in Södermalm Square.

I tried to interpret Johnny's expression while Sis was standing there and going on about the steps and how she'd get dizzy and be sick and God knows what else on a set of steps with handrails wherever you look. He must think she was the end. But actually, Johnny was the only one of us who didn't even sigh when Sis started getting all hysterical. And when I whispered in his ear, while we were walking down Götgatan, that let's face it, I told you she wasn't quite right in the head, he just shrugged his shoulders: Well, vertigo, you can't help that.

Dad coughed up 55 öre each for the journey of 5,300 metres to Björkhagen. We'd timed it nicely, cos in a month from then, on the first of June that is, they were putting the prices up – 50 öre for one zone, and 15 öre for each extra zone, and that meant our trip would become 10 öre more expensive. That would be the fifth time they'd shoved up the prices since I'd been around, but this was the first time they were going to put up the price when you went from one zone to another. A bit more than two hundred and fifty million passengers were fleeced for a hundred and ninety million kronor or thereabouts in 1954, but that wasn't good enough: they had to put up the prices yet again.

OK, so now it was the last day of April and the trip was still 55 öre. When we got to Björkhagen, we got out and found ourselves in an enormous big field with a good view of the bonfire.

When they'd finished singing and hip-hip-hooraying, Johnny took me to one side and said this was his last question for today, really, and I could tell him where to go if I felt that way, but why all this messing around? Was it all something to do with Jesus?

But I knew my duty, and I didn't tell my friend Johnny where to go. On the contrary, I'd begun to catch on to how enormously important it all was. So I said I didn't really know, it could be, but it's all so complicated, I'd better ask my dad.

I sidled off and did a tour of Dad, who was bellowing out some joyful Spring Song or other. Got back again, and explained to Johnny that it was an ancient ritual to greet the spring, nothing to do with God or Jesus, just the old King of Winter, who'd done a bunk. Boreus his name was, and then there was the sun that was getting hotter and hotter. It's a celebration, Johnny, an ancient feast-day, when people rejoice cos winter's gone at last.

Johnny looked at the heathens prancing about at Björkhagen, and nodded, and said, Wow! They're a funny lot, this crowd, say what you like.

The cop's very interested in all this. Everything I dare to tell him, or he can drag out of me. I keep noticing how he's always tricking me into telling him things Johnny certainly wouldn't want me to tell him.

But Johnny, what you wouldn't want doesn't matter all that much now. Everything changed and took on a new light when you floored me. Your battered face, being away all that time, not wanting to go to the camp, not knowing anything about religion . . . all that.

It all comes tumbling out of me, cos there's so much I just don't understand, and cos the cop seems to know nearly everything already: he just keeps nodding and recognizing everything, as it were.

The wounds healed, the bruises changed colour and faded away. Questions about them stopped a lot earlier. A thin, white scar across his left cheek, not disfiguring at all, was the only visible reminder. Reminder of I didn't know what.

Johnny returned to being more or less his old self, quieter perhaps. Not so blasted brilliant at everything all the time. On his bicycle, yes, but he'd quietened down a bit otherwise. Maybe even Johnny got older, though he claimed he didn't recognize that.

Even so, all the time, non-stop, it was deadly dangerous having Johnny around. All of sudden, in the most ordinary of circumstances, everything could get turned upside down and you'd find your life was at stake.

In May, we spent lots of evenings smuggling diamonds from Maria Magdalena Church to South Station, or vice versa. You weren't allowed to go east of Södergatan or west of Timmermansgatan, you couldn't cross over Hornsgatan to the north or the railway line to the south, and you couldn't cycle. Even so, it was hard for the border guards to control the whole area. What made it just about possible was that the smugglers had to cross over St Paulsgatan and had to cross over Högbergsgatan. Those were the only streets that had no secret underground passages, so this was the real problem for the smugglers. If you could get over St Paulsgatan from Number 14 to Number 19 without being seen, for instance, having first got into Number 14 through a window which was always left open at the rear of the building, and then along a passage in the basement, from Number 19 you could go underground all the way along Kvarngatan and up and down lots of exciting stairs and passages down below, and only see daylight streaming in when you were nearly as far as the corner house in either Högbergsgatan, or, if you turned off right at an awkward point, in Björngårdsgatan.

I took Johnny with me along that route. He was so thrilled he nearly ruined the whole point of the enterprise: getting the diamonds to the barrier at South Station without being caught.

What wizard passages! What secret caves! It's great, matterfact! Johnny in his element, shouting, banging on walls, and peering down narrow corridors and wondering where that one went to and what about that one then.

I had to keep hushing him up over and over again. Södermalm, up above our heads, was inhabited by those awkward types, with or without uniforms, who like to go around listening for any kids having fun underneath their houses. If so, the culprit has to be hounded out, given a good hiding and a telling off, have his name taken, reported and made an example of for suspected criminal activities, clapped in irons and flung into even deeper dungeons to cure him of his interest in the underworld.

In the school rules concerning order and good behaviour, it says in paragraph fifteen subsection four: Even outside the school premises, pupils will behave in seemly fashion.

Johnny could do what he liked, but I had to be careful about following the instructions in the school rules about order and good conduct. Any complaints from the general public about boys in our class went straight to Mr G.G., and a complaint from the general public about Christopher Nordberg would fit perfectly into Mr G.G.'s view of the world. From then on I'd have to spend the rest of my schooldays trying to explain what I could possibly have been doing in passages underneath buildings where I didn't live. Mr G.G. would know all right, and interpret it in his own way.

Johnny calmed down a little bit, perhaps, but he'd never seen anything like it!

Don't you have anything like this around Bjurholmsplan then? I wondered, then kicked myself on both shins, bashed my head against the wall, bit off my tongue and would have given anything not to have said that, but h a d said it, me, stupid barmy daft idiot that I was, and when I turned round it wasn't only quiet behind me, it was empty as well.

No Johnny. Not a trace of Johnny, no sound of footsteps dying away, no sign of Johnny in the beam of my flashlight – no matter where I sent it, it just reported that Johnny wasn't there.

I started shouting, but then I thought, For God's sake shut up!

Cos it was simple, really: as he'd disappeared in a trice without a sound, he must be standing up against a wall not far away, round the nearest corner to be more precise. There weren't any deeper passages around here to slink into, so there was no chance he'd slipped off into a side-alley and was wandering around lost somewhere under the cliffs of Söder. So I waited a bit, then retraced my steps and peered round the nearest corner where he just had to be, according to all the laws of nature. But he wasn't there. He wasn't round the next corner either, nor the one after that.

I started going more quickly, cos I was beginning to suspect Johnny had yet another talent which would go well with all the rest of them: an ability to move without making a sound. Maybe he'd got away by taking advantage of the noise I'd made myself. This talent of his wasn't very suitable around here, just now, cos there were lots of nasty little snags down here you ought to be aware of before you started wandering about on your own. I really had to catch up with him before I got to the Pentagon, which was where five passages met. When you were coming from the north, you could pass by without any problems, without even noticing there could be any problems. That's exactly what we'd just done. I didn't say anything at the time, cos I'd just been telling him off for making such a godawful row. But now, coming from the south, he'd have been faced with four identical openings. If he took the wrong one, he really could get into trouble. Specially if he'd switched his flashlight off so as not to be seen. There were black holes in two of the passages, crumbling round the edges and with no protective barriers. I've never dared to have a good look.

Needless to say, I didn't catch up with him. There I was at the Pentagon, with no idea which of the four openings Johnny'd chosen. So I ignored all the risks involving nosey-parkers, private detectives, complainers, Mr G.G. and his investigations, and I yelled out, Johnny! Come back! You've taken the wrong one. You'll never find your way out! And I hoped he'd believe me and turn back before he fell down some hole where it would need dogs to find him and the fire service to pull him up again.

I shouted again, cos there was a life at stake, Johnny's life again, which he laid so little store by. I yelled my head off. It's dangerous, I added. And when Johnny eventually appeared out of the darkness, with his flashlight off, of course, I felt so weak at the knees I had to sit down.

Johnny sat down beside me. Neither of us spoke for ages. Then I tried something I'd never managed before: Sorry.

Johnny leant over towards me and rested his red head on my shoulder. I told him we'd followed him to Bjur—holmsplan once. But that was all: only Bert and me knew. And it was just that once.

Johnny muttered something about it not being a prohibited area, but it wasn't much to show off about either, matterfact.

What about that bicycle repair shop? I wondered.

There was a big hole down there, said Johnny, pointing at the passage he'd just come out of. I had a good look down, but I couldn't see anything. Where does it lead to?

Right down into hell, I replied.

Then we sat there for a bit without saying anything. Till Johnny said don't forget he had promised to tell me the whole story one of these days.

I just managed to remember in time that I hadn't heard that promise before, so I was sort of pleasantly surprised. But if he fell down a hole before he got round to telling me, then I'd never know.

In that case it wouldn't matter anyway, matterfact, Johnny reckoned.

Does everything really have to be such a big secret?

It wasn't that everything was secret, matterfact.

I'd have liked to hear how things really were, matterfact. But there was no mention of that.

But Johnny, everything w a s secret in fact, no matter what you said then. To know one of these days, maybe get to know one of these days, what's the good of that?

We didn't say any more about it, but went out into Björngårdsgatan, and walked straight into the arms of Bert and Pecka. But it'd no doubt have been just the same if we'd taken the Högbergsgatan exit.

There was another way of getting through, more awkward and more secret. We took it one night in the other direction. In through the front door, I'm not saying which one cos there are still loads of secrets here that can't be told on any account. Right up all the stairs till we came to the attic door. Special knock, then wait a bit.

Johnny was shuffling his feet in time to a chorus of, Why are we waiting?

We were waiting for Daft-Georgie, that's why. He's the secret. He's been my secret ever since I happened to find out, many years ago and by chance, that he lived in a box room up here. He was the one who called himself Daft-Georgie, but it always seemed to me he was no dafter than anybody else.

I used to sit up there quite a lot when I was six or seven. Listening to his fantastic tales. He'd been around a lot, said he'd been around a lot, worked in a circus, on a boat and then in a circus again, and seen most of the world. I can't say for sure if it was all true or not, but he was good at telling his tales, was always the main character and the hero in stories that c o u l d easily have been true. Cos this straightforward, uncomplicated world I had all around me isn't all there is, I knew that even then.

There were times when I was up there all day long, and when I eventually got home, Mum'd be going mad with worry; but I never let on where I'd been. Then as now, and presumably as for ever, there were horror-stories going the rounds about Dirty Old Men and what they could do to young children who didn't look out for themselves. Daft-Georgie more or less fitted the bill as far as those horror-stories were concerned, and I knew our meetings would soon end if I said anything about who he was and where he lived.

I trusted him completely, and he never laid a finger on me. If life had been a horror-story, I could well have disappeared, I suppose. Nobody would have come looking for me up there, and when they eventually managed to find me, it would have just been another Dirty-Old-Man story come true. I reckon Daft-Georgie's part of a happy-ending fairy story, cos there are some of those as well. I wonder if lots of lonely men turn into Dirty Old Men because that's what's expected of them.

Anyway, he opened up and when he stuck his stubbly fizzog round the door, Johnny took two steps back into a hiding place that wasn't there. Daft-Georgie croaked out his usual password, Now then, Chris me old lad! Let me in and beckoned to Johnny, who'd suddenly gone all hesitant. Ah! Got yourself a girlfriend since you were here last, have you? Jay-Jay, eh? Well, well, what d'you know!

This was Johnny, I had to tell him, and we were only going to nip through.

Jay-Jay! Daft-Georgie chuckled away and reckoned he knew what he knew about that little poppet all right, so there was no need to call her Johnny, oh no. Anyway, just creep on in. And he crept after us himself so he could unlock the door on the other side.

Halfway along there was a recess with a window and a pretty good view over the rooftops. We stood there for a bit, drinking in the view. All of a sudden, Johnny unhooked the catches, opened the window, took hold of the bottom sill, leaned right out . . .

For God's sake, are you out of your mind! I gasped, pulling him back in, cos I swear it looked as if he was about to leap out into space.

What's up? Couldn't he admire the view? Johnny was amazed, but made allowances for my sensitive nerves and didn't stick his snout quite so far out.

Then he started counting and mumbling and pointing, and it suddenly occurred to me he was mapping out a route over the rooftops to Maria Magdalena Church. Climb up there and then balance along there and slide down a bit and then jump over to that one there and pull yourself up that thing and then a bit more balancing and sliding, and there you are. All that up in outer space, six storeys from solid ground.

I explained, tried to explain, that no matter what it looked like from here, we had St Paulsgatan between us and the church. Just a little eight metre long jump, Jesse Owens style, but without a run-up; not really on, is it?

But I could see the mad idea had already taken root in that red skull of his. There were loads of wires and cables over St Paulsgatan, holding up the street lights and all that. A whole carpet of wires, no problem. And if there was a bit of a problem, Johnny would hold my hand.

If anybody needed holding by the hand, it was Johnny himself. Holding by the hand and tying up and locking in, that's what he needed. Those wires were four or five metres up. But we were h i g h u p! Rooftop level!

You could jump. Climb up and down the drainpipes.

To my horror, he stuck his leg out of the window and got ready to launch himself out.

What about me, then! Being weak was my only chance, as weak and scared as I really was in fact. A waste of time being strong and a tough-guy. Weak, and keen on the only life I've got. Johnny's own life was worth nothing.

Johnny stared at me in surprise. Wasn't I coming with him, then?? It was the best way. He'd give me a hand.

He'd have to carry me all the way then. There wasn't a single bit of the route he'd mapped out I could manage.

Johnny was all eager-beaver. Climbed out and walked a few metres along a ledge. Look, it's dead easy.

I was panic-stricken. Daft-Georgie was standing next to me, but he'd no advice to offer. Clapped me on the shoulder. Don't worry, she'll make it all right, will Jay-Jay. Easy as pie.

I daren't! I yelled. That was the bald truth. No matter how much help I got, I'd never dare to go out on to that roof. And I yelled like a madman and cried openly and put all I'd got into it and threw all my self-respect to the winds. I daren't go out there. And I daren't walk through the attics all on my own. Johnny, please Johnny, for God's sake, don't leave me on my own! I'll die, Johnny! Can't you hear me!

And can you believe it, he did hear me! And he came back. And he jumped in through the window, a neat little jump. And he hugged me as I stood there shrieking my head off. Good God, Chris, I'm here now, calm down, what's got into you!

But I'd been going on all cylinders and it was ages before I could calm down, so Johnny was really upset about what he might have done to me.

Daft-Georgie scampered back and forth, listening to see whether the row had brought folks running up to his attic, but nothing like that happened. When I'd got back to something like normal, he gave Johnny a thump round the earhole and ushered us out through the door on the other side and bolted the door behind us. He was going on about that being the last time he was ever going to let me in. Johnny took his thump as par for the course and let himself be bustled out, and there we were, right at the top of the stairs.

Now the danger was over, the most exciting question

139

was which one of us was going to be the first to say what. It was Johnny who broke the silence with a little clap on the shoulder: That's OK, Chris. Pat pat. Getting dizzy. Vertigo. You can't help that. It's something you just can't do anything about. Pat pat. That's OK.

He turned on his heel and went downstairs and out in the street and round the corner and round the blocks to the church. I was two paces behind him. No sign of the border patrols, and we handed the diamonds over to Sten. Johnny unlocked his bicycle and rode off without a word.

I spent the next two days worrying: Is he annoyed or isn't he? He wasn't, at least he wasn't when we next met, cos everything was normal, the laughs and the nudges came when they should, there was nothing awkward between us, and life went on as usual.

I was the saddest person in the world on Saturday, the eleventh of June, the day after school broke up. I'd been stupid enough to ride down to the quayside and see off all the kids going to the South Side Grammar Summer Camp. Happy faces wherever you looked, and what was I doing there? The boat left, and all those happy faces were in for a guaranteed happy summer. But what about me? What was I in for?

At the end of May, Johnny disappeared in a puff of smoke.

The Friday before Whit Saturday, he'd been with me round to Bobby's, to see the fantastic model railway set-up they have there. It's pretty impressive. It used to be Bobby's dad's, but the old lady started moaning cos grown men are not supposed to play with toys, they're supposed to join the rat race and bring in the lolly. So it came down to Bobby and he's been adding to it, managing his inheritance, as he put it. Now his dad could play with it as much as he liked, cos that meant he was being together with his son, and it's a smashing thing if a dad can be together with his son, even Bobby's old lady could see that.

All that might seem a bit involved, but I spelt it out for Johnny before we got to Bobby's. And Johnny caught on all right. He'd dragged his feet a bit at first. Didn't really want to go to Bobby's place, cos Bobby had been a bit frosty when it came to Johnny, ever since he'd clobbered him one last autumn. But this was a pretty classy model railway that you just *had* to see, and if Johnny could bring himself to mutter something nice about it, it might be possible to bury the hatchet. And that's exactly what happened. Johnny was full of praise and spotted and appreciated all the subtleties and fancy bits, and after ten minutes we could all feel the ice melting and see the sun glinting on the waters and Bobby had found somebody who really appreciated the important things in life.

The next day, Whit Saturday that is, Johnny was supposed to come round to us quite early, cos Dad had promised us circus tickets and Mum was going to rustle up something for dinner beforehand. But Johnny didn't turn up. So there was no special dinner, which was just as well as it happened, cos Mum didn't make anything special; no doubt she'd forgotten she'd invited him.

And so Dad's annual tradition was cancelled: no Circus AIR première for me this year. Circus AIR, no animals, just humans doing fantastic things: Magic Magico with his supernatural tricks; The Bats soaring weightlessly through the air in just as supernatural fashion; Miss Juvenile, defying death on the slack rope and broken trapezes; Jacob and his Bone-Crushing Brothers who smashed each other to smithereens – you could see how they bashed each other and hear how their guts were being shredded, but then they'd bounce back up again as if nothing had happened.

I knew it all more or less off by heart, but even so, I'd been looking forward to it with the same eagerness as always. But it all came to nothing, cos this time Johnny was supposed to be coming with us. And Johnny didn't turn up.

Sis was generous and offered to come along instead, after the latest possible departure time had already passed. But I ask you – Suzie? No thanks!

Mum came to the rescue on this one, out of the blue. What's all this nonsense! she said, staring at Sis. Suzie shrugged her shoulders, bit her lip, and decided she'd better shut up. And so we stayed at home, the lot of us.

Is this right? The cop's holding up a photo.

Miss Juvenile is balancing on a one-wheeler on a tightrope. The photo is taken from below, focused on the lace panties she's wearing, and her face is bathed in the spotlights. The little panties are the most important feature, that's obvious. The whole set-up reminds you of Sten's dirty magazines with flabby tarts and legs apart, showing all they've got, and you follow their legs up till you arrive at something that seems to have got there by accident, and the tart and the photographer would both have loved to show you a bit more, if only . . .

I can see this photo, black and white, is what Circus AIR based this year's poster on. Drawn by some artist, in colour, and much clearer, it was posted all over the town for a fortnight before the first night. Now the cop's showing us the original, I can see the artist made a good job of it: Miss Juvenile was more than a pair of panties on the poster, she looked more attractive, and her balancing act seemed more dangerous. The photo was designed to attract old men who like looking up girls' skirts. The poster was aimed at those of us who like dangerous balancing acts.

The background, which is just spotlight beams in the photo, had been filled in by the artist with drawings of The Bats in free fall.

Dad explained it all to me once upon a time, when I wondered why these circus girls who all seemed to be about as old as I was were so extremely clever. These young girls were subjected to incredibly intense training from a very early age, Dad reckoned, so that their development into young women was delayed. They looked as though they were about ten years old, but in fact they could easily be twenty. What a life!

When he said, What a life!, I expect I looked like I'd been twisted into a question mark; and Dad had plenty more to say for himself, so he kept going on: This was exploitation, dressage, worse than cruelty to animals. In modern Sweden, this kind of exploitation of children (it means *using* children: I looked it up in a dictionary) is forbidden by law, but it used to be different in the old days, and it still was different in other places in the world. Not for nothing were we renowned as a welfare state, where the worst of the injustices had been reformed and banished. There was no exploitation of children here.

But foreign artistes here on visits were different, of course, and Swedish audiences encouraged and applauded the fruits of cruelty to children. The only thing we demanded by law was a safety net. That wasn't something they demanded abroad, and they weren't used abroad either. That's what the circus manager boasted, in any case.

Dad looked pretty grim when he spelt it all out, but let's face it, he still used to take me to the circus première every year even so.

They must get fantastic pay then? I reckoned.

We had no control over that.

To tell you the truth, all that background stuff couldn't undermine my reactions when I saw the performance. It's only now, when the cop is showing me this picture of a pair of lace panties in position right at the top of a pair of legs, that my thoughts start buzzing. And I've just been taking a look at some of Sten's secret pictures – no question of panties there, I can tell you – so that explains how it all falls into place.

I nod. Yes, that's right, the Circus AIR.

Why do I have to spell out the obvious for them? Does this cop think there is more than one Circus AIR with an opening night on Whit Saturday?

No sign of Johnny. Not that day, and not the next one either. The days passed by, days I'd intended to spend planning a summer together with Johnny. I didn't manage to find the time to hunt him down those early days in June either, cos that swinish Mr G.G. staked his claim to loads of time, energy and concentration when he presented us with a just and honourable opportunity to query his grades before he submitted them. He announced he intended to award me B-minus, which provoked an incredulous reaction throughout the class.

144

Even Mr G.G. noticed it, and he raised his eyebrows. Any problem here?

Objection! I said, an English word I know even though Mr G.G. hadn't taught us it.

I knew all my marks off by heart, and I reckoned that if he was going to be really strict, I might only manage an A-minus, but an A wasn't absolutely impossible. Bergman and several others had already patted me on the back, a congratulation in advance for the A they were convinced was bound to come.

And then Mr G.G. says, Nordberg, B-minus.

Mr G.G. peered at me, his gaze betraying no sign of appreciation of my correct pronunciation and use of the word objection. He thumbed through his Black Book of Horrors, pretending to add up. He must have been pretending, else he was useless at counting.

Twenty-three, he said.

Hedlund, in the middle of the back row, had also been counting. He was our accountant. If anybody deserved to be called Catalogue, Hedlund did. We report all recorded marks to him. Just occasionally he gets contradictory information, in which case he notes down both marks and then probes and queries till he gets the right version. Every mark has its own date. If necessary, then, his columns can be put alongside Nilson's and Öström's checks on Mr G.G.'s activities. We hadn't got that far yet. This was just the point where Hedlund whispered:

Forty-three!

You could hear it, clear as a bell, and then there was a pause, and then Mr G.G. croaked out his standard comment, Come off it boys, this won't do. I'm a bit too long in the tooth for that one.

He used to say that with a so-called humorous glint in his eye. But there was no sign of it at all this time.

I think I know best what it says in here, he said, without lifting his eyes from his Black Book.

He pretended to count again. Then he repeated his twenty-three, in English, and looked at me questioningly.

I could feel Dad's promise from last autumn pounding through my veins, and I knew that now was the time to clobber Mr G.G. once and for all, even if it meant losing my mark in English and my conduct mark as well.

Forty-three was the figure I'd worked out myself, without having discussed it with Hedlund at all. So I said, a bit too impulsively perhaps, but my heart was beating twenty to the dozen, I don't accept that twenty marks have just disappeared out of that book of yours.

The world can be absolutely dead silent at times. This silence piled up in our classroom in the last week of the spring term, and thirty-five first-formers and an English master held their breath. Deathly hush.

Mr G.G. called me out to the front. He covered up all the columns of marks apart from mine in his Black Book and invited me to count them for myself. I did so, for appearance's sake, counted up all the figures, all of them noughts and ones, and totalled them to twenty-three. Mr G.G. requested me to look very carefully and see whether I could find any trace of alterations. When I hesitated to bend over and have him breathing over me, he was kind enough to lift the book and hold it in front of my nose.

Well, Nordberg? Any sign of alterations?

I moved a bit so the light was shining down my row of figures, but there was no trace of any changes. The marks were all noted in red ink, and nothing suggested they'd been interfered with in any way at all.

Well, Nordberg? Any sign of alterations?

When I shook my head, Mr G.G. asked Nordberg to be kind enough to say in a loud voice, so that all Nordberg's friends could hear it, that Nordberg could see no sign at all of any alterations, and that Nordberg would then withdraw his accusations.

I said, in a loud voice so all my friends could hear, that I hadn't accused anybody of anything. I just said I couldn't accept that twenty marks had just disappeared. I had no intention of taking that back.

The look on Mr G.G.'s face was not nice to behold as he asked Hedlund to read out the marks he had in his list, slowly and clearly. Hedlund read them out. In time with his voice, Mr G.G. ran his chubby finger down my column of marks. The only similarity was the number of entries. Then Mr G.G. looked first at me, then at Hedlund, then back again. He was obviously waiting for some comment, but I was too busy memorizing the position of the most interesting difference between Mr G.G.'s list and Hedlund's: the only place where Mr G.G. had a higher mark than Hedlund. The sixth mark from the end was a one in Mr G.G.'s book, but Hedlund had a zero, the only zero in his list. The rest were ones and twos.

Mr G.G. was waiting for an apology, he said, cos this isn't how it goes when the flak starts flying. But there's no more to be said, is there?

On the contrary, I reckoned. I thought it was time we brought in some grown-ups for comment. What we pupils have to say isn't worth a fig.

That really put the cat among the pigeons. Neither me nor Mr G.G. was interested in letting it drop now. He marched straight off to the Headmaster's office. Actually dared to leave us on our own for a few minutes.

That sixth mark from the end had been given on the twenty-second of April, according to Hedlund's list. Nilson looked up his notes for the twenty-second of April and discovered it was the day I'd been three minutes late. I'd forgotten about that!

That night I told Dad all about it. He asked whether I was absolutely sure, completely sure, and this is the most important thing of all, Chris, are you one hundred per cent certain that Hedlund's figures are correct?

A hundred and ten per cent certain, I said, thinking how Einar Theodor would be driven to an early grave – well, maybe not all that early – if he could hear me coming out with figures like that. Not even in fun was it permissible to exceed the hundred per cent barrier. That was absolutely forbidden! Here was me putting my mark in maths on the line as well!

The thing about Einar Theodor Strand, you see, is that he tells you all kinds of things that have nothing to do with the course, and according to the rule book, they're things you don't need to know. Reasonably enough, he doesn't set us any questions on that stuff later. The best bet, then, is to forget everything that really belongs to the advanced course, or at the very least to say nothing about what he's been telling you. If you do say anything, and you get it wrong, like with this hundred and ten per cent business, well, then you're really for it! A boob like that pulls down the general impression you give, and might affect the mark you get for the maths course you're actually supposed to be doing. A speech for the defence along the lines that you were only joking, and all that hundred and ten per cent business was just a . . . well . . . er – that'd be no good either. You don't joke about mathematics.

You can think what you like about all this. That's how it is, that's all there is to it, in a school with a history and with traditions from the days of the old Foundation School.

Well! Einar Theodor couldn't hear me, and just now it was Mr G.G. and my English mark I was concerned with. Dad took the next morning off work and went to see the Headmaster, after which INTERVIEWS got underway.

It must have been round about now Mr G.G. discovered I was more or less an English-speaker. Dad had imported Mum from England once upon a time. That's why I'd been there quite a lot, staying with my aunts. Most recently last summer. And the summer of '53, and '52 . . . We very nearly decided to stay there for good a few years ago, but both Sis and I started to pine for home so badly and so noisily that our good parents came round to the fact that we belonged in Fredmansgatan. There may well be nothing to beat a few months in nice, quiet English surroundings, but not a whole lifetime, not when your whole life's at stake. My home is my castle, and my castle's in Stockholm.

Mum reckons I speak English better than she speaks Swedish. And her Swedish isn't something I need to be ashamed of. It does sound a bit odd now and then. Specially when she gets really mad, then she can slip up a bit. Mind you, so do the natives when they get really het up.

I'd have given anything to see Mr G.G.'s face when he found out about that.

Without any warning, I was called in and addressed in English by a native-speaker, answered in English, and we had a polite conversation that went on for quite a while with Mr G.G. sitting in a corner looking daggers and his jaw sinking down to his knees.

I also had to explain what I'd been doing during break plus those three extra minutes on the twenty-second of April – in Swedish. This time, when it wasn't only Mr G.G. hanging on my every word, I thought I'd nothing to lose by telling exactly what had really happened.

This elevated company had no idea who Johnny was, I could tell that all right. It was sufficient to call him a friend who'd disappeared and been away for a very long time, then turned up out of the blue, and I just lost track of the time. I reckoned there was no point in going on about how he'd been beaten up and all that. Who knows what that might have led to. Dad just sat there, with one foot in my camp and one in the investigators', as it were, and evidently didn't see any need to spell it all out.

Only Mr G.G. found it remarkable that a friend of Nordberg's turned up at about nine o'clock on a Friday morning. How did Nordberg's friends manage to organize their school attendance? And really meant What kind of a rogue is Nordberg if he has friends like that – unless it was a pack of lies, as usual?

But Dad confirmed that it was true. The friend in question had in fact turned up that morning, and since we were all so pleased to see him, it never occurred to us to ask about school. We got the impression he was on holiday Friday and Saturday, but as he hadn't actually

149

said that, it must have just been something we assumed, but that's how it must have been, mustn't it?

By the time he got that far, nobody could remember what it was that must have been, and I took a good look at my dad with his fantastic fantasies and started to wonder if this was the same bloke who'd once instilled into me that you should always tell the truth no matter what. It was time to modify that maxim: you should always tell the truth in so far as the facts can be checked. You can elaborate on the rest as much as you like.

It wasn't only me they spoke to. There was Hedlund as well, and Nilson and . . . Good God! yelled Nyborg the Elder as he came racing up. I hope you've got copies of all the material? Nilson nodded, Calm down, and went in to see the Headmaster. But Nyborg the Elder marched up and down wringing his hands, he was in a much worse state than any of those involved, till he saw Nilson come out again complete with his papers and with his head still in place.

If he's as nervous as that, he'll never get his book published. Sooner or later he'll have to submit his manuscript, and he won't trust anybody enough to let them have that. If Nyborg the Elder's nerves are a result of the experiences he wants to share with the whole world, I reckon I can understand there must be certain experiences that can damage you for life.

Interviews. Checks. Interviews. Then, when our figures and information had been examined, we pupils were all sent packing and nobody said anything about what was going on behind the closed doors. The adrenalin that had given me my strength drained out of me, and I was wandering about in a cold sweat, feeling sick and trembling like a leaf.

This wasn't all over and done with in a day, I can tell you. But on the last day of term, Mr G.G. grabbed me in the corridor and muttered something about there having been a mistake, very odd, but, er, well, in any case, I was going to get an A, that's what Nordberg deserves after all, eh, haha, make you feel better, eh, haha again, and I'm sorry this regrettable thing, hum, yes, well, hope that's the end of it . . .

You old devil, I thought, but didn't say it out loud I must stress. He'd had me on tenterhooks all week when I could have been enjoying myself, or looking for Johnny. But I didn't feel like doing anything at all as long as this cloud was hanging over my head. So it certainly wasn't the end of it as far as I was concerned. I couldn't give a toss about what he thought of me, and I asked Mr G.G. in a loud voice, so that all my classmates could hear, if he would kindly repeat what he had just said. And if he'd mind explaining how mistakes like that could come about. But Mr G.G. wasn't prepared to be that obliging.

When I got home, I asked Dad what had been going on, but he said it was a sad business, and it must be awful to be a teacher in a class where a gang of the awkward squad was keeping an eye on every move you make. Our notes were very trying for Mr G.G., said Dad.

But it was a good job I blew the whistle when I did in any case, I hope, cos I was blowed if I could make out where Dad stood in fact. Oh yes, he reckoned, it was a good thing I'd blown the whistle cos blokes like Mr G.G. need keeping an eye on. But it would be best for me to let it drop now, though, cos in spite of everything Mr G.G. was only human after all, and there was nothing to be gained by pushing him any further.

Just what had he been up to, though, I wondered. He must have been fiddling somehow or other. But Dad thought I should just let it drop. If you dig too deep, you get your hands dirty, said the Chief Clerk.

I reckoned he was probably right, even if he was keeping quiet about the details. So I tried to let it drop. But at the breaking-up ceremony, when the certificates were being handed out, and I got mine from Mr G.G., I didn't bother to notice that he was holding out his hand in expectation of it being shaken. All my classmates duly bowed before Mr G.G. and shook his paw. Have a nice holiday and thank you for all you've done for us.

Not me, though.

Did Johnny often disappear? the cop wondered.

Often? Well, this was the second time.

The third at least. Eh?

Third?

He was missing 9.12.54 to 10.1.55, you said. And again 28.2 to 22.4.

Oh, yes. Though he told me first in December. This was the second time he'd just disappeared. The previous time he didn't come back for about two months, the twenty-second of April as I said, and he'd been beaten up.

As I dragged myself back home along Skeppsbron after seeing the boat off, I asked myself if I was prepared to find him as battered as that this time as well. I'd settle for anything, I reckoned. As long as he turned up.

But Johnny didn't turn up. Days turned into weeks and before we knew where we were it was Midsummer. Dad could see I was upset and pointed out that after all, Johnny didn't actually *promise* to stay around town all summer, did he now?

That's a pretty peculiar way of playing with words, if you ask me. If I said I'll thump you one if you spit into my milk, and you are all nice and leave my milk alone, and I thump you one even so, you'd be a bit cheesed off, and quite right too, I'd have thought. But the way Dad was twisting it round, what I said didn't mean I wouldn't thump you one if you didn't spit into my milk. So there's nothing odd about my behaviour at all.

OK, Johnny hadn't said anything special about this summer, except that he didn't want to go to the camp. Right then, as Dad said, he might have gone off to the North Pole or to America, and he might even have landed up in the camp against his will. Anything might have happened, but that's not the same as *wanting* to go to the camp.

Anyway, I reckon that *not* saying anything means

152

there's nothing special to say. Dad thinks Johnny was the type who only tells you the answer to the particular question you've asked. And if you didn't ask, Johnny, are you going to be in town this summer?, there was no need for Johnny to supply that information.

I protested it could well be that Johnny shut up like an oyster when Dad or any other grown-up asked him anything, but I was his mate after all, wasn't I?

And how could Dad explain away that he'd disappeared as early as May? It wasn't just a question of the summer holidays.

What is it a question of, then? Why don't you go round to his house and find out? What?! You don't know where he lives! For God's sake!

Come Midsummer I was sufficiently fed up to let Dad ring the South Side Grammar Summer Camp and ask whether there were any vacancies out there. No, there weren't. On the contrary, they were over-subscribed. There might possibly be something when the change-over date came round in mid-July. So Dad put me on the waiting list for any vacancies that might crop up. That was the best he could do for the time being. That, plus the fact he *didn't* remind me that staying in town that summer was my own choice. Not that there wasn't a taste of What-did-we-tell-you in the air, but neither Mum nor Dad made any reference to it. Mum asked if she should get in touch with one of my aunts and see how things were on that front, but hang on a bit, Mum, hang on, something might turn up.

Nothing will happen, surely, but it takes time for letters to go back and forth.

Yes, OK! But hang on a bit in any case. Summer's a long time, after all.

And what a summer it was! That incredibly warm, sunny, fantastic summer! Everybody was gasping in the heat and saying what a smashing summer, isn't it!

Not me, though.

I was freezing. Freezing cold through and through. I missed Johnny so much, I was ill.

Dad got more and more annoyed as the evenings went by and he was forced to look at my miserable fizzog. He churned out the same things time after time till one night it got too much, going on about how was it possible to be the best of pals without knowing what the other bloke was called or where he lived, something as simple as a surname, I mean, even if it was only Svensson it might make looking for him that bit easier, but nothing, nothing, what's going on here, haven't you ever asked him what his full name is?

Anyway, it got a bit much, as I said, and that evening I broke down and started bawling like I haven't done since I was a little tiny kid. Dad stopped muttering and mumbling and consoled me instead, and tried to patch things up as much as he could. He took me to Gröna Lund Fun Fair and we listened to Evert Taube. It was a nice thought, but what's Evert Taube compared with Johnny!

We took in the Crazy House and the crazy Tunnel of Terror and the crazy Big Wheel and the crazy Toytown Train and the crazy Hot Dogs and all the crazy things on offer at the Fun Fair.

Oh, how I longed for Johnny! I missed him so much I was ill.

Even Sis was nice for a bit. Then all of a sudden, she packed the whole of her life in a trunk and flew off – even with her vertigo she flew! Flew off to Paris, Paris dans La France.

It sounds daft, but the place seemed empty after she'd gone.

Her secret mission had been going to French lessons, I was now told. Can you imagine why anything like that had to be such a big secret? But that's the way it is: once you suss out what secrets are, they're nothing special after all. It was some time before I caught on to the fact that Sis's secret mission was only a secret for me. Mum and Dad would never have let her go off on secret missions into the Big Bad City night after night. Obviously they knew what she was doing. So I'd been thinking her secret mission, when it was revealed, would prove to have something to do with me. But it was French lessons, was it, vocab, expressions, exercises night after night. Tests, exams, and in the end With Distinction. Everything a secret as far as little brother was concerned. Sis didn't even say anything about it after her With Distinction. Beat that if you can. And will somebody please tell me how Sis managed to survive classes night after night, all year long. She's not exactly your Miss Egghead. At least, I'd never seen her in that light.

She wrote lots of letters. To Dad, and Mum, and even to me. Every time she ended up with the same question: Have you looked at Johnny yet? You must soon. It doesn't take long to forget how to speak your own language once you get abroad. *Have you looked at Johnny yet?* I showed it to Mum, and she saw straight away it wasn't right. Oh dear, she muttered, stroking my hair.

What you have to bear in mind is that Sis only got a C-minus in Swedish when she left school. It looks as if her chances in French were a bit more rosy. I'd never have believed her if she'd told me that. Why didn't she say anything?

She seemed a bit better by letter than in person. Even so, I missed her somehow. God knows, I cried my eyes out that summer!

And Millie! When I got home at night, he used to sniff around and ask where Johnny had got to, but Johnny was never there. I couldn't give Millie what Johnny used to give him, and before long Millie started to pine, and just lay there, staring into space.

It was no good just hanging around town, and before long I was nipping down to Ringvägen and catching the swimming party special Yellow Buses to Lake Flaten. It could be I was just going back over the happy memories of summers I used to spend there before I started going to England; I think I must have been seven when I last used to go to Flaten regularly. But I was a bit old for it all now, and nothing they put on there was fun any more, cos I missed him so much I was ill.

I took the scheduled buses after a bit. When you went on the Swim Specials, it was all get in line and who's missing, and there might be up to forty buses full of kids bubbling over with joy, and then all the swimming teachers and the life-savers and endless kinds of leaders counting all the children and lining them up and then counting them again, and the poor little mite who was in the loo when they all got so worried they started ringing for somebody to drag the lake, and the poor little swine hardly dare show his face and put things right again. No, it was a bit too lively for me, and some of the leaders were inclined to be over the top, and two o'clock was when you had to be there and counted and in possession of the slip proving you'd survived the horrors of Flaten. Then you were shipped home on buses dripping in sweat, back to the vibrating town where there was a whole long, hot day in store for you.

I went out on my own, then. Paid 45 öre, half fare, cos I was only eleven after all. The conductors would grin knowingly, but play along all the same: of course I was only eleven; a bit on the big side perhaps, but then some kids are.

At Flaten I would live it up on the grown-ups' side of the fence: the area around the café and the boat hire landing stage. You could get a rowing boat for one krona an hour. I used to row out into the middle of the lake, more or less, and let the sun shine and the boat drift while I just lay back and listened to my body growing up. I wouldn't get away with being eleven next year.

There was a girl in charge of the boats, about the same age as Sis. I used to sit on the beach and chat to her sometimes, waiting for a boat to come in or a bus to take me home, or for nothing in particular. It was just easy to chat to her.

My brother's called Johnny, she said when I told her what was in my mind most of the time.

She was red-haired and a bit freckly and I could only whisper when I asked her how old her brother was, but he was older than she was and she laughed in a nice way when she saw how disappointed I was. And I tried to laugh back, cos I could see my hope was childish, but I burst out crying instead, and the girl was all horrified cos she'd laughed when she shouldn't have, or so she thought, and I felt really stupid, sitting there bawling in a public place, but that's how it was all summer, I missed him so much I was ill.

Time and time again I saw Johnny just a bit away on the beach, in the queue at the café, up on the diving board . . . and my heart gave a painful leap, but then when I got a better look it was always somebody else. I had long conversations with the empty space by my side, where Johnny should have been. I said some really marvellous things to him and got some wonderful answers.

There were no spare places at Värmdö in the middle of July, but it didn't matter any more. The papers were full of stories about kids going missing from Children's Island, girls who were then found dead somewhere or other. Some weren't found at all; people searched all over for them, and just hoped they'd done nothing more than run away.

Värmdö isn't the same as Children's Island was Dad's comment, all calm and collected, but I had no idea how far apart the two islands were, and wasn't sorry I hadn't gone there.

Mum was worried about me going to Flaten on my own in these dangerous times. On my own is hardly the right expression, I objected, thinking of how chock-a-block the beaches were. But some days there was just no holding Mum, or maybe she just wanted to get out and have a bit of sun herself: she insisted on going to Flaten as well.

Sorry, Mum, but those days were pretty disastrous. She used to natter away when I wanted to think, and eat when I wanted to swim, and swim when I wanted to read, and we had to be together all the time, and it was all non-stop moving around blankets and air mattresses and wet towels and dry towels, and don't lie so that the sun is shining on to your book, and put some dry shorts on straightaway, and don't try and read with the sun in your eyes, and turn over so as you're not burnt to a cinder, but the one who was fiery red before you knew where you were was Mum from the shadows of Fredmansgatan; I was the colour of ginger biscuits already.

I'd never dreamt anything could be so complicated as a day on the beach with Mum. I could feel the ants crawling around the ends of my nerves the moment she announced she was going as well first thing in the morning. So it was a good job it didn't happen all that often.

I tried to explain that Flaten wasn't Children's Island either. Mum had no need to be worried. I could manage on my own, I could manage better, much much better on my own. As I wasn't a girl, these loonies weren't interested. In any case, what on earth could the looniest of loonies get up to in the midst of all those people at Flaten?

Actually, there were loads of girls with hardly anything on at Flaten, if that's what they were after. The littlest ones running about with nothing on at all. I could raise my eyes from the latest discussions about the sex murders in the newspaper any time I liked, and gaze straight into a bit of fanny on some little kid only a couple of steps in front of me. No matter how much I studied them, I just couldn't work out what could tempt some old bloke into 'outrageous behaviour', which is what the papers claimed they did.

Outrageous behaviour. You just got vague answers if you asked what that meant. But it led to death and newspaper headlines. You had to guess the rest. A young kid always has to guess the right answer to some things.

158

The graffiti on the loo walls at Flaten provided all kinds of useful information. But they were hard to make out sometimes. They looked like Swedish, but you had to read them differently from the way you usually did. A sort of code a bit like the one I used at home for the secret section of my card index. Mind you, my technique was better. I used to write things so that anybody reading it would never guess there was some hidden meaning there. The code they used on the loo walls at Flaten made it quite obvious there was some hidden meaning there. You got curious. You solved it by guesswork.

What the papers meant when they wrote that some strange bloke had committed 'outrageous behaviour' with the seven-year-old everybody was now looking for was something you could work out eventually, even though no grown-up seemed to want to explain it.

No matter where Children's Island was in fact, the horrible goings-on got that bit nearer the day the police fished a suitcase out of the lake at Alby, and found a missing five-year-old in it. A girl, of course. That's what happens when we get a hot summer, the police reckoned, and the newspapers reckoned, and when all the searching and investigating didn't get anywhere, after a while they all seemed more interested in a lot of submarines that kept coming and going around the Swedish coast. Russians, everybody thought, but the Russians shook their heads and said, *Nyet*. So they were secret submarines.

Circus AIR got some free publicity for a bit when one of The Bats fell. There was a safety net, safety nets are compulsory in Sweden, and that's what saved her. So safety nets were a good thing, weren't they?

Oh no, not at all, reckoned the circus manager. Safety nets weren't a good thing at all, cos if there was a safety net the artistes would relax and get careless, and then this kind of thing happened.

There was a photo of him smiling and trying to smooth it all over. Anything more like Mr G.G. when he was forced to give Christopher Nordberg an A you couldn't imagine, complete with eyebrows, the lot. Why not, I thought. Mr G.G.'s twin brother a circus manager, and Mr G.G. himself behind a desk, what's the difference?

The newspaper devoted most of its thoughts to the fact that the Bat girl was flying through the air again only two minutes later. Still, it was the first time anybody had fallen in the history of that circus.

There was plenty of time to read through the papers as the days dragged by at Flaten; normally, I'm not all that bothered about the state of the nation. I used to read, and doze, and my fevered brain mixed up what I was reading with what I was dreaming, and made up all kinds of exciting new worlds till I ended up with a terrific story:

All these kids who kept disappearing like that were kidnapped and stuffed into black submarines and transported through unknown seas to distant shores where they were locked up in secret camps, in Siberia for instance. Or in another galaxy. There they had to practise day in and day out, and after ten years or so, maybe fifteen, they were put in a circus and sent to perform all over the world.

Their families had stopped looking for them ages and ages ago, and now, ten or fifteen years later, nobody recognized them any more.

Why didn't they run away, then? I had to make the story watertight.

At first, they were too little to catch on to the idea of running away. Later on, they were used to that way of life and they had nowhere to run away to, they didn't really know where home was. Somebody was giving them food, carefully measured portions full of calories, somebody they were tied down to, who'd whip them if they caused any trouble.

The more I elaborated on the story, the more likely it seemed to get. The girl in the suitcase in the lake at Alby had been thrown out. Kidnapped, talents tested: too clumsy, dump her.

Anyway, my explanation was no more sick than the one the newspapers put forward, that the country was full

160

of sex maniacs who screwed little girls then flung them on the tip.

And when these circus stars finally faded away? How long can the human body cope with strains like that? At first, she gets better and better. Then she holds out at the top for a while. Then she starts going downhill, but she's still useful. Maybe the delayed development into a woman that Dad was on about catches up with her eventually.

When Dad said woman, I pictured something pretty solid, like Mum for instance. A woman like that doesn't fly weightlessly from one trapeze to another. Mind you, she was quite slim at one time. A bit like Sis – Dad's shown me the photos.

Anyway, I had two different endings for the story. Either the camp murderer would slit the fallen star's throat and fling her into the dustbin. Or else she became a sort of camp mum, looking after the newcomers and helping to train them. The latter, I hope. It sounded a bit better.

Maybe it wasn't really true that this fall was the first time anything of the kind had happened in the history of Circus AIR. A fall might be a sort of natural farewell for people in this job, if there wasn't a safety net. Maybe clapped-out circus stars were ending up like this nonstop abroad.

Camp mums could be real mums, come to that. There are blokes around as well in the circus world. Jacob and his Bone-Crushing Brothers, for instance. Breeding stock for new generations of circus kids. I preferred that idea to the one where all of them are kidnapped.

There must be statistics that could give a few pointers. Number of kids lost a year? Number of bodies of unidentified young women found? At intervals of fifteen or twenty years. Number of circus artistes died? In Sweden, and in the whole world?

If only I'd needed data on the population as a whole. At the beginning of the year, Sweden had 7,234,664 inhabitants, of which 3,544,020 lived in towns, and of those 776,947 lived in Stockholm. Or the number of births last year, 105,084, and 69,078 deaths, and 20,817 immigrants came to Sweden, and 13,822 emigrants left . . . I had all those facts at my fingertips.

But missing persons!

In *Amazed*, people who disappeared without trace were explained as having slipped into one of the alternative worlds. Such things happened because there was an error in the cosmic mathematics, or they might have been whisked away on purpose, by slant-eyed men who ruled the fifth dimension.

If circus stars were recruited like that, it wasn't even necessary to let them perform at home in their own world. They could be sent out to the third or fourth alternative world, where nobody would ask any questions.

Somehow or other, the statistics for missing persons must be hidden among the figures for the changes between this year and last. And so on, for years back. It seemed a pretty big job, something for a specialist – field: mathematics; department: statistics.

Too big for me.

But your imagination doesn't need exact figures. To cobble a story like this together, your imagination, mine at least, only needs the vague kind of statistics newspapers use, numberless statistics: Summer is the time for mysterious submarines; the time for missing, assaulted, murdered little girls. The warmer it is, the more of them there are. Maybe the heat reduced the barriers between the alternative worlds.

What about when their circus career was over, though? Assuming they survived? There couldn't very well be any kind of a normal life outside the circus and the camp in Siberia for anybody who'd got mixed up in this other existence to start with. She wouldn't have been to a normal school. I mean, what good would reading-riting-rithmetic be to somebody like her? She'd forget all about her normal years as an ordinary little kid. Or maybe the memory was still there, hidden away deep

162

down, and it would jump up to the surface all of a sudden if somebody in the audience looked like MUMMY!

I was moved to tears. All these tragic fates for those poor women! I *was* ill.

Dad thought it was a good thing I'd started reading newspapers at last. Apart from the comic strips and the sports results. He used to call my lack of interest indolence, and pretend to be all worried. Mum would point out how old I was. It seems to be a game they play, when they both have the same cards every time.

Anyway, when I got home and came out with my perfect story about life in a circus, Dad tapped me on the forehead and asked if I'd got a temperature. Mum was a bit more polite. She pointed to the map of the world in the hall: nothing you can think up in your imagination is so peculiar that it couldn't happen somewhere or other out there.

I just stared at the patchwork of the world, and wondered where the camp could be.

Dad didn't really think Flaten was a risky place for me to be. Apart from the danger of getting sunstroke, of course.

He kept giving me a bit of dough for the journeys, a bite to eat, and the boat hire fee. It would have been dearer if I'd gone to the South Side Grammar Summer Camp, so he was saving anyway.

You got a bit of discount on the cost of a boat if you were out for several hours on end, of course. And it was cheaper still once I'd got to know the girl in charge. After a bit, her brother Johnny took over, and he didn't give any discounts. The weather was too fine for that, he reckoned.

Dad coughed up whatever I told him it cost, and thought I was getting rather a nice tan out there at Flaten. I looked healthy enough. But I missed Johnny so much I was ill.

All that long summer! Why didn't you send me a letter, at least? A stamp only costs twenty-five öre, and you knew my address. Just

163

one little letter, Johnny. Full of lies about everything, or just some blooming big truth, anything. What a difference that would have made.

One evening at the end of July, I finally summoned up enough courage to walk the short distance from the buses to Bjurholmsplan.

If Johnny had been in there then, he'd have realized I had to see him, surely? Two whole months, for God's sake? I missed him so much I was ill.

If I'd seen him, I'd never have been able to keep control of myself. It feels horrible when you know you're blushing, but the state I was in, I'd have let it happen even so, if only Johnny had turned up. But he didn't.

I checked the outside. Was it a cycle repair shop, or was it a cobbler's? Who knows? The part of the first letter you could see on the sign was so small it could just as easily have been a C as an S or an O or a G. What you could see of the last letter might have indicated another S, but there was nothing to stop it being an R, or even a B. Where the fifth letter should be you could just make out what could have been an L, but there again, it could also be an E, or a G come to that. The rest was shrouded in darkness. Encased in filth, more like it.

The agents fixing the transition between the alternative worlds had done a pretty good job here. I'd never be able to show it sometimes said CYCLES and sometimes COBBLER on that sign. Or anything else that might fit on some other occasion, like CIGARS or ORANGES or COCKLES . . .

I opened the door, no problem. When I went in, it was a cycle repair shop. There was a smell I recognized, a mixture of asphalt and resin, of tar and pine needles, the same smell as Johnny had left behind in my room last winter and spring, the smell I'd forgotten about, but now it conjured up a picture of Johnny before my very eyes, so clear and unexpected I could barely hold back the scream that bubbled up inside me without warning.

Out of the darkness came this bloke looking like Boris Karloff's version of Frankenstein's Monster; Boris Karloff is what he looked like. Playing the monster.

He stared at me in that cold way monsters do. I wanted to run for it. But asked if Johnny was in. The Monster just kept on staring. After a year, he said, Johnny bloody who?

What can you say to that? Red-haired Johnny, green-eyed Johnny, freckle-faced Johnny, Johnny Tangerine? I settled for, Red-haired Johnny, he's called.

The Monster was red-haired as well. Not the same unruly mass of fantastic flaming thatch as Johnny, though. This swine was a sort of rotten red, been lying with his head in the ground decomposing for seven years. Dug up by Frankenstein.

He kept on staring. Had he gobbled Johnny up?

He's had his bicycle repaired here, worth a try, that. Should jog Frankenstein's memory. Dig a little deeper.

Never heard of nobody called Johnny! declared the Monster, taking a step towards me. Limped as well. Dragging one foot behind the other!

I ran out into Bjurholmsplan quick as a flash. The Monster was evidently nailed to the floor, he didn't come after me. I stood a few metres away and had a good think, but I didn't come to any conclusions.

Apart from the fact that something was wrong. There was something hellish odd about Bjurholmsplan, and something even odder about the cycle repair shop, and oddest of all was the Monster.

Now I'm opening the door of the . . . cobbler's. Inside is a shoemaker, an invalid, and he looks at me with that face of his which has been so depressed for so long: My son, whom I'm so fond of, isn't at home. He'll be back from school shortly. But then we're going to our chalet

166

out at Kortenslund near Bromma Airport, where I keep
a little axe and a sheath knife. It'll be a long time before
we get back.

The cop is obviously very interested in the Monster. So,
I actually went in and talked to the man, did I? And he
didn't know anybody called Johnny?
  That's what he said, yes.
  Can I describe him?
  Have you ever seen Boris Karloff?
  Well, yes, but . . .
  I can't get any closer to what he looked like than that.
  And the green Studebaker?
  That's right! I'd noticed, despite all my hard thinking.
It wasn't there.
  Sure?
  Certain.
  OK. Then what?

The next day I gave up Flaten and turned to research
instead. I got on my bicycle and pedalled as far as the
Forest Cemetery, cos this business needed clearing up
now. I asked a bloke with a rake, but he didn't know, and
I asked a girl with a rake, but she didn't know either, and
I asked an old man with a rake, and he scratched his head
but he didn't know, laddie, but you could ask at the
office.
  The office?
  The Graveyards and Burial Grounds Administrative
Centre.
  Where could I find the Graveyards and Burial
Grounds Administrative Centre?
  He scratched his head and had no idea, laddie, cos
they usually put places like that in Timbuktu, but look it
up in the telephone directory. The Graveyards and
Burial Grounds Administrative Centre. The Greater
Stockholm Graveyards and Burial Grounds Administra-
tive Centre.
  Where could I find a telephone directory?

He scratched his head and hadn't a clue, laddie, but ask at the corner shop just outside the gate.

Over at the Graveyards and Burial Grounds Administrative Centre they were not too keen on seeing little boys who have cycled themselves red and sweaty through uncharted areas of Stockholm. Thirty-three degrees centigrade in the shade, claimed the thermometers, and what it was in the sun God only knows cos they don't make thermometers that can go that high.

Every goon I stopped to ask the way was a tourist and laughed at me in Greek.

Don't know, not vershtanden, but then there was this Negro complete with camera, binoculars and map of Stockholm, with all the streets and squares in an alphabetical index which directed us to look at square G7, and so we cracked it. Before we parted, he took a picture of me: Wow, you sure am a typical little Swedish kid, yes sah!

There was a dragon at a desk and she most certainly did not approve of little boys coming to disturb her work by asking about graves.

You see, I must know the date of the funeral or interment.

I could give her the date of the funeral all right, the fifteenth of April, so that took her back a bit, the Dragon that is, and she was forced to start thumbing through the biggest ledger in the world. The whole population could rest in peace in that book, with their final journeys carefully annotated.

It was the Forest Cemetery, plot number E10412, Karl Hildur Andersson and Per Anders Andersson under the same number.

And how did I get to plot number E10412?

You could tell from the glint in the Dragon's right eye that my ignorance was shocking, always assuming I wasn't just having her on. Plot number E10412 was in section 50, of course.

I was so bold as to enquire how to get to section 50. A

168

whole big section and I didn't know where it was.

The Dragon said nothing but just pointed to a map on the wall. With the whole cemetery spread out in front of me I could see how it was divided into sections and segments and lots of little squares. As I noted down the position, the E-graves and section 50 and the best way to get there, I cursed myself for not having asked Dad's advice. He'd have been able to tell me straight away I should come here. Then I could have come in the morning, in a clean shirt and bow tie, before everybody's blood started boiling in the Administrative Centre sauna. But I was getting a bit fed up of Dad tapping me on the forehead and his, Isn't it getting a bit too hot for you down at Flaten? He'd done that once too often, so I wanted to sort this thing out myself. He'd only have started asking about what I was up to.

I took a chance and asked the Dragon if she might have happened to see the name of my other friend in the ledger as well. John Anders Andersson.

She sighed, no: hissed, asked for the date of the funeral or interment, but I didn't know for sure. Some time in June. Or thereabouts.

Which made her close the ledger on all the dead, and a sweaty bloke at the next desk grinned. If all your friends are called Andersson you'd better get used to the fact that you'll lose them after death.

His twisted smile indicated the comment was meant to be funny. I wondered for a moment whether I ought to make Sweaty Socks wet his pants by bursting into tears. But two important questions remained on the agenda.

I turned back to my dear old Dragon and asked whether there was, I mean for John Anders Andersson, somewhere a bit nearer, in the south, where I could ask next time.

Dragon suddenly became very helpful, and could inform me straightaway that as it was the Forest Cemetery we were talking about, I didn't need to come here at all, no, I could have gone to the Southern Area Graveyards and Burial Grounds Administrative Office in Enskede, that was a lot nearer.

It dawned on me then that if only I'd turned round and looked in the other direction when the old man was scratching his head and pointing the opposite way, I'd have seen all the signs and arrows: OFFICE, INFORMATION, and the nice friendly-looking little hut full of happy, smiling locals who would willingly have told me all I wanted to know.

Anyway, here I was at the very heart of cemeterial care. My last question was whether Dragon could tell me who to go and see if I wanted to open up a grave.

That was even worse than letting off a real rip-snorter of a fart in here. I'm surprised she didn't faint on the spot.

When Sweaty Socks had stopped shaking and she, Dragon, had regained control of her face, she asked in the faintest of voices whether I was referring to grave number E10412.

I didn't quite understand what that had to do with it, but yes, it was grave number E10412 I was talking about.

I could see the little dragonian hand crawling towards the telephone, ready to get straight on to the police: There's a madman loose in the Graveyards and Burial Grounds Administrative Centre. She must have realized she had made the worst mistake of her life when she told me how to get to plot E10412, cos she suddenly yelled out with both voice and face completely out of control, YOU MUST NOT DIG UP THE URNS!

Now I was really sorry I hadn't let Dad look after the whole business, if he'd agreed to do it. The very idea that somebody would tell my dad what he was allowed to dig up and what he wasn't was absurd and ridiculous. I'd have loved to see the prats here at the Junkyards and Very Old Clowns Administrative Centre just try telling Mr Chief Clerk Nordberg what his dead mates ought to be called, when he came to ask for the address of a friend, a dear and tragically departed friend, of my son, of my son here, of whom I'm very fond. The Dragon would have coughed up the information before you could blink, and she could assist the gentleman to open the grave herself if he so desired, sir.

Anyway, I didn't let them get me down, cos I know that's the way things are, and I know that one of these days I'll be growed up. And when I am, I'll come back here and in a loud voice instruct them to dig out information about my uncle's sister-in-law's grandfather who died in mysterious circumstances, run over by the last of the horse-drawn trams some time in 1905, and was shoved into the ground God only knows where, possibly somewhere in the Stockholm area, and I've no idea what he was called, but I'm called Nordberg, Managing Director Nordberg, and I want the old boy found!

No, I didn't let them get me down, but I shouted out under my breath, Pass, Chris! Open goal ahead!

Said to Dragon, Oh, they're in urns, are they? In that case I'm not interested. It's the bodies I want to see.

Withdrew with all flags flying. No idea how they sorted it all out at the Graveyards and Burial Grounds Administrative Centre.

The way back was just as hot, but not as long. Straighter, as it were. At Medborgarplatsen I took a break and nipped in to the Milk Bar and filled up with sausages and eggs, yes please, sunny side up, and beetroot and milk, and a slice of bread and butter, real butter in a little packet, and cheese. Life almost started smiling again, but it was hard going along Skanstullsbron and Nynäsvägen for the third time. I didn't have all Johnny's fancy gears to smooth the way. Amazing how hot it could be here in the Polar Regions.

The map on the wall of the Graveyards and Burial Grounds Administrative Centre must have been upside down or back to front or coded in some way or other, cos I went wandering around all the graves dragging along a bicycle that was more and more unwilling to follow me. It just didn't want to be pushed, and it was especially unwilling to be pushed in a cemetery, but for God's sake, you don't ride a bicycle round a cemetery.

171

I wandered deeper and deeper into the vale of death, reading Beloved and Sadly Missed on stone after stone. Amazing how many there were, crosses and stones and white doves with their stony heads bowed. A Last Resting Place, Our Dearly Beloved, Here Lies, Beloved, Sadly Missed, Born, Died, Born, Beloved, Died, Sadly Missed, left and right of one newly raked sandy path after another.

Here and there I found a letter or a number denoting a section or segment, and tried to remember how it had looked on the map, but nothing seemed to fit when you saw it at ground level. The rakers had no idea where section 50 was, of course, and all other members of the human race were bowed in prayer at some grave or other.

But in the end, as I got closer to the far side, near the wall along Tyresövägen, the section numbers started getting higher, and hey presto! Here was both section 50 and segment E. This was obviously the Unknown Soldier's part: a lawn dotted with little wooden crosses and no connection with real life apart from their numbers, stamped on the back. E10412 was different from the others in that nobody had bothered about the grave since it had been dug. Actually, there had never been any mention of relatives. The odd thing was, it was so overgrown and unkempt, looked as though it had been there ever since the war or thereabouts.

I didn't reckon it was any of my business to look after the grave, but I did wonder about the trick of burning the bodies. You couldn't very well think of a better way to cover up the evidence. The Agents from the Alternative World had won every trick yet again. Anyway, it's true to say I was no longer interested in opening up the grave.

So, it was a hard day and it ended in disappointment and empty hands, but then, what had I expected? My bicycle had turned into a concrete sculpture when I dragged it out of the cemetery and into Tyresövägen, and don't think for a moment that all the day's goings on had banished Johnny's freckled face from my mind. Not a bit of it. I was just as miserable as usual, and tired now on top of everything else. All my strength had gone, and it was a very long way home, and so I sat down by the roadside and cried my eyes out. As I said, that's the kind of summer it was.

When I'd got over it, I tried to hitch a lift, but nobody wanted to pick up a grubby little lad with a bicycle. Well, there was one bloke in the end. But the prat wanted me to do him a little favour first.

Little favours, Chris! Watch out for little favours! If some stranger comes up to you and asks you for a little favour, don't even ask what it is. Remember what I've told you. We don't want to read your name in bold print in all the headlines.

So I said I'd just go and tell my dad, who was over there by Mummy's grave, that I was getting a lift. The prat was off before I'd got halfway to the gate.

So there was nothing for it but to climb up on the sculpture and hang my heavy legs astride it and force it on its way home, but on the way past Medis I stopped again and nipped into the baths and took a long, cool dip in the pool. I'd always wondered why places like that kept open during the summer, when there were ice-free bathing beaches all over the place. Now I knew.

On the way home after my dip, I found myself free-wheeling down Högbergsgatan in a dream when I suddenly woke up and realized that I would have to gather a bit of strength if I was going to get up that hill. Just when I'd got myself down to a nice comfortable temperature.

As I passed the Kvarngatan steps memories of Johnny's stepracing came surging over me. I saw him come flying down that last stretch in and out of the old girl's bags, his face glowing with intense concentration, then landing and careering over the railings and leaving his bicycle behind and flying through the air . . .

I stood there staring across the street at the tangerine

ball rolling over and over and waited for the screech from the trolley bus, till I came back down to earth and remembered where I was. Odd, that bit with the face. I'd been watching from behind, from up above, when it actually happened, but here, today, he was coming towards me with all his features razor-sharp and his hair flowing back revealing his bare forehead, a naked, white forehead that had never seen the sun.

I know I've never actually seen him like that. Where did I get the image from?

I gathered my last reserves of strength and dragged myself and my concrete bicycle up the steps. I just never learn that this way, the shortest from Kvarngatan down to Högbergsgatan, is the longest way from Högbergsgatan to Kvarngatan.

On with the blinkers when I get to the top. It's very uplifting I don't think to live next door to a school building as big and imposing as South Side Grammar during the summer holidays. Everything's so quiet and brooding, much worse than anything the Forest Cemetery can come up with. Windows are squinting in all directions, the clock's stopped at a quarter past two and the whole fortress is sighing and whispering:

LIBERA SUM. DORMIO.
QUI FUGARET SOMNUM MEUM CAPUT
EIUS PERDEAT

In Latin, of course, cos the Municipal Grammar School for Boys hasn't caught on to the fact that there are three science specialists for every classics buff in that ancient and most worthy seat of learning, and that those classics buffs will die out before long since they have just decided to introduce a new non-academic stream for the boys of Södermalm who can't count and who've been going into the classics stream so far even though they're no good at languages either, just cos it's easier to learn languages than maths if you're no good at either.

Like the staff, the school building is marooned in times

174

past when every gentleman had to know Latin as a sign
he was educated. Nowadays you're better off if you know
a bit about atoms and can count and understand
formulae, the universe and the Alternative Worlds. Still,
to make sure progress doesn't get altogether out of hand,
they get in a few ancient relics to teach maths. In the
science stream, at least.

After dinner, I sat for a bit thinking about Per Anders
Andersson's card. Indicky card, as Johnny calls it. Then
I noted down:

> BURNT. E10412, sec.50, together with KHA.

Master shoemaker Karl Hildur Andersson was so fond of
his son, he wanted to take him with him into the kingdom
of death. There they both were now, with the same
address: E10412. Was KHA satisfied now, then?

I took a new card and wrote down:

> SECOND PROOF:
> PAA burnt to ashes.

On second thoughts, I reckoned that wasn't actually
proof, it was just . . . I tried to find the right word in the
dictionary, but when you really want something, it's
much harder to find it.

By Jove but you're working hard! Don't you take a
summer holiday like everybody else? Dad wondered.

This was a holiday job. What's it called when it's not
proof but just sort of suggests proof?

Did I mean circumstantial evidence? What are you
trying to prove now?

I changed both the FIRST and SECOND PROOF to
CIRCUMSTANTIAL EVIDENCE. Neither of them
was really proof. They were just circumstantial evidence.
Evidences? Pieces of evidence?

Just think. There was a bloke today who wanted me to
do him a favour.

At Flaten? I hope you went straight to one of the guards!

Not at Flaten. I told Dad how I'd been cycling all round Stockholm today. Have to get to know this dump somehow.

You've got time yet, said Dad. Plenty of time. What sort of a bloke was he?

The evenings were long, but there was nothing doing in the streets then either. The gang was scattered all over the place, living (let's hope so at least) at various camps. Apart from Bert. Bert was fifteen now and had started work and was hard at it during the day. He'd changed, cor had Bert changed! He was doing something interesting over at Kungsholmen, so I hardly ever saw him. We did bump into each other a few times in July, and once or twice in August. Every time he looked more and more like a stranger, and he gave me increasingly distant looks. Last time he had a bird hanging round his neck and a fag in his mouth, and he pretended he hadn't seen me, even though I knew he had. So I pretended I hadn't seen him either, but he knew I'd seen him. We know each other. Knew, I mean. Now he was away. That's how it goes with old pals.

It was less than four months ago he'd had a go at George who was puffing away at a Boy while we were waiting for the rest of the lads to turn up before going in to the baths, i.e. we were waiting for Harold as usual. George had a future as a sportsman to think about, and Bert was as upset as a youth club leader on his high horse. Smoking was the next worst thing you could do, after boozing, which was really rock bottom. So, it took just under four months to slide down to the bottom rung but one. I didn't want to know what came next.

Bert's departure meant the end of my innocence, if I can call it that; my naive belief that the lads were at the centre of my life, and would be till the day I died. One day, just after I'd seen Bert for the last time, it was clear to me, as clear as if I'd read it somewhere, that the future, my future, depended on what I could get out of South Side Grammar. I'd have to drop the lads soon. It wasn't only that your outlook on life is different on one side of the line from what it is on the other. The viewing stations are at different heights. I think the height is what really matters. It's your parents that dictate the height you start at. From then on, you start your own building.

This was another thing I discussed at length with the empty space beside me. *Do I have to drop you as well? Or have you already dropped me? Come and collect your Tizer at least! Say goodbye to Millie.*

You didn't answer. But I could hear your voice, I heard your voice so often but then when I turned round, you were never there.

Such was my summer holiday.

I thought I was crying non-stop all that summer, not least in the evenings when my loneliness caught up with me in bed in my room, the room that really was my own room now, with no Sis faffing around and getting on my nerves. I just cried my eyes out, and was lulled to sleep by the music Werner, the old-age pensioner, provided to sweeten the air of summery nights. He'd asked rather considerately if it was all right, as it was summer, even though it was on the late side, and Mum said, Oh yes, of course, it's just nice.

He'd sit there in the twilight, without turning the light on I reckon, and fill the whole house with sad sonatas, one after another. It's a mystery how anybody could fit a grand piano into that place, but there it was all right and Werner knew how to play it. I don't know what the pieces were called, the ones he used to play, cos there was no humming and hawing between records telling you if it was in K flat sharp and who was waving the baton round. But those were the Nights, Summer 1955, Lullaby for Chris, tired, sad, and missing Johnny so much he was ill.

Before the autumn term started, I plucked up enough courage to go to EPA and stock up with a few pens and pencils and a writing pad. Big, A4, with squares for drawing graphs, holes for filing, and no perforations, cos the pages just fall out if they're perforated. When the pad's full you detach the pages from the spiral and put them in a ring binder. You use the labels to give each binder a title. I bought three ring binders as well. I like binders.

I could have bought most of the stuff at the school shop, from the caretaker. His prices were a bit lower, but there wasn't as wide a choice. I wanted to choose my colours for the binders, and I didn't want to have yet another argument about the pros and cons of perforated pages, cos as we don't sell pads without perforations here it's obvious pads with perforations are much better, so you obviously ought to have a pad with perforated pages. And if I didn't want a pad with perforated pages because I wanted to wait until the whole pad was full before I put the pages into my binder, the fact is that lesson notes and homework and all the rest of it come in various subjects and they're spread over a long time, so of course it's more practical to be able to tear out individual pages whenever you like and sort them out into different ring binders, and so pads with perforated pages are just what you need. But I wanted to put my notes in my ring binders when it suited me and not when the blooming pages decided for themselves they were going to come apart. Cos that's what happens when I turn over a bit too energetically, they just float off and play at gliders and they land under the sideboard and hide and get all dirty. And the pages that don't come loose by themselves never do come loose, not even when I tear them along the perforations, least of all then, cos they're a law to themselves and the pages tear in the most unexpected places and always right through the middle of my most important notes. But the caretaker had never heard of his useless perforated pads behaving like that, despite the fact that I used to complain every time I felt bound to buy them the previous year. There was no shaking his view of the world: if the perforations didn't work, it was me who was odd. OK, I was odd, and I used to get a terrific thrill when I eased the spiral out of my pad, a thrill I lost out on altogether if I used the perforated sort.

Anyway, I wanted to have everything ready in good time before term started. And so, I went to EPA. That was where I discovered something I didn't know you could buy on the open market. I thought teachers were given a copy each, handed out by the teacher's employer, whoever that might be, and tabs were kept on it, or so I thought. But not at all. Anybody who wants can evidently buy as many copies of the Black Book as they like.

At last, I caught on: so that's how Mr G.G. did it.

On the other hand, I didn't think I'd ever be able to understand w h y he did it. And t h a t he did it. Wasn't Mr G.G. a bit long in the tooth for such games.

I reckon it's part of the story to report that when the new term started on Mon. 29.08.55, at 13.30, we lads who turned up to the classroom marked 2C were not welcomed by the worthy Mr G.G., but some new bloke. Worthy Mr G.G. had disappeared into thin air, not just from our class, but from the Municipal Grammar School for Boys on Södermalm. Or South Side Grammar, as it's usually known.

Teachers move on every year, I expect, that's reasonable enough. No doubt the way it goes when the flak starts flying.

I reported to Dad, who just looked blank. So blank I knew straight away Dad knew all about it, and had known since June. But what he actually said was that he'd forgotten all about Mr G.G. And had thought I'd forgotten him as well.

Have I forgotten Johnny? asks the cop.

No way. You don't forget Johnny. You force yourself to stop thinking about him, once you've realized there's nothing you can do about his mysterious absence and silence. You've got to, so you force yourself to stop crying and talking to yourself, and to others as well come to that, cos it only makes people stare and wonder which loony bin that mumbling whispering weirdo's escaped from. You force yourself to stop all those things that cause you pain. You distract yourself with vast clouds of triviality. Writing pads, for instance. You go to the flicks and try to switch your mind off. But nothing helps really: you can't forget Johnny even so.

The lads got together again as soon as there were enough to get together. We eyed each other up and down to see how much we'd grown, and soon knew all about that and everything else for the whole lot. George's face lit up as he told us he'd sailed over one-sixty-nine three weeks ago, and then done it again four more incredible times. We tested him straight off. We believed him, even though he only, only haha, managed one-sixty-five just then, and we gave him nine out of ten and promised him the extra point when he'd cracked one-sixty-nine in front of witnesses. He was going in for the local championships now. Bound to win in the '43 class, everybody reckoned.

Bert had left now, and to my amazement there was something in the air suggesting the lads were expecting me to take over. Maybe I should take that as a compliment: Catalogue Chris wasn't regarded as a complete and utter twit even though he did go to South Side Grammar. That's not the way things were looking last spring.

I didn't have any such ideas myself, as I've said. It's

one thing feeling you're on the way towards dropping your old mates. Quite another to say to them, Right, lads, I'm going to concentrate on my career now. I'm going to let you down now.

I just couldn't do that. Instead I went on and on about some maths stuff I barely understood myself. If the lads thought I was round the twist, they'd soon have second thoughts. Personally, I thought Sten was the best bet. A dead loss compared with Bert in his better days, but nobody could match that. Johnny maybe, but I knew Johnny would run a mile from any posts which might threaten his freedom.

The lads asked after Johnny, of course, thinking I was bound to know where he was. I told them Johnny would be coming, he's got a few things to see to, he's coming all right.

On Monday evening, when the autumn term started, I was all on edge, dead sure Johnny would turn up just as he had on the first day back at school last year. But Johnny didn't turn up.

A year with Johnny, I thought. Take away a month around New Year, two months around my birthday and Easter, and three months in the summer. What did that leave of the year? Half a year. Evenings for half a year. About five o'clock to ten, sometimes eleven at night, for half a year. Say six hours a night, which is on the high side. An eighth of a year, that's what's left of a year with Johnny.

It was only then, the evening of the twenty-ninth of August, that I finally understood. It had taken me a whole year! What was Johnny up to for seven-eighths of his time?

What's he up to? The lads wondered.

Johnny'll be coming, he's just got a few things to see to, he'll be coming. Day after day.

I didn't believe, despite my searches that summer at the cemetery and the Administrative Centre, I didn't believe for one moment that Johnny was really dead, or that he'd disappeared in the real sense of the word. I was certain he'd turn up again. So I'd decided that when he did so, I wouldn't ask him a n y t h i n g. I'd just tune in to his wavelength, and if he was going on as if we'd been together the day before yesterday, I'd do the same. If he wanted to tell me what he'd been doing all summer, I'd let him, and if it had been a smashing time, mine would have been as well. If he'd cried himself to sleep every night because he missed me so much he was ill, it'd have been just as bad for me.

It was time to put that into practice when Johnny Tangerine came out of nowhere, racing along St Paulsgatan on Monday night, one week after term started. He came like a flash of lightning, as August Strindberg's supposed to have said, but not about Johnny I shouldn't think. If Strindberg had seen Johnny on a bicycle, he'd really have had something to write about.

He came just as unexpectedly as first time, and blocked me, and it was 18.32 just as it should have been, and in a flash, there was the same still life as last year: the green eyes and freckles and the blazing inferno on his top-knot and the big white smile and the gap where there should have been the other half of a front tooth, on the right. From where I was.

When I compared the two pictures, I could see he was thinner now. And prettier. Yes, prettier, sorry about that!

The scar on his left cheek wasn't on last year's picture. It was now, though. But it was only just visible.

Just like last time, I got that strange feeling again: Where have I seen him before?

Hiyah! My name's Johnny. What's yours?

I took a deep breath, the biggest and deepest ever taken, and gave his incredible bicycle a thump. It didn't have any pennants any more! And I yelled out, What the hell do you think you're doing blocking my wheels, you rotten swine!

Then we let our bicycles drop and started wrestling on the pavement outside Number 21 St Paulsgatan, van der Noot's Palace, till our feathers were flying and smouldering in the evening sunlight. And we laughed and we cried, and we tickled each other in between bursts of thumping, which didn't hurt at all, and we wrestled and hugged each other, and the lads stood round clapping and cheering on I've no idea who, and Johnny was back, and I just knew he'd disappeared because he had to, and that maybe that's all I would ever know about it, but now he's here, so make the most of it and get a feel of him before he disappears again!

Then Johnny went over all the bicycles in sight and started adjusting saddles and handlebars that were too low, and moaned about all the things we'd let slide: How the hell can anybody make such a godawful mess of a set of wheels, Sten! Get some oil on that treadmill before the whole thing grinds to a halt, Harold! Has this little monster been on the rubbish dump all summer, or what, Pecka! How can the old girl have got as rusty as this after a summer like we've had, Bobby! For God's sake, what a shower!

I got the thumbs-down for my tyres, but there was nothing he could do about them just now.

His magic spanners flashed and sparkled, and the lads looked at each other and let him get on with it, but I thought: Something's happened. Something's happened to my eyes this summer cos I see what I haven't seen before: Here's Johnny doing all the things Johnny does, but it's not Johnny. All this performance with the bicycle spanners is play-acting, while the real Johnny is standing alongside, or even further away, testing to see whether we'll buy it again this year as well.

When he'd finished we all jumped on board and flew off like a swarm of bees towards Liljeholmsplan and back, and when we got back in a new world-record time we were all gulping ten litres of oxygen per second the way sportsmen do, all except Johnny that is who just laughed as if nothing had happened, waved, and disappeared in the direction of Götgatan before anybody could breathe a word. Disappeared in typical Johnny fashion, on Johnny's incredible bicycle, in a flash of tangerine flames down Götgatan, and away towards mysterious, rotten old Bjurholmsplan.

Sten held his paw out and said, Congrats, Chris Catalogue.

What do you mean, congrats?

On passing your exam, of course, Chris, that swine Chris.

What on earth are you on about?

Everybody heard you call your bike your wheels, and everybody thought you pronounced it perfectly. So congrats! You can stay with us for another week now.

I was surprised how much it hurt. That was Bert's old ploy. And Bert was no longer with us. Sten had no business to be playing at being Bert.

I cleared off home and announced that Johnny's turned up again!

Mum peered round behind me, no Johnny, have you fallen out?

But I reckon I had something in my eye or round about there, when I said no.

Dad was surprisingly sour and said that was terrific, cos now we've just missed Circus AIR's last performance in Sweden as well.

But rats to the circus, I've grown out of circuses, they catch children and all that, and I'm never going to a circus ever again! Johnny's back again now!

Dad tapped himself on the head and said he'd hoped I'd got over that summer's story about circuses by now. But never mind. He'd used to go to the circus for my sake, and if you don't think it's fun any more, I can always find something else to keep me happy.

That quietened me down a bit, cos when I'm doing something together with somebody else, I like to think we're both having a good time, generally speaking. But

184

now I was hearing that Dad had only gone to the circus for my sake. That was a bit hard to take.

Anyway, he produced a little notebook and a stub of pencil and he shoved them into my hand and instructed me that the next time you see Johnny, you just write down his name and address, and his telephone number if he has one. If you don't, I'll do it the next time he comes here, get it?

I got it all right, but I wasn't looking forward to doing it. When I had Johnny in front of me, I could never bring myself to ask him questions. And so night after night went by, but as long as Johnny made no move to come back home with me, there was no problem. After a few days, it looked as though he'd soon be asking about Millie, so on Friday night I made something up, and it looked pretty authentic I reckoned:

Jan Anders Andersson,
Bjurholmsgatan 23.
No telephone.

I'd no intention of handing the page over to Dad, and I wasn't going to let him copy it either. I just wanted to have something written down, something I could wave in front of his face, if he asked me.

And he did ask, of course. And I waved it around. And he wanted to see it properly.

But the information was top secret. A black spaceship had landed from Andromeda, and the Andromedans were looking for Johnny, cos he had, well, actually, that's also top secret as well, but there mustn't be too many people who know where they can find him. So I promised. The information can only be revealed in the most exceptional circumstances.

Dad reckoned I got more childish the older I became. Stop reading that *Amazed* stuff and go back to something simpler. *The Statistical Year Book* and Donald Duck and stuff like that.

Et Consortes, Dad, not Donald Duck and Stuff Like That.

185

All right, all right, but make sure you don't lose that piece of paper, and don't eat it up either, cos Andromedans can read chewed-up human handwriting ten times easier than they can read ordinary script.

So, I could fool him after all.

That's the way it is: if you tell the truth, and say that this is very serious, deadly serious, he's my mate, my very best friend in life and death, and our friendship depends on him being able to be who he is and that I don't ask questions and that he can rely on my not saying anything, well, if you say that, or something like that, then you get pressurized, and all your ideas are childish, and Johnny is crushed, and everything is ruined, and don't worry about it, there's lots of other nice friends in the world. But if you spin some cock-and-bull story about the level of a six-year-old, you get that little tap on the head, but you can keep the most important things to yourself even so. When I grow up and my son comes home with his mate and they have their friendship and their secrets, I'll leave him in peace, I won't interfere in what is his business, no matter how peculiar it looks to me from my grown-up point of view. Maybe they'll let me share it then.

And so Johnny was spared an interrogation. I really don't know how he'd have managed if he'd been questioned by Dad. The Chief Clerk spends all his time investigating things, and he knows how to get at facts. Mind you, he uses different methods from Mrs Nordberg, his wife, my mother.

He is fooled sometimes, though, just like her. By me.

It was hard enough for Johnny when he finally came and knelt down beside Millie's cage: That blasted mole has gone and forgotten me, matterfact!

A nasty mood came over me and I said that was impossible, cos guinea pigs have the best memories of all the animals. You must have offended him.

Never!

They're also the most easily hurt animals in the world.

186

You must have said something to hurt him, that's for sure. Or just told a lie. That'd be enough.

Johnny whispered to Millie, S-s-sorry, Millie! Hugged Millie, W-w-what's the m-matter then, M-M-Millie? Stroked Millie, but Millie just snorted and said he wanted to be left alone.

Dad reckoned I was right. Very sensitive animals, guinea pigs. Just think! And Millie being so friendly with you was a guarantee that you were an honest person.

But going on like that wasn't fun any more, as I should have realized when he started stuttering. Johnny headed straight for the door, without a look at anybody, and disappeared.

He's your man, said Dad, and I set off after him.

But a thunderbolt as the front door slammed, no sign of any bicycle down there, Fredmansgatan deserted in both directions. I was out-distanced, and it was hopeless.

Did this lead to another disappearance then? asks the policeman as I just stand there without saying anything. Partly cos I'm waiting for another bus to roar past, and partly cos I am remembering how furious Mum was with Dad when I got back upstairs again. I don't want to go into that.

I got dragged into her anger as well, and she went on and on about how inhuman we were, when we knew how things were with Johnny, poor kid.

I felt as though I'd been twisted into a question mark again, and looked to Dad for help, but he got out of the way, cos Mum in that mood is not his idea of good company.

How are things with Johnny, in fact?

I managed to slip that question into a gap when Mum had run out of steam for a couple of seconds. What kind of a poor kid is Johnny then?

Johnny's the kind of poor kid lots of other poor kids are all over the world, who are exploited for all kinds . . . all kinds of . . . purposes. But in the ideal homes of the welfare society young kids like that are reformed out of

187

existence according to official information to obey. They don't exist. And if some slip through the great welfare security net even so, the public just put up with the claim that they *don't* exist.

The Swedish people applaud the boasts of the politicians and pay up. Pay up fantastic good taxes, so they don't get their impressions clouded by proof that need really does exist. Everybody helps to keep the painful truth under the covers.

She has a few problems with the Swedish language, Mrs Nordberg does, my English mother, when she gets as worked up as that, but what she was getting at was quite comprehensible. Quite comprehensible.

If only I could understand what she was getting at. What could my imported mother see that Swedes couldn't see?

Had I forgotten what his face looked like last spring? How did it get like that, do you think? What right have you to put Johnny on the rack? You know nothing about the summer when he's been away. What did you chase Johnny out into just now, do you think? What's in store for him when he gets home?

And so on. It sounded pretty overwhelming, but I didn't really get it. Did Mum know something special about Johnny, or was she just going on like that from pure inspiration?

No, Johnny didn't disappear, I tell the cop, cos Mum's outburst is a sort of family affair.

He just stopped coming round to our place. So I did lose out on that.

Dad asked if he should apologize for something or other. Mum reckoned that was only right. I didn't know. It was all such a mess. Johnny was different, somehow, and yet just his old self in other ways. I don't know how to explain it.

Can we have a look at this then? The cop holds up Johnny's bracelet.

Johnny's bracelet.

Johnny! Now I k n o w something awful's happened!

Warning bells were ringing in the background. Look out! Look out! deep down inside me at first. They were getting louder every time the cop produced your most intimate belongings, one after another. And the questions! Watch out! Watch out! The leading questions, the images they conjured up. Warning! Warning! Details I hadn't noticed before. And now your bracelet. Now the sirens are screeching. Something awful's happened! Somewhere or other something awful's happened!

What's the matter, laddie? The cop looks me straight in the eye. Start at the beginning. We've got time.

Oh no we haven't got time! No time at all! Lives are at stake now, Johnny's life again, though he doesn't value it much, and I've been wasting all this time going on about all this stuff, I myself chose to start from the beginnning and not from the end, but I didn't know then, the idiot copper started with the bicycle and the Tangerinos instead of producing the bracelet straightaway, but now I know better and I yell that there's no time to waste, no time to waste at all, and show the cop my own bracelet, and the cop seems to believe me, maybe because my bracelet is exactly the same, only mine has a neat J punched on it where Johnny's has a C, and you don't need to be Sherlock Holmes to work out how the two bracelets are connected, and as they are connnected, and as I'm shrieking, in any case I can feel myself bursting and a shriek is spreading all over the street, as I'm doing that, and not putting it on or doing anything the least bit forced, the cop believes me, believes there's no time to waste, but first we'd better have a word with your parents, and he goes up the steps with me, while his mate drives the cop car round the block, at least I guess that's what he's doing, and when we get home he mutters away to Dad, while I put on something a bit warmer, and Mum gives me a hug and everybody behaves in such an odd way, curse them, this is no time to be odd, and when Dad says, You've got Johnny's address, and I'm forced to tell the truth about that, then Dad says, my fantastic dad!, *at last Johnny, at last I realize why you like him so much*, he just says that's a pity and the cop asks if Mum or Dad want to come as well, and they look at me and then at each other and then at the cop and then at me again and they're just about to say, Yes all right, Dad is at least, but instead he says, This is something Chris can handle himself, I reckon, we'll wait here, there's not much we can do, we can't change anything, and if you need us you know where we are, Chris, and so we set off, No, just a minute, the number! shouts the cop when we're halfway down the stairs.

What number?

The registration number of the Studebaker.

Back up again and dig down into the drawer.

Thanks! We've been looking forward to getting this.

And now, this time, we go down to the car, where all the lads are standing wide-eyed, wondering what's going on.

You don't *know* Johnny, lads. You don't know him at all!

Where Swedenborgsgatan runs into Adolf Fredrik's Square, the lads used to stand around just so we could have the pleasure of enjoying a bit of hatred. There are a few Nobs living round there, you see, and Nobs ought to stick to Östermalm or somewhere even more distant so they don't get in your way. So when the Mighty Mercedes-Benz With Private Chauffeur glided up to the kerb, the comments came thick and fast, bombarding the ears of the Nobs who were actually using their legs for a while to transport them as far as their front door. Most of the bombardment was aimed at the pale, well-mannered boy of about our age, running the gauntlet without raising his gaze.

The Nobs didn't pay much attention to us; we were just a phenomenon which manifested itself occasionally, nothing to worry about as long as we didn't assault them physically, which we never did. Pecka, who's still a bit childish, once opened his claspknife and was thinking of decorating one of the fancy cars, but we all stopped him. We had a good idea how Justice would react.

It was while we were engaged in one of those hate sessions I happened to notice that Johnny didn't take part in such things. He was some way off, messing about with his bicycle, and my new eyes realized he obviously didn't belong to the gang stirring things up outside Number 4 Swedenborgsgatan.

I went over and asked him if there was anything wrong, but it was just a routine service.

I worded my question a bit more precisely.

Johnny stopped pussy-footing, pointed at the gang and muttered something about little kids, daft carrying on, kindergarten stuff, matterfact, if you really want to know.

Then he jumped on his bicycle and would have been away if I hadn't been ready for him this time and held him back and asked him what he was so sour for.

Johnny wasn't sour, it was me who'd asked, matterfact, and he just answered, and was there anything wrong with that then?

But of course he was sour, he kept out of the way and called us little kids . . .

No, that's just not true, matterfact, cos it was when I *asked* that he'd *answered*, otherwise he wouldn't have said a word. And he wasn't keeping out of the way either, he was just standing waiting for us to finish playing, but then you never do that do you, so if you'll just l-l-l-et go of my back wheel, or do I have to th-th-thump you one f-f-first, then I'll hop it, cos it obviously p-p-puts you out if I'm not g-g-giggling with you while you're playing with your b-b-buckets and sp-sp-spades.

I heard all right, and knew it was starting to get dangerous for me if I stayed within range of him; but I wouldn't let go of his back wheel even so until he'd promised not to run away from me: Promise properly, Johnny, no fingers crossed or anything like that.

God but you're a p-p-pest! I have p-p-promised.

Then I got on my bike as well and we rode around for a bit, but without going anywhere near Bjurholmsplan. There were 66,061 cars in Stockholm, A-cars from the city itself that is, and goodness knows how many B-cars from the suburbs as well, not to mention a certain Studebaker. But at this time in the evening, Södermalm was a velodrome for the silent cyclists.

Johnny changed mood gradually and was OK again, and I like him so much it hurts. Just think if I could pin down Johnny, the real Johnny! When he's distant and acting peculiar like that, it hurts as well, but in the wrong way.

Johnny stood for ages outside the ironmonger's in Götgatan, lost in a dream and full of awe at the sight of all those amazing tools they had on display and his lips formed soundless technical terms which I don't even dare to try and repeat. My dream, my secret dream is that one day Johnny will say, Get out a dozen of your indicky cards, Chris, cos now I'm going to teach you the names of all the things that exist in my world, things which I know about and you don't.

That wasn't going to happen today, though, and after his moments of devout meditation we carried on up the street for a while.

Let's go in here! Johnny proposed, out of the blue. We've never done that before.

It was The Crown, the café in Götgatan. Right at the top of the hill, the crown in other words.

I protested wildly, we couldn't go into a café for crying out loud, you know that full well, Johnny, come back home and have a sandwich instead. Doesn't cost a dicky bird. Nice company. Nice surroundings.

But Johnny had a bit of cash, oh yes, and he was going to treat me just this once. We'd got enough nice company to keep us happy, and it looks pretty posh in here, so lock up your bike and come on in!

Johnny had a bit of cash?

That was a sentence which couldn't possibly exist in the Swedish language. How had it managed to get there?

I protested a bit more, but what choice did I have? Just clear off? Ask for details first? Whatever else you do, you don't ask your mate, when things are a bit sensitive anyway, Johnny, where did you get the cash from?

And so I felt obliged to go into The Crown with him. I had a feeling I hadn't had since I used to go to tea-parties at my aunt's place: trousers too big and shirt too small, and smelling of sweat among sensitive noses.

But as for Johnny, he didn't seem to feel a thing! His self-confidence wasn't just an act. Had somebody been and substituted a new Johnny since last summer?

There were so many Johnnies already. Johnny

Tangerine, one of the lads, number one maestro on a bicycle. The Johnny who's my and Millie's friend, Gentle Johnny, thrilled to bits with Donald Duck. Though that version seemed to have faded away now. A third Johnny, the secret, private Johnny I so longed to know, *do you exist?* Thinking deep thoughts in the void by my side, all summer long. He'd probably never existed, in fact?

And what about this Johnny? Johnny with a bit of cash. Johnny Posh, treating you to drinks at a café. He didn't seem to fit in at all. Did I want him?

I'd finished my painful cup of hot chocolate and was just wondering how on earth you got out of a café with your honour intact when Johnny leant over the table towards me.

Next Thursday I'll show you a secret. Thursday OK for you?

As he was being so formal about it, fixing up exact times and everything, I got my diary out and pretended to check all the important meetings I had, but what luck, eh! On Thursday I happened to have a vacant slot, so I expected I could fit in a secret that afternoon. Johnny was peering at my diary upside down, and he pointed and asked if hol. meant that I was off school on Friday, matterfact?

Hol. meant I was off school, yes indeed, there's a clever boy! You must have Friday off as well, don't you? Everybody's off next Friday and Saturday. It's good old half-term which they've shifted to the end of the month and fixed so that we miss out on Thursday.

That's perfect, matterfact, reckoned Johnny, and got me to book Friday as well. You'll be staying the night.

But Johnny! All a secret?

Why not?

I tried to explain about having a mum who worried and a dad with principles, and the effect it would have when I went home and said I was going out and would be spending the night somewhere, don't know where, and all the rest's a secret. It'll be thumbs down, for sure.

What did I mean, worried, and principles?? Johnny'd be there. What could possibly happen?

I laughed my head off at that, right in the middle of The Crown. So long that Johnny was surprised and turned a bit sour on me, and in the end he said, You can pull it off all right, if you really try.

If you want to, he added, a bit shy all of a sudden.

But I wanted to all right, and now it was Thursday and we were racing southwards out of town on our bicycles.

Mum had been doubtful, in spades, but Dad had faith in the good influence Johnny and I have on each other, though God knows where he got that from, and the autumn was still warm when they said Yes. And then there'd been a sudden cold snap yesterday. But that hadn't changed anything, seeing as everything had been decided already.

So Mum had made enough sandwiches for four to last a week, and stuffed them down into a rucksack with a couple of Tizers that Johnny had ordered, and a blanket. And a toothbrush! Oh, come on, Mum!

Johnny didn't need a blanket, he reckoned. He wanted to be a free man. You could tell a man was free cos he didn't lug stuff around with him wherever he went. A free man managed all right with Tizer and the amount of Mum's sandwiches I had in my rucksack.

We whizzed along through Hammarbyhöjden and yelled rude comments at the pale weedy kids from the suburbs who'd never seen a real lad from town on a real bicycle before, else why should they be pointing at us and screeching things we couldn't hear, those creeps on the pavements, as if they wanted us for something, but we'd disappeared over the horizon already, down streets with funny names.

Tyresövägen through Enskede was the road to the secret at the end of the world, but at Pungpinan, right outside the cemetery entrance where once upon a time, one lost summer, I'd cried my eyes out over a lost friend, there was such a hell of a bang from my front wheel that all the corpses came rushing up in a panic asking the way to the right hand of God the Father.

A king size puncture! The whole tyre in tatters. But no problem, Johnny was at hand, get on with it, Johnny!

This time though he could only scratch his topknot and it was obvious right away that it was hopeless. There was no chance of mending the inner tube and the tyre was in ribbons. It's had it, matterfact. How can anybody be so stupid as to ride out for a picnic with a tyre like that?

But Johnny, I rely on you to look after my bicycle. What sort of a job do you call that?

Johnny checked right and left, but no spare wheels came rolling past today. We shifted the rucksack from the luggage carrier to my strong back, hid my bicycle under a fir tree in a thicket to the left of the road, and asked the corpses to keep an eye on it so the local light-fingered gentry wouldn't find it.

Johnny pumped a bit more air into his back tyre. It's at times like this you need a luggage carrier, matterfact, he muttered in annoyance.

I had to sit right at the back end of the Vienna roll and look after the pedalling. Johnny squeezed in front of me, got hold of the handlebars and covered all the levers and handles, and yelled, Full steam ahead and anchors aweigh! and so I started pedalling, cor but it was easy, and God only knows where Johnny put his feet, but off we went anyway.

The first bit, going downhill, I tried hard to see where we were going, but it was very awkward, threw us off balance and wasn't worth it, so I gave up.

I held on to Johnny's waist for dear life, yelling, Do your stuff, I can't see a blind thing!

Just give me enough speed so I can steer, he shouted back at me.

I held on to his back with my teeth, pedalled away, and could feel how he was changing gear at just the right moment. Cor, how easy it was to ride Johnny's amazing bicycle! It was the first time I'd been on it; in fact, as far as I knew, it was the first time anybody but Johnny had been allowed on his Holy Bicycle.

He smelt of tar and pine needles, and his muscles were hard because of the peculiar position he was forcing his body into, and he leant on me with part of his weight once he felt we were balancing OK, and I pressed myself up against him with a similar amount of force and hung on round his waist.

Le Chatelier's principle! I yelled.

Eh?

Le Chatelier's principle. When the conditions change on a reversible reaction, the equilibrium is adjusted to reduce the effect of the change.

You're mad! shrieked Johnny. Stark raving mad!

The fact that we didn't fall off has less to do with Le Chatelier's principle than Johnny holding hard on to the handlebars, cos I was pedalling faster and faster, my thighs were rubbing up and down along Johnny's hips, his bicycle was too low for me, too low for him as well come to that, but that's the way he wanted it, and so my knees went backwards and forwards like pistons along Johnny's sides, and the friction nearly set my trousers on fire, and the movement made his Tangerinos slide down and his shirt work its way up, so after a bit his back was all bare, all white and naked, it had never seen the sun, and I had my face buried in a knot of a shirt smelling of tar and pine needles, the shirt Crimsonita, and I was pedalling like hell, cos I remembered Johnny's lesson showing that you wobble less the faster you go, all that about centrifugal forces and gravitation and going round in circles, and I was scared stiff of falling off any minute, but I also felt secure in the smell of tar and with my arms round Johnny, and when I heard his chest vibrating because he'd stopped singing, Chris is mad . . . I have a mad little Chris on my bike . . . Chris is mad . . . , and had started singing some wild, secret song or other, I disappeared into another world, with Johnny pressed hard against my body, jammed between my legs as I pedalled away, and this crazy song, which the wind

197

snatched away but which vibrated in his body and mine as well, cos in that world we both had the same body, his arms, my legs, his legs, my arms, and the same thoughts, swaying along with the song, which we were singing together, only with his tongue and his vocal cords and his chest, and the smell of pine needles and tar till Johnny put the brakes on, suitably gently, and unfolded his legs so the bicycle didn't fall down.

Let go! I could hear it miles away. No, I didn't hear, didn't understand, nothing to do with me.

Let go, Chris! We're there now!

Odd! It was Johnny shouting, but it wasn't until I got an elbow in the belly that I realized I was involved somehow, and carefully loosened my grip. Johnny turned round and looked me in the eye. His lovely freckled face, etched by the wind now.

He didn't smile at all, just looked deep at me for ages. Could he see something special?

Come on, Chris. We go up here for a bit.

I recognized where we were: we were outside the bunker built into the hillside at Flaten. I never came here last summer, but at other times I'd whiled away the occasional summer day here, in among the secret shadows of the war. At least, that's what I associated the bunker with. If in fact it has more in common with big underground warehouses, I still prefer the more exciting version I thought up as a seven-year-old.

I felt too muddled to say anything about recognizing where we were, hadn't shaken off that other world yet. I just followed Johnny, who was leading his bicycle along a winding path up the hill opposite the bunker, right up to the top and way into the forest.

He stopped and gestured grandly, and there was the secret: a magnificent hut.

I was really impressed, and went round and round it, sighing, Just look at that! and, Just look at this!, noting all the fancy touches. The situation was perfect: you couldn't see it from any direction until you were right on top of it. When I eventually crept inside, it was obvious you could snooze away here in peace and quiet, all nice and dry, even if there was a hurricane blowing outside.

What a really smashing hut, Johnny! The hut of huts! What a terrific secret to have tucked away!

We sat down and started the evening with a sandwich each.

She's pretty good at this, your mum, Johnny acknowledged, his mouth stuffed full.

It wasn't the first time he'd given Mum the OK, but it was the first time he'd actually put it into words. It suddenly struck me that Johnny didn't have a mum. You could just feel it, somehow.

She's got such a marvellous dialect, said Johnny, thoughtfully.

Accent. I put him right.

Eh?

Accent. An English accent: Dad's imported her.

Is she really from E n g l a n d !

What was so special about that?

Yes, that's why she has an accent. Remember, dialect is what you and me and people from the south have got.

I haven't got a dialect! protested Johnny.

Too right you ain't got no dialect, I agreed, piling it on. Depends wot yer comparing it wiv.

Accents and dialects are great, though. When you stick your neck out and reckon: Ah hah, Norrköping. And all that.

He stopped dead.

Oh, so Johnny had been around a bit, had he? Slipped up just then. So used to that kind of thing he could stick his neck out and reckon Ah hah, Norrköping, when he heard that dialect. Why keep it all a secret?

Mind you, I hadn't let on about going to England now and then, even if it wasn't exactly a secret. It seems a bit much, boasting about foreign trips in front of the lads. That kind of thing's more suited to the classroom. But I'd kept quiet about it there as well, as usual. That's why my classmates were so impressed by my English. By not letting on about the simple truth, I'd got plenty of admiration to make me feel good.

What was the big secret Johnny was keeping under his hat? Was he really a rich man's child, in disguise so he could study low life?

‘ But that didn't really fit. Not even when I thought back to how relaxed he'd been at The Crown. Cos that didn't fit in with anything at all. There was too much about Johnny that just didn't fit in, no matter how you tried to explain it. But the idea of a rich man fitted in worse than anything else.

I hastened to fill the silence before Johnny caught on that I'd noticed what he'd said. Of course! Coming back home after a summer in England was like having a dip at Medis after a hot Wednesday. For your ears, that is. At last, people seemed to be talking properly.

So you can speak   E n g l i s h, then!

Fancy being able to impress Johnny with *anything* at all. But why English?

Johnny rolled over on his stomach and gazed longingly at the bulge in the rucksack that spelt Tizer: And GeeGee hates you even so.

I was going to point out that Mr G.G. had never found out what I knew before he started hating me. But then time stood still, and the room started going round instead. Johnny?

Yes?

I've never told you anything about Mr G.G., have I?

He thought for a bit. Yes, you must have, surely? I reckon . . . Mebbe not, though . . . Anyway, I know GccGee. You'd never have believed that, eh!

Certainly not! Never believed, never dreamed, never suspected.

But he's gone on about Nordberg, he has. It's thanks to him I know you're called Nordberg. You should hear him going on about it! Cos Nordberg is no fit company for me: I'll beat the living daylights out of you Jayjay, if you go around with Nordberg any more. And then it'll be Nordberg's turn.

Good God, Johnny! He wasn't lying there and telling me Mr G.G. was his dad?

No! Hell, no! Johnny roared his head off, and tried to twist his freckly fizzog into a G.G. expression. Dead like him, eh?

Dead on, I reckoned, but I thought, Too young, too lovely, too far, far away. I wondered for a moment where I'd got that from. But explain, for God's sake!

What d'yer mean, explain. GeeGee is . . . how shall I put it . . . matterfact . . . well . . . a friend of the family, you could say. Not my friend exactly, but . . .

So tomorrow he'll beat the living daylights out of you?

Huh! Johnny sat up straight. Nobody beats the living daylights out of me, matterfact.

What did you say he called you?

Jayjay. Yang Jayjay.

Good God! Are you a Chink?

Eh? You're half English and you don't know what yang means?

I stared at Young J.J. and thought of Old G.G. and wondered what was going on, and asked myself what a friend of the family could mean.

It seemed about time to change the subject, cos for some time now I'd been closer to Johnny's Secret Home than ever before, so he might go into reverse gear at any minute. But listen, Johnny. Next time you come round to our place, just take a look at the door if you want to know what I'm called. It says Nordberg. At about knee height, or thereabouts. On the letter box. On that brass plate hanging over the hole in front of the letter box, I mean. Seen a letter box before, have you?

Oh, you mean one of them?

Exactly. What does it say on your door? Young Johnny J . . .

Haven't a clue. It doesn't say Nordberg, though.

Anyway, now it's time to vote. Tizer for afters, or no Tizer. Thrift is a virtue, so we decided to save it till the next day, or maybe the night, if it was cold.

Something to drink was a good idea though, so our next decision was to go down to the bathing beach and enjoy a dessert from some tap or other.

I asked Johnny when he'd found time to build his palace, and he said offhandedly he'd done it last summer. He'd been at Flaten every day, travelling on the Yellow Buses, but he'd managed to slip away before they caught him and made him play all their uplifting games.

This last summer, you mean?

Exactly.

I was in a bit of a rush to get out, cos I didn't want Johnny to see my eyes, not even my face, cos I could feel something was happening there that was hard to hide, much too hard, and I didn't want Johnny to see it. But Johnny came out as well, of course, and I worked away on my face, trying to hide it, specially my eyes, and I tried to go down to the beach with Johnny without saying a word, cos I didn't trust my voice either.

If Johnny had been on the Yellow Buses one single time last summer, I'd have seen him. You can't miss Johnny!

So, there was something else that didn't fit. And the lie he came out with wasn't really a lie either, cos a real lie has to have just a little bit of a chance of being taken for the truth. There was no chance at all here, cos the kids who go to Flaten in the summer have no chance whatsoever of keeping out of the way for whole days on end, I knew that, and everyone else who'd tried it knew that. Everybody except Johnny, of course. And so Johnny just hadn't tried. And so he was telling lies, and so there was something special about this hut, something which Johnny didn't want me to know about, and something special about last summer, something which Johnny didn't want me to know about, and there were all kinds of things about Johnny that Johnny didn't want me to know about.

It was a good job Johnny didn't press me and ask why I wasn't saying anything. I know I wouldn't have been able to keep a straight face, and it was essential to keep a straight face now. But Johnny was good at keeping quiet and leaving other people in peace, so by the time we got down to the taps I'd managed to get my fizz sorted out and made up my mind, as I had to do of course, that for the time being I wouldn't mourn the fact that Johnny, my friend, my best mate, was spinning a web of yarns. I'd been let into a secret, but I'd landed myself with a new riddle.

I put this new bit of the puzzle away in the same box as all the others. I thought that one of these days, I'd be able to piece together his true face. But at this stage I was beginning to suspect I shouldn't be in too much of a hurry, that there wasn't all that much of a rush to get the puzzle finished. After all, everybody knows that once you've finished the puzzle, there's no fun left.

Anyway, I pretended to be cheerful again and we splashed water over each other and chased after each other and did press-ups on the exercise frame and Johnny did most, of course, even though I'm actually stronger than he is, but he managed to force his tough little body to do six or seven extra on pure will, so what can you do?

The café was closed of course. The rowing boats were chained up, and reminded me of a summer which Johnny suddenly wanted me to remember differently. I wished the boat girl was sitting there, cos I wanted to show her Johnny, the real Johnny, and I wanted assuring by her answers that I hadn't just imagined the whole summer.

Yes, of course *you* were here, Chris. And you went on about him over there, Johnny, who *wasn't* here. That's how it was.

In a nutshell, Flaten was dead. Apart from a bloke standing near the trampoline, smoking. The Monster? The distance transformed somebody who may have been innocent into the Monster's twin brother.

I looked over at Johnny without making it obvious just as he was gazing along the shore. If it had been the Monster standing there, Johnny would have surely reacted in some way. I insisted on linking Johnny and the

Monster, even though the Monster denied having ever heard of Johnny. The link was unknown, and so was the reason why he denied there was one, but there must surely be something. Johnny didn't react at all now. But there must surely be something.

Up at the camping site, we found a hut. A pretty tenth-rate affair, and whoever built it had cheated with planks.

Amateurish, was Johnny's comment. It's not meant to last.

We took a few steps towards it and caught a glimpse of a floor, which, despite the regulations nailed to the Flaten notice board, had not been dismantled when the tents were taken down. There was a bloke and a girl lying there, against other regulations, convinced they were invisible, either that or they didn't care either way. When we realized what they were up to, we withdrew discreetly.

Well, to be honest, it was Johnny who withdrew. As for me, I wasn't fully enlightened on this fascinating topic and I'd have had nothing against broadening my education for free, but as I say, it was Johnny who withdrew. The education you can get from Sten's magazines is veiled in mist, and everybody just giggles when Sten snatches back his precious possessions before you can get any further than noting that tarts have breasts and blokes' tongues hang out when they touch them. Me, I refuse to buy *Pinup* and *Health and Efficiency et Consortes*, which would really be the simplest way of studying them in peace and quiet; but where would you keep them? Even if you plucked up enough courage to venture into the Newsagent and Tobacconist's and point to them. And as for paying the old girl behind the counter!

We didn't say anything about what we'd seen, but the silence was a bit awkward for a while, till we came upon a ball in the ditch just behind the little grass pitch. We tried a bit of dribbling between the goalposts as the sun was setting.

This was something Johnny wasn't much good at, at

least. He had no skill at all, just kick and rush; and if he found himself in front of an open goal with the ball at his feet, he'd just give it a little prod and nothing happened at all.

This was fun, and out here at Flaten, it was OK to laugh, but in the yard at South Side Grammar it would be a real nightmare if you had to have somebody as useless as Johnny in your team. From a creeping suspicion that great Johnny's ball sense wasn't all that fantastic, they'd realized he was absolutely useless when it came to anything of that kind. Maybe he was brilliant on a bicycle, but he was a complete duffer as soon as he came anywhere near a ball. Out of respect for Johnny we didn't laugh, didn't smile, didn't make comments, didn't sigh. But it hurt. By God, it hurt! With an atmosphere like that, of course, we didn't get round to playing much football. And now that Bert had gone, there was nobody to kick us into playing anything remotely resembling matches.

Out here at Flaten though, with nobody around, I could laugh, Johnny allowed it, laughed himself, and made fun of this important game which, understandably, he didn't take very seriously. Still, we got pretty hot, so when we'd finished kicking around and booted the ball into the bushes, I suggested we should take a quick dip.

You go ahead, said Johnny. I want to keep warm ready for the night.

There we were again! Every time we were going swimming at Medis, Johnny had some excuse or other; and now here was a new one. He didn't want to go swimming in Flaten either, but he couldn't blame it on the chlorine out here.

So I had a dip. In the buff, of course, as there was nobody around. The Monster's twin had disappeared, and the couple at the camping site presumably wouldn't have been shocked if they'd happened to come past just now.

By Jove, it was warm! Johnny sat on the jetty as if he was a lifeguard. Stick to where it's shallow. He sounded like a lifeguard as well.

Hey, *can* you swim? I put it to him straight.

Course I can, he snapped. As far as you like, matterfact.

I was just going to tell him to prove it then, when I remembered how he'd done his tightrope walk over Södergatan, and various other things Johnny had to prove. No thank you, I don't need proof!

I said nothing, which is what wise men are supposed to do, and played whale a bit longer, which is what wise men aren't supposed to do; but I wanted to show him how great it was in the water.

For crying out loud, don't swallow that sewer syrup! was all Johnny had to say about that.

Anyway, I got out eventually and stood there on the jetty, letting the breeze dry me; it took quite a while at this time of night, and I started shivering. A jetty's ideal when you've just come out of the water. You don't get sand between your toes, sand that gets into your underpants when you pull them on later, and then itches and tickles unless you can get a shower pretty sharpish.

Johnny was sitting right out at the end of the jetty, staring stubbornly at the café all the time, and in the end I asked him if he was upset.

No, what d'yer mean?

He sounded genuinely surprised, but even so, I thought it would have been more convincing if he'd looked at me instead of talking to the café. I myself am not so good at keeping quiet and leaving other people in peace, even if that is a quality I admire in others, so I went up to him and tried to make him look at me, but he just turned away. So I sat on him.

Blimey, he was mad!

He jumped up and gave me a hell of a thwack just over my ear, and I didn't know if I was coming or going. He was as white as a sheet in between all his freckles and yelling away at me, but I've no idea what he was on about cos I was seeing stars, and I very nearly fell back into the water, but then he grabbed me, groggy old me, and flung his arms around my soaking wet body, and whispered, S-S-Sorry, C-C-Chris . . . s-s-say you'll f-f-forgive m-m-me! right in my ear, the one I could still hear with, and what voice I had left mumbled, Course! Course! and asked, But what on earth did I do anyway?

He led me over to my clothes and I got dressed, cos I was dry now, the last bit of damp was in his Crimsonita. But the thump had set me off sweating, and I was all shaky, and Johnny was muttering s-s-sorry and all that, and I was saying, Course, course, and I suppose I meant it, but after we'd gone a couple of metres over the grass, I blacked out.

I've no idea how long I lay there, but I woke up to the smell of tar and pine needles, and Johnny was lying pressed up against me with his arms round me, crying so much he was shaking, and then I burst out crying as well, I felt so awful. But Johnny was thrilled to bits and gave me a whopper of a kiss, just as unexpectedly but naturally as when he'd flung himself on The Ostrich that time.

Anyway, that was enough of bawling. We washed our faces under the tap, and tested the loo which was still perfectly usable, though it was too dark now to study the inscriptions on the walls.

We'd started a new chapter now, Johnny. Once you've cried together, the world's never the same again.

Finding our way back to the hut in the dark was no real problem. Well, maybe I shouldn't say that, because Johnny did the map-reading. I probably wouldn't have found it on my own, cos you couldn't see it from any direction, and there were no landmarks visible in the dark woods.

It was pitch black inside. Johnny fumbled around and produced a flashlight from a corner, but when it had glowed orangey-yellow for half a minute or so before going out, it had to be said that the organizer had slipped up on one detail, in fact.

Johnny hit on the idea of moving his dynamo to the back wheel and pedalling up a bit of light that way, but we both reckoned it wasn't really necessary. It was easy to find the rucksack, and we managed to stuff a sandwich into our mouths without a searchlight.

Mind you, it was pretty awkward laying out the blanket in the dark. I was really glad we had a blanket with us now, cos it wasn't all that hot since the sun had gone down. Yesterday's cold snap looked as though it was going to repeat itself. We just had to hope it wouldn't drop below freezing, not inside at any rate. Cos we'd promised not to use matches even if we were freezing to death. The hot summer had really dried out all vegetation, especially up in the hills. All round us were brown trees looking as if they'd burst into flames at a touch. We just had to imagine a nice warm fire.

Don't you want to share the blanket? I asked the darkness, even though I knew the free man from the hills would say no thank you to any kind of cissy stuff.

But lo and behold! Yes, please, after a silence that echoed round every free hill there ever was. And he crept up close on the blanket.

We folded the edges over us and rolled about and shuffled around for a bit, but discovered what we had to discover, namely that in circumstances like these the best way to lie is with one arm over the other bloke's chest, and the other under his head, holding on tight in order to keep warm, and there it was again, his smell of tar and pine needles, and a bit of idle chat about this and that, getting vaguer and sleepier in the warmth we were giving each other, and though it was pitch black I can almost swear blind that when Johnny muttered something about trying out the hut in winter one of these days, I could see, floating freely in the air, his white smile with the gap where his front tooth should have been. On the right. From where I am.

Then we slept pretty badly, both of us. It was cold from the ground, and on our backs. Once or twice Johnny's rusty voice muttered into my ear, Time to turn the bacon, and so we did. But then I couldn't use his arm as a pillow, and it wasn't long before my stomach felt cold without the warmth Johnny had supplied, and I couldn't lie on my right ear, which was aching something awful.

It must have been more or less the same for Johnny, apart from the ear, cos pretty soon he turned over and I turned over and we went into a clinch again. This time we intertwined our legs as well.

Johnny raised his hand and gently stroked my ear: Does it hurt?

It's not too bad, I lied. And Johnny sighed.

The warmth came back again, though now my back was cold, and the tar and pine needles swept over me and I was whisked away into that other world again and I could feel my dick hardening and growing. I'd been afraid of that all the time, ever since Johnny had started talking about spending the night together, but now that it was happening, I didn't mind. Johnny must have noticed, but he didn't say anything, and I was glad about that, cos I don't find it easy to talk about such things. It's all very well joking in general terms about life's secrets, and pretending that such things don't affect me. But talking about yourself like that, seriously, and just when something embarrassing is happening you can't do anything about, I don't think I could manage that. And Johnny had never been known to either joke or say anything serious about the area inside his underpants.

Anyway, he didn't react in the same way now, or I'd have noticed, of course. But he was awake, at least as long as I was, and in his freckly silence, and all the tar and pine needles, I just lay in another world and couldn't care less that my dick was pressing up against him.

I kept waking up, so I must have got a little bit of sleep. On one occasion I was woken up by voices.

Or so I thought.

When I listened, though, it was all quiet outside, so I wasn't sure. Had I just dreamt the voices? My sore ear was buzzing and wasn't reliable. In my dream, the Monster and Mr G.G. had come striding up and were

209

going to get Johnny and me. We hid behind the Studebaker, which was all transparent and was parked in our courtyard at home, in front of the outside loo. The Monster was pointing straight at us, saying something about us being there, but Mr G.G. said they might just as well turn back.

Johnny wasn't breathing at all. He had let go of me. In my dream, he'd been lying on his back with a little axe in his hand. Now I couldn't see how he was lying. Couldn't hear him. But I could smell the tar and pine needles.

Did you hear anything? I asked.

Was he asleep?

No, he was holding his breath.

Was he pretending to sleep?

No, he was keeping quiet.

No, he whispered after an age. Pressed his bonce against my chest. I didn't hear anything. He hugged me tight. There's nothing there.

Johnny was frightened. It was catching.

They won't find us, he breathed.

Who won't?

It was three centuries before he breathed again. They won't find us.

It was another three centuries before he dropped his guard, softened up, loosened his grip on me a little bit and started breathing again like you do when you're asleep.

In the dawn light I could just see, behind Johnny, the little hiding place with the burnt-out flashlight standing open. There was also a little axe and a sheath knife in there. Tools for building a hut?

I examined Johnny's right wrist carefully, very carefully, as it lay naked before my eyes. What had I expected? It didn't tell me anything special about Johnny, apart from that he was very skinny. And it occurred to me that this bloke who was so ginormously tough that everybody gave into him could nevertheless feel so little and skinny and helpless, lying tight up against me as he was now. In his sleep, with all his defences down, his pretty girlish face was turned towards me, close by, naked, all soft and open, but even so I couldn't read out of it all the secrets that just had to be there. The world hidden inside his red head was so close by me, and yet so far, far away. There it was again: Too young, too lovely, too far, far away. Yet again, I wondered where it came from.

He woke up, as if my looking at him had singed his skin. I saw his pupils grow and could feel his muscles twitching until he came down to earth, his pupils went back to normal, he went all soft and cat-like, and laughed at me: Cor, you're so big at this time of morning. And he licked his chapped lips, and I did the same; a delayed mirror, I was.

We rolled apart and guessed at what time it was till I looked at my watch, my self-winding, waterproof, shatterproof wristwatch which also told you the date. The date was FR 30 SEP, and the saint's name for that day was Helge, I informed Johnny, though that last bit of information wasn't displayed on the watch.

Yes, OK, but what time is it, Chris Calendar Clock Catalogue Card Index, what time is it?

Twenty-two minutes past five, pip, and Johnny had guessed nearest with his dead on half past five in four seconds from now, compared with my bid, which was a quarter past six. What had fooled me was that I knew sunrise was at 5.51 at Stockholm's latitude, and now it was light. Knowledge plus ignorance equals a faulty answer. My ignorance was that I'd always thought it was dark until the sun rose. It was only now I realized what really happened, in that way the penny drops and you suddenly k n o w that it was just as obvious it would be light for quite a while before the sun rises as it was for it to be pretty light for quite a while after the sun sets.

We left the hut, and softened up the joints that had been in contact with the ground all night. Johnny jogged off and was out of sight for a while, but I kept within sight of the hut. My feet felt as if they belonged to somebody else, and my back had been through the wars. Still, once round the hut and a morning slash in the bushes, and life started to come back. Johnny returned from his jog and reckoned his morning stiffness was a sign of old age coming on.

But you're never going to get any older. A pretty good dig, though I say it myself.

His hair was blazing away all round his head.

It occurred to me I'd never seen him in the morning before, apart from when he was fast asleep and shattered that time at home. Never like this! He was one of those people who are always pale in the morning. His skin was snowy white in among his cheeky freckles, and the fire in his hair brought a wave of joy flowing forth from my innnermost oceans, and it broke on the shore in bubbles of laughter I made no effort to conceal.

He eyed me up and down and wondered what I was laughing at, and I asked what he was laughing at, cos that hair of his shouldn't be mentioned, but he was laughing cos I was laughing, he said, and so I laughed at him laughing at me, and in the end we just laughed cos we were laughing, that's all, and we boxed each other till we had no strength left. Then we crawled back in and gobbled a couple of morning sandwiches and half of a Tizer each.

When Johnny took the bottle out of the rucksack, to my horror and shame, my toothbrush followed it into the light of day. I'm never going to hear the last of this, I thought, but it just shows you how little I knew Johnny, yet again. He took one look at the toothbrush lying there, and I could see his ears changing colour.

Attack is the best form of defence, I reckoned, and I asked him if he'd never seen a toothbrush before.

Good God, course I have, twice, or three times, at least.

Don't blame me, it was my gormless mum who put that in.

Gormless?!?!?! For crying out loud, you haven't a clue, have you! God, Chris, you're a lucky blighter!

Oh yes, course, the luckiest boy in the world. But what on earth do I want a toothbrush for out here in the wilderness?

But come off it, I hadn't a clue what a smashing mum, old lady, mother I had.

It suddenly occurred to me that all this was because Johnny didn't have a mum himself. I wanted to change the subject, but Johnny kept going on and on, het up, morally het up, indignant, as I believe they say in better-class circles, till I groaned, Stop it, stop it! I promise to tell her I'm sorry when I get back home, sorry Mother, I did you an injustice, you're a treasure.

He did actually stop at that, and we completed our simple breakfast and established that Life, with the biggest possible capital L, should be like this: sleeping under the open sky in the middle of the jungle, wrapped up in your worn-out panther skin, getting up at dawn and howling at the hazy disc of the sun . . .

Johnny howled like a true sun-worshipper, and we decided first to go down to the lake and watch the sunrise, then nip over to the Haunted House at Ekudden.

We got the time just about right for the sunrise, but the direction was wrong, so that was rather less than a total experience.

Ekudden next. I suggested we should swim over there, seeing as we'd already gone down to the shore and could see the headland not far away over the water. But Johnny didn't want to, of course. We should walk all the way round, through the thickest undergrowth. There was an old hut he'd built that he wanted to have a look at on the way.

Either he forgot about it, or else he looked quicker than your craftiest Indian, cos there was no more mention of that hut, and I didn't see any sign of it either.

The haunted house crouched broodily in the morning sunlight, which only succeeded in sending darkness in through all the broken windows and doorways, where the doors themselves had holes instead of panels, and pointless padlocks round the handles.

You had to be careful how you went, cos it wasn't last week when the place was last repaired, and it wasn't exactly newly cleaned either. You could fall through the floor any moment, and the stairs especially were unreliable. The place was supposed to be haunted, with disembodied heads wandering about on their own, and detached hands grabbing at your throat . . .

The stories sounded a bit far-fetched, in fact, and the morning sun didn't give the right atmosphere. Actually, there wasn't a single interesting item left in the house nowadays, but needless to say, we had to go in and look round even so.

Johnny told all kinds of bloodcurdling stories about what had happened here in the murky past. They were the same old stories. The alarm bells started ringing just as I was about to fill in an extra detail for him, and I didn't let on I knew all about Flaten. Johnny was supposed to be the one claiming to be at home there. And he obviously did know quite a bit, in fact. Very odd, all this!

No ghosts appeared, so we wandered out into the garden.

Just think, as from tomorrow no one'll need a ration book any more, I remarked, out of the blue.

Yes, so I heard, said Johnny, without a moment's hesitation, as if he'd been thinking about exactly the same thing. A real stroke of luck, eh! One book less to read.

I tried to work out the joke, to work out what wave-length he was on. But he didn't look as if he was trying to be funny at all, so in the end I asked him if he knew what the ration book was.

He hesitated for a millisecond, and that green look of his gave my face the once-over, but then he chuckled and said he'd just guessed, had I noticed, and what kind of a book was it then?

I explained about the ration book for strong drink, and Johnny said well then, they used to need a book, but now they don't need a book any more, so that's a good thing

214

isn't it, just as he'd said?

I didn't say anything, of course, but I reckoned I'd just witnessed the Oddity of the Week. But it was some time before I caught on to why I thought it was extra-peculiar, and then maybe it wasn't so peculiar after all. It was Bert who'd said Johnny got beaten up at home. Without spelling it out, it was the same as saying they got drunk at Johnny's place.

Now, in the garden of the Haunted House, it dawned on me that getting beaten up at home wasn't necessarily the same thing as the family being boozed up. It also dawned on me that maybe Bert's explanation wasn't right. Perhaps Johnny hadn't been beaten up at home after all.

That was something, at least!

It seems a dead cert that there's no boozing going on at home if a bloke doesn't know what a ration book is. Hadn't Johnny heard Martin Ljung's monologue about the trip through the jungle?

Martin Ljung?

The comedian Martin Ljung was the explorer, and when he got to the sea he was attacked by sharks, and so he painted a message across his chest, in great big letters: THE RATION BOOK WILL NO LONGER BE NEEDED FOR SPIRITS AFTER THE FIRST OF OCTOBER. And I'd like to see the bloody shark that'd swallow that! was how the monologue ended. Not heard it?

Explorer. Who the hell has time to listen to Cultural Corner!

Suddenly, Johnny burst out, You k n o w so much! Where do you find time to learn it all?

What could I mutter by way of a reply? I was flattered, but I could feel Johnny was really talking about himself. And he went on: couldn't I teach him a bit about all kinds of things. Not all that indicky card stuff, but a bit of everything.

Of course I could! If he would teach me a bit about his bicycle repair world. Terms. Words, that is.

You mean like spanner? Crankcase? Lynch pin?

For instance, yes. But then he shouldn't get upset if I suggested there was something he didn't know.

What did I mean? Johnny never got upset, did he? Never?

Never because of you, Chris.

The garden was full of apple trees with hellishly sour apples. If that was the kind they had in Paradise, I bet Adam and Eve were glad to get out of there.

In a field just north of the house, towards where the chalets were, was an abandoned tractor that we nosied around, and on, and in.

Not much good as a jungle jeep, matterfact, reckoned Johnny, pulling and pressing all the knobs and buttons without anything interesting happening. When he pulled at the radiator curtain, though, the chain broke off and came rattling out, while the curtain clattered down at the front.

A lot of old rubbish, matterfact, like everything else nowadays.

Mind you, the chain might come in useful, Johnny reckoned, and took it with him.

We wandered around the chalets for a bit. It wasn't really early morning around Stockholm's latitude any more, and the whole area was mined with suspicious, gaping old codgers, ready to defend their dolls' houses with cudgels if we looked too closely at their precious possessions. But we were two free men from the hills, on the recce, taking all kinds of risks as we reccied around in the slums. As long as the old codgers didn't offer sanctuary to that swine Liberty Valance, they'd be safe enough. If everything was calm, it could continue to be calm. Our men, waiting up in the mountains above the mists, could lie low till we gave them the agreed signal. No signal, no blood.

In the midst of all this let's-pretend, I happened to catch sight of Johnny's eyes, unexpectedly. Watching me.

I got that same feeling again: Here's Johnny, but he's not here. He's standing to one side, keeping an eye on things. Is Chris having a good time? It's for your sake we're here today, Chris. Dad goes to the circus so that you can have fun. You are having fun, aren't you?

Anyway, it soon passed and I was back with the old codgers again and their rubbishy apple trees, and they couldn't tempt us into any kind of manoeuvre. Not just because there were lookouts hidden behind every curtain, but just think of the bitter fruit we'd tasted not long ago. The whole place must be poisoned.

We got lumbered with a nattering old bird cos Johnny came out with something about how fantastic the old lady's roses looked, when you think how late in the year it is. What a thing to say!

The old bird went rabbiting on about names of roses and Ah hah, it wasn't too late for them as know what they're doing, the key thing is the nights, you see, the night temperature, it was a bit dodgy the night before last, but the wily old girl had been ready for it. This kind you have to do this with and that one you have to do that with, and Johnny kept putting in an Oh! and a Really? until in the end she asked us in for a glass of strawberry squash and ring-shaped biscuits, and she got more and more miserable as she told us how the old man had died, then the cat, then her sister, then her brother-in-law, and all the rest of the family tree.

Just when Johnny must have been running out of remarks to make, she flung her front paws in the air and reckoned here she was talking nonsense and spoiling a nice day for two nice lads, and that wouldn't do now, would it, both us and her had other things to do, hadn't we, and where do you come from, by the way?

From Flaten.

Oh, Flaten. Are you staying there?

Yes.

Isn't it a bit cold at night?

Yes, 'tis really.

We were more or less thrown out after that.

217

Didn't know you could be so polite, Johnny!

Johnny didn't answer, said nothing at all, to be more precise. Not for ages, and then he muttered something about everybody having something to tell.

Yes, yes, that's no doubt true, sure, I nodded, looking intelligent. But I didn't think that was the kind of thing Johnny would say. It would have been less baffling if he'd said, now it was all over, what the business with the old lady was all about. It evidently wasn't about anything except the obvious: listening to her for a bit.

Johnny steered us through the woods without any problems, he must have had a built-in compass and map. Me, I was lost the moment I set eyes on a forest, but just as I thought the whole world had got lost, there sure enough was the fence round the Flaten area, complete with hole for us to climb through.

There was a commotion going on up at the camping site, or rather, the end of a commotion. There were fire engines everywhere, and loads of people.

Cops, said Johnny. Let 'em get on with it. Keep your head down, for God's sake!

But I wanted to know. Johnny hung about in the background, didn't want me to go any further, but he didn't stop me either.

It was that rickety little hut, the amateurish one, that had burnt down and taken with it a bit of the surroundings. Only a little bit, cos luckily they'd discovered the fire before it had really taken hold properly.

A constabule grabbed hold of me and wanted to know who I was, and where I came from, and what I was doing there. I was a little, little laddie, out wandering through the wood, for our poor teacher's resting, and a man is made of mud.

He took my name and address, and the following Saturday I read in the papers that the fire had probably been caused by children playing with fire. A twelve-year-old boy passing by was asked to explain what he was up to, but was unable to help with enquiries.

218

And Dad said, Hum? when he read that, cos by now he knew we'd been at Flaten, but I certainly was unable to help with enquiries and just ran off as quickly as I could, hoping the constabule wouldn't be all that prompt in checking out the name and address I'd given.

Johnny, who'd been totally invisible for a while, appeared out of nowhere and asked what did they say and what did you say and then what and cor, pretty good, you led 'em up the garden path, matterfact.

What do you mean, garden path? I hadn't done anything.

Course you hadn't. Just you try and prove that.

Johnny could give me an alibi. I could give him one.

I? You? You? Me? Good God, do you believe in fairies? Johnny knew full well that if the cop needed us cos he wanted somebody to pin something on, nobody could care less what we had to say. That's why he hadn't come forward with me. Never talk to the cops! Never to the cops, I'm just telling you.

But that hut business was pretty odd, I reckoned.

That's the kind of thing that happens, was Johnny's view.

We wandered around in our bare feet, out of sight of the firemen and cops. They were packing up anyway, and it was soon quiet and peaceful again.

The easiest way of hanging on to summer is pretending it's still there: wander around in bare feet and shorts and no shirt till the blizzards come and prove otherwise. Johnny managed to get as far as the barefooted stage today. He otherwise stayed fully clothed as he always was. I've decided ages ago that what I'd heard somewhere or other is right and that redheads are oversensitive to sunlight. If the freckles all over their faces get backed up with red burns all over their bodies, redheads are probably wise to keep their clothes on.

There was no urge to do anything special this time. Minigolf without balls and clubs is a bit of a dead loss. The football pitch just lay there, remembering the summer. The café was boarded up, and there were no chairs forgotten outside. The boats were chained together. No oars. In a word, the place was dead.

Didn't I want to have a swim?

We're here so that Chris can have a good time, after all. Does Chris want to have a swim?

I felt whether I had any urge to swim wherever it is that such urges usually come from. It was all pretty calm there at first, but when I saw the silhouette of the diving boards and springboards, something clicked after all. I flung my clothes off and dashed up to the fifteen-footer.

Johnny yelled something that sounded like, Chris! You can't!, but I know best what I can and can't do. Johnny was presumably airing his well-known aversion to water sports again.

So, I went on climbing and took no notice of his shouts. I was nearly on the top step when I saw he'd whipped off his tangerinos and was wading out into the water at high speed. By the time I was ready to dive, he was standing right underneath the springboard, just where I would hit the water, with his Crimsonita hoisted up over the waterline, which was about up to his waist, and he was yelling at me, his face white as a sheet, C-c-can't you s-s-see now, you s-s-stupid b-b-bastard, that I'm s-s-standing on the b-b-bottom just where you'd have . . .

I could see all right.

Any desire I had to dive in from any height at all drained straight out of me. I climbed down again, trembling like a leaf. Johnny didn't use that time to stand still and meditate out there in the water. When I got down, he'd disappeared, and taken my clothes with him.

I felt a right fool. What was the point? Was I going to be punished by having to get back to the hut stark naked? Flaten might have been deserted so far, but you could bet your life it'd be full to overflowing now. Nosey admirers all the way up to the back row of the gallery.

Before I'd had time to set out on this embarrassing

trek, Johnny reappeared and flung my clothes at me. My pants were soaked through, cos he'd changed into mine before he took his little dip.

You've got to p-p-pay somehow, was how he explained that detail away. Don't think I'd wet my p-p-pants for a p-p-prize n-n-nitwit like you.

He was pretty annoyed and angrily rejected my thanks.

I could manage all right without underpants, if that was really going to be the whole cost of having my life saved, but I couldn't manage without Johnny, so I apologized for being a nitwit, for existing at all, for doing what I did, which was wrong.

Johnny came round after a bit, gave me a wink and slapped me on the back: Let's forget all about this Flaten hell-hole and pedal back home.

On the way back to the hut, I gathered together my latest impressions and decided I might have been seeing ghosts where there weren't any. After all, Johnny had seen what I hadn't seen, even though I'd been at Flaten all summer: that the diving boards had been towed in to the shore. That meant he just *had* to be pretty familiar with the place, no matter what. Perhaps he'd come out with that lie about the Yellow Buses cos he came here every day on his bicycle, and he'd done that cos he couldn't afford the 45 öre here and the 45 öre back again, maybe he didn't even know he could travel half fare, and didn't know that a season ticket on the Yellow Buses plus entry to all activities in the Children's Section at Flaten was cheap, but he probably thought that if he'd said he cycled here every day in that hot weather, I'd have realized he couldn't afford it, and being poor is so shameful that every single lie is more honourable than that, and even though it was ages ago I'd realized Johnny was poorer than I could ever understand, we hadn't laid our cards on the table yet, so he didn't know I knew that. When I pieced together what I'd realized alongside what I suspected, the lie about his summer became comprehensible to me, though the performance he'd given at

The Crown became even more depressing: Johnny wanted to be a free man. But he wasn't free.

If you wanted to believe, as I did, that he really had been here at Flaten this summer, you had to accept that fate kept us from bumping into each other. Maybe there wasn't all that much fate involved. Him up here in the woods, avoiding all the reservoirs with their poisoned water, and me down on the beach, or out in a rowing boat.

That's probably how it was. If you examined this explanation too closely, perhaps all the details didn't really fit, but I decided that was more or less how things were. I was so keen to have simple and natural explanations.

It wasn't time to leave Flaten yet. We had to eat up the rest of the sandwiches and empty the other Tizer first.

While our stomachs were coping with that pleasant task, we lounged around, feeling a bit sleepy now. I'd rolled up the blanket and was using it as a pillow. Johnny lay at right-angles to me, on my perpendicular bisector in fact, with my stomach as a pillow. I was stroking his thatch, quite gently. It was soft, and felt thick and cool between my fingers. Johnny was moving his nut from side to side, a bit like a cat dictating how you stroke it.

I can hear the Tizer bubbling away in your cellar, he informed me.

That was all either of us said.

I was just about to nod off, when Johnny woke me by asking if I could keep a secret.

Couldn't I just! It was an insult to ask!

But he meant a real secret. A Real Goddamned Secret. So big that the question wasn't an insult at all, I gathered, but rather the biggest compliment he could pay me. Not just one of these common or garden secrets, about the hut of huts and little things like that.

There he was, Johnny, my friend the perpendicular bisector, pulling himself together. Taking a deep breath. Sitting up straight. Taking another deep breath. Wow, but it was hard going! And then he slumped down on me again. And took another deep breath. And got ready to tell me a Real Goddamned Secret. And turned away from me then back then away then back again, and my stomach was taking a real pummelling. He worked hard on how to begin, which word he was going to start with, and it was, Well . . . , and that was all. And I could see the black chasm widening, saw the darkness inside there, and all Johnny's demons holding him back and yelling, Shut your gob, Young J.J.! If you blab, we'll kill you! Then it'll be Nordberg's turn.

And I could see how everything would soon, now, engulf me and carry me away, cos Johnny's agony was genuine and breathed hellfire, and was too great to bear alone, and the Blackness grew and grew and hovered over me and started to swoop down, and I jumped up and yelled, I'm d y i n g ! I'll *die* if you go on like this!

He sat up and gave me the oddest look the world has ever seen and he'd lost his stride altogether, that was obvious.

Who cares! he said, and you could tell he was trying to make it seem couldn't-care-less and a bit of a joke, this who cares, but inside me somebody was busy with a chainsaw and sharp chisels turning and a hammer crushing, thumping, saying again and again and again, yes, yes, yes, you always spoil the lot, lot, lot, Chris Nit, Nit, Nit.

OK then! Johnny took charge. Tell us about life at the summer camp instead.

What was he on about? Did he mean the South Side Grammar Summer Camp?

Of course! What else did I think?

I turned back the pages, back, back, back, till I could hear Johnny rubbishing everything to do with summer camps. Sis came and Johnny went and I had to talk to Mum and Dad. I thumbed through to the beginning again, but I couldn't find anything to show Johnny must have realized I hadn't been out to Värmdö camp. I didn't think anything had been said in Johnny's earshot all May. Maybe he really did think I'd been out there.

I looked deep, deep into Johnny's eyes. Was all this a big ploy and double bluff, from start to finish? I was supposed to say I'd stayed behind in town, and then Johnny would suddenly admit he'd also been there, in the same town, quite unnecessarily, and then I'd have to defend myself and explain why I hadn't said anything about changing plans last spring, defend and explain while Johnny got away with it and didn't need to explain anything at all. He was obviously in charge, compared with the position he'd have to take up the day he was faced with the question, as he would sooner or later, What did you do last summer, Johnny?

Built a hut? Oh yes, pull the other one. One thing was clear, and spoilt all my simple and natural explanations: the whole thing smelt fresh, September fresh, and it would have been finished in less than a week once Johnny got going, with all his skills.

Looking deep into Johnny's eyes produced nothing new at all. Unless you think that in a way, the fact he didn't look away was an answer. He just looked straight at my left eye, without flinching, without breaking the very long and very audible silence by asking why I was staring at him and not saying anything, when he'd only asked for something very straightforward.

Was this a poker game?

I chose my words carefully: Well. Nothing to tell, really.

I cut through the bond between us by closing my eyes. Had to turn away as well. Not as good as some people are at keeping a straight face, me.

As I lay there with my eyes closed, it suddenly occurred to me that if Johnny was in good faith, that long stare plus the long pause plus my answer plus this turning away and closing my eyes must have looked pretty peculiar from his point of view. Maybe he was sitting there thinking I was the oddest bloke the world has ever seen, and a real pain in the neck as a friend.

The thought buzzed around in what passed for my head: Just think if Johnny has been in good faith all the

224

time, and that everything he said was true, but that I misunderstood him, cos I couldn't get it into my head that the world is as odd as it must be if everything Johnny says is true. But the world is more peculiar than anything you can think up in your imagination, as my worthy Mum always says.

I mean, look at the way in which Johnny became one of the lads and how we became friends, and tell it from Johnny's point of view. Where does that put *me*, then?

It was true Johnny had come up against a wino in Götgatan. When he told Chris about it, Chris burst out crying. Sensitive type. Chris didn't want to hear any more; in the middle of the night he screamed at Johnny that he wanted to be left alone. What got into him?

When Johnny was discreet enough to melt into the background during the summer holidays, so that Chris wouldn't feel embarrassed cos he was going to the marvellous Summer Camp while Johnny had to hang around town in all that heat, Chris just forgot all about Johnny. Not a postcard, not a word all summer. And then, afterwards, he didn't want to say anything about it. If that's not pretty sick, then you tell me what is. Well, OK, it eventually came out that he hadn't in fact been out to Värmdö, but claimed he'd been hanging round Flaten every single day. But come on, Chris, we all know that can't be true, cos Johnny was out there building huts all the time. If you'd really been there as well, he'd have seen you. What were you really doing? Never mind, OK, we'll let it drop then.

But what about that business after summer, when Johnny came back and was going to establish contact again, and tried to have a session with Millie? Both Chris and his dad started going on about how Johnny was the world's biggest let-down, who hadn't given a toss about Millie all summer. Funny lot, those Nordbergs!

Yes, that's a point: Nordberg. I don't believe Chris has ever said what his name is. He just left that for his mate to work out for himself.

W e i r d was what he called me, Johnny, just before my birthday. You're pretty weird, Chris, you really are.

Maybe I was, from Johnny's point of view?

Johnny had started doing something, and when I looked to see what, I saw he'd got the chain from the radiator curtain and had taken some tools out of his saddle bag. He was sitting there mumbling and messing about. What was going on?

Try this.

He threw something over to me, which turned out to be a length of the chain. It was fastened together with a piece of metal forming a charm, and a neat J was punched on it. So well done that it must have been punched elsewhere. I fitted it round my wrist and was one bracelet the richer.

Johnny held up his right hand, and there on his wrist was an identical length of chain, but this one had a neat C on it. So well done that it must have been punched at some other time.

He took my hand and put his charm up against mine. He grasped my arm and I grasped his arm, noticing yet again how skinny he was. He produced, from down inside him somewhere, the Text, which he now read in a hollow voice, gazing all the time straight into my left eye, which started smouldering:

> As long as you are my best friend,
> as long as I can be yours,
> the charm will shine, as now.

> If mine goes dull I'll know:
> You don't want to know me.
> If yours goes dull you'll know:
> I'll obey. I'll go.

> If one of us is in danger
> the charm will glow,
> and hurt the other's hand
> until help comes.

If your life is at stake
then let the charm go.
It will hunt me out,
and I'll come.

You do the same
if mine comes to you.
Listen, wait for the sign
and come quickly.

He went all quiet. Then asked, Will you promise?

Cold fingers were running all over my spine.

I promise.

C, as in Christopher, as in Caesar, as in Certain, as in Comrade.

J, as in John, as in Jewel, as in Jaguar, as in . . . I couldn't find anything suitable!

You will sooner or later, said Johnny with a grin. A little smile I'd never seen before.

He had a J-suggestion in reserve, and if you find it really impossible, I'll tell you one of these days. But we've got to do it right. You're not exactly short of words, so you'll manage it all right.

The rest of the chain was hanging over the entrance to the hut.

This is where the Certainty comes from, he said solemnly. Here is where you find . . . Then he lost his inspiration. That was just as well, cos after what had just taken place between us, anything would be a flop.

Anyway, it's just the thing to strangle intruders with.

Johnny wheeled his bicycle to Tyresövägen. We got on just as we had the previous day, and we were by the graveyard before you could say corpse. On the way there, another of the real-life details dawned on me and disturbed my simple and natural explanations: When I hung on tightly to Johnny, I could feel his Tangerinos were wet. Or damp, to be exact. Just about as damp as they would be if he'd been swimming with his underpants on, wrung them out as much as possible, and put them back on in that state.

Course, I thought it was nice to know he hadn't in fact paused to change his underpants when my neck was at stake. But why did he want me to think he had?

My bicycle was still there, so you can go back to your graves now, ladies and gentlemen.

I unlocked it and we walked back to town. Not through Hammarbyhöjden this time. The suburban wimps might have been around to see our inglorious return, recognize us, remember the less than complimentary things we'd yelled at them and call out a brigade of several dozen warriors before we had time to clear their boundaries.

Oh no, along Nynäsvägen, and past the sports field at Johanneshov, where we paused to watch some grass-green Hellas athletes training to become even better.

Grass-green? Are you barmy? They're olive-green.

OK, OK.

And then Skanstull bridge down to Götgatan.

All the time, all the way from the graveyard and into town, I had to keep a tight rein on my tongue, which wanted to jump out and talk about that horrible summer day when I'd cycled along this route four times, twice there and twice back again, in a hopeless and fruitless search. My tongue wasn't allowed to talk about that, cos I still didn't know what I'd really been looking for that day.

We didn't say much at all that last bit over the bridge. I was thinking to myself about all the things that had happened in the course of this last day. And I made an important decision: as soon as I got home, I'd sit down with pen and paper and write down everything I knew about Johnny, one point at a time. Everything I knew was true, and everything I knew was a lie. Truths and lies. Lies which were trying to conceal the truth. Truths which could throw light on the lies. I thought I could see a pattern. The thought: He wants to be a free man but he isn't free, was jostling alongside something a certain

228

family friend had said, and various other ideas were flying around in my head yelling out, Look at us! I would go home and capture all of them with pen and paper. I needed my best nib in the pen and a big sheet of paper. One of my little cards wouldn't be enough.

Come on, this way! said Johnny when we got to Ringvägen, pointing to the right with his head.

I thought, Now something has really changed! Johnny's going to take me home with him!

It wasn't quite like that, but nearly. Johnny marched off to shady Bjurholmsplan, and took hold of the handle on the door to the even shadier workshop. I stopped him and asked for help, I must have some help now, you must help me to solve a mystery.

Johnny went along with the interruption and looked at me. Waiting.

I went through the whole rigmarole: Bert and me behind the Studebaker there, and you going into the cycle repair shop. Cycle repair shop, cycle repair shop right until Easter. Then it was a cobbler's shop. A closed cobbler's shop. Last summer it was a cycle repair shop. I was here last summer, did you hear about that?

You weren't here last summer.

Johnny insisted, staring hard into my ravaged left eye. Once again it flashed through my mind, all that business about everything being the other way round, and that Johnny was right and bona fide, in which case I must seem round the twist. But the flash didn't help this time. I *was* here last summer.

I was not here last summer. Johnny has no doubt at all. The rest was so straightforward, you must have the whole of your head stuffed full of card indickies not to catch on, matterfact.

Oh, yes? Couldn't he stop kicking a man when he's down. Out with it.

Easy. You got it wrong.

I got it wrong. When exactly?

Johnny shrugged his shoulders. It was all crystal clear,

229

matterfact. Everybody makes a mistake sometimes. It's nothing to get all het up about. Get a new card indicky card, and come again.

I put my hand on his, as he was just going to turn the handle: What is there in there? Now?

Johnny turned right round to face me. His green gaze looked me up and down. He didn't say it, but I could hear it all right: Are you out of your mind, or what?

Johnny? Do you know Per Anders Andersson?

You can't know somebody who doesn't exist, he answered straight off, still giving my face the once over. Was I in a bad way?

Did you know him then? When he did exist.

What did you say his name was?

I've never been to a psychologist or any other kind of shrink. But I imagine they behave like this. Say peculiar things, and look the patient straight in the eye in order to check his reaction.

Per Anders Andersson, I said again.

Johnny was still looking hard at me: I've already told you, you made a mistake.

I had to think over those words a bit. Then that was enough of mysteries, and enough help in solving mysteries. Johnny opened the door and went in. It was a cycle repair shop inside.

The shiftiest of Monster fizzogs gaped out from the background, nodded briefly at Johnny, but stared sullenly at me, hellish sullen he was.

Chris needs a tyre and inner tube.

The Monster nodded at the shelves and disappeared behind the curtain. Why did he hate me?

Johnny got what he needed. We went out and Johnny ripped the bits of tyre off the front wheel and put on the new inner tube and tyre. Before I knew what was happening, there was a whole new front wheel in place.

We exchanged some more words. As follows:

Me: Doesn't he like me?

Johnny: Who do you mean?

Me: Your dad.

Johnny (roars of laughter): That's not my dad, you nitwit!

Me (taking a trip as far as the flower bed and back): Who is it then?

Johnny (less amused now): For God's sake, but you're determined to chase up my dad today, aren't you! I haven't *got* a dad, if you really must know.

No dad either! Could you live, could you breathe, without a mum or a dad? They were a bit of a pain now and then, the way they were always trying to teach you manners and that, true, but could you manage without both of them?

He'd finished the wheel. Flashed his tools around and whipped the back wheel off as well: This'll go west tomorrow. Disappeared into the workshop. Back out again complete with tyre and inner tube.

Then he explained it all at last. Explained while he was juggling with his tools that this bloke, the shifty Monster, that is, had taught him all he knew.

About bicycles and things?

That's why Johnny kept coming and going here. Helped out a bit. Got a bit of lolly for his . . . what should you call it? . . . his little favours. You get by.

Oh, I see.

Don't know about any Johnny, he'd said, the Monster. Odd way of putting it, in fact. Don't know about any Johnny.

Does he call you Young J.J. as well?

Johnny nodded. Everybody does.

I don't! I never do!

I know! said Johnny.

No dad. No mum. No name.

When you don't ask, the answers come. Now, tomorrow, or in fifty years' time, but they come all right, to those who wait in silence. Cos now Johnny let slip a little bit more than he needed to, he'd already let slip quite a bit, and didn't need to say anything at all. There was a little bit more, which wouldn't have come out, I reckon the day before yesterday, for instance.

I live here. In principle.

I took a look at the caked-up, filthy repair shop window. Did he really mean *there*, or in a flat upstairs, behind, at the side? For God's sake, he must have meant upstairs, or behind, or at the side!

No dad. No mum. No name. No home.

A room and a bit of lolly for little favours.

Is he all right? was all I could think of to say. What a daft question to ask! But I just didn't dare talk about all the other things piling up all around me.

Johnny listened to the hub, and adjusted the wheel with enormous care.

Yeah, course, he said eventually, very quietly, when I'd already decided he'd forgotten me and the conversation we were having. It didn't sound at all like Yeah, course.

Then in a flash: his battered face last spring. And I went all cold!

Johnny had finished. Disappeared inside. Came out again. You're not exactly an oil-painting yourself, he said out of the blue, holding up a mirror. I could see an ear like a red cabbage and a blue-black stripe across my cheek. It was pretty obvious the whole port side was out of action. I'd never be able to explain that away when I got home. Pity I don't have your thatch to hide it all under.

But you just couldn't mention hair to Johnny. Just watch it or you'll get a dose on the other side as well, he muttered.

What was I going to say when I got home? What on earth was I going to say?

That was no problem, matterfact. Say what the hell you like. Tell 'em just what happened: Johnny blew his top. We had a fight. No good? You bumped into an elk in the dark then.

Or I came up against a wino in Götgatan.

That was unnecessary! Oh boy, was that unnecessary! The moment I'd said it I knew straight away. It was unnecessary in spades.

Johnny gritted his teeth and turned the bicycle the right way up in one jerk. I had to grab hold of it, or it'd have fallen down as he turned on his heel and disappeared inside with the mirror and his tools. I let down the stand and was about to follow him, cos we couldn't end the trip like this. But then he came out again, luckily enough, cos I didn't want to go in at all. Enormously interested in his own bicycle now.

I've got to get through to you, Johnny, got to get through now, must explain myself, must explain for you, but you were so incredibly busy with your bicycle so I grabbed hold of you and lifted you up, light-as-a-feather Johnny, and pushed you up against the wall, just held you there against the granite blocks. You didn't try to defend yourself, just let your arms dangle, looked away, suddenly looking frightened.

Johnny! Were you frightened of me?! Let your arms dangle and waited to be thumped, without trying to defend yourself.

I had him up against the wall, but what should I do with him there? Thump him, he thought. What sort of a bloke was I, when Johnny, my friend, thought that?

Johnny! I keep saying the wrong thing all the time . . .

His green, green eyes came round to meet mine.

And when I begged him, Forgive me, Johnny, forgive all of me, yet again!, to my horror those green, green eyes started crying. And it was unreal, incredibly strange, to stand looking straight at Johnny like that, and he was crying without hiding his face, without looking away from me. I didn't know where to put myself, what to do with myself, what there was I could do to cope with all this p a i n , which was washing over me in long black waves, and which I didn't understand, couldn't handle.

Good Lord, but how he must be suffering!

I knew and I felt and I realized that I would never understand. I would never, never understand!

And now here I am in the cop car, cruising along Götgatan and down towards Bjurholmsplan. It's the first time I've been in one of these vehicles, and it'd feel pretty remarkable if I didn't have so many other things to think about just now. Twelve and nearly two-thirds I was the first time I rode in a police car. I'll remember that.

Why didn't you come to us? asks the cop. When you saw all that. Or tell your parents, who realized quite a bit.

He can say that, and I still haven't told them about the trip to the hut. But that's the kind of thing only a cop can say when he hasn't caught on that you lead quite an ordinary life, where nothing much happens really, and what does happen has simple and straightforward explanations, and the cop isn't exactly a friend you turn to.

It was bad enough on Monday night when Dad said, Well, young man, and dumped the newspaper in front of me. The police were appealing for the twelve-year-old boy who had been passing the camping site at Flaten on Friday to get in touch with them. The newspaper maintained the police had promised the boy didn't need to be scared because he'd given them a false name and address. There had been an obvious smell of paraffin at the site of the blaze, which the police had not mentioned before for technical reasons connected with their investigation. So there was no question of kids playing with fire, but the boy might have seen something of great value.

I'll come with you, said Dad, cos I was really trembling like a leaf. But tell me all I need to know first.

I said there was nothing to know, that I hadn't done anything and didn't know anything.

In that case, why had I given a false name and address?

On the way downstairs, my answer was that it was a sort of impulse, really. But by the time we were walking across the South Side Grammar school yard, Dad's protests had wrung out of me the fact that Johnny had been against me going anywhere near the cops. He was sort of scared, and so I thought . . . well, I don't know really.

Ah hah, so that was why they only referred to one boy.

234

But did Johnny have anything to do with the fire, then?

Of course not. As we were walking across Götgatan, I asked him how much I ought to say in fact. Dad thought I should answer everything the police asked me. And don't start making things up again. Stick to the truth, if you've got nothing to hide.

But I didn't want to give them Johnny's name.

It took Dad all the way to the post office in Folkungagatan before he said it was getting pretty complicated now, all this Johnny business. But if you're really sure you two had nothing to do with the fire . . .

A hundred and ten per cent.

. . . Then just call him Johnny. As usual.

When I told them what I'd come about, they sent for somebody from somewhere else, and when he arrived, I recognized the constabule from the previous Friday, and he was grinning away at me and said, Hi there, Bengt-Göran!

Horrible! said Dad, shaking hands with the flatfoot. Couldn't you find a better name than that?

The flatfoot kept on calling me Bengt-Göran, with first a guffaw and then a wink every other time, till I was sick and fed up to death of Bengt-Göran. I realized straight away that he was coming this favourite-uncle line in order to get me on his side, but I went along with it, at the same time as I cursed myself for being so easily fooled.

He didn't think for one moment that I or my friend, Johnny, wasn't that his name?, had anything to do with the fire. But try and think whether you saw anybody else around. That morning or the previous evening. Or during the night. Did you go out at all during the night?

I thought for a bit and remembered the bloke who had been standing smoking by the springboards that evening. But I only saw him from a distance, so that was useless.

Not at all, nothing was useless. A bloke you say. A doddery old bloke? Tall? Short?

I had the impression of somebody tall and thin. He took a couple of paces and limped a bit. I reckoned he'd be about thirty at most.

The flatty politely noted down all my guesses. Didn't ask where I'd got the age bit from. It was the tall, thin bit and the limp that made me think of the Monster. But I didn't say that.

Anybody else?

Oh, yes. There was a couple not far from the hut.

A couple? Two persons?

How could I put it? I felt myself blushing. Repeated that it was a couple, in fact. On the floor, er, they were lying there, sort of. I mean, er, how should I put it . . .

Ah hah, young Bengt-Göran, said the flatty with a loud guffaw, and winked, then laughed out loud again. They were screwing, were they?

I nodded. It was obviously incredibly funny, cos the flatfoot filled the whole room to overflowing with his guffaws before deciding we could take it they didn't start the fire, and there was no point in trying to get hold of them either. Anybody else?

That was all.

Nobody during the night, nobody in the morning?

No, there was just us. Though . . .

Yes?

We did hear voices once. During the night. Towards morning. Before it started getting light.

That was very interesting. You could see that. Men or women? Cheerful, angry, upset? Lots of them, a long time? Nearby or far away?

But I couldn't help him at all. I'd woken up hearing the echo of what could have been voices. My mate hadn't actually said he'd heard anything. But if it really was something, it was two men's voices. Angry maybe, or irritated rather. Quite near, and hushed.

For somebody who didn't hear anything, I'd heard an awful lot, the flatty reckoned.

It sort of followed on from something I'd dreamt.

What had I dreamt then? Could I remember that?

But there was a brick wall there.

Listen, Bengt-Göran, hahaha. You think you hear voices, eh? OK. But then you must have heard *something*.

An o-sound, or a word, or half a sentence, I don't know what. But not *just* a voice, that's for sure. Something the voice says. Anything at all? No matter how silly it might seem. Something crude about screwing, perhaps? Shall we send your dad out for a minute? Any words at all? Any sounds?

We might as well turn back, I said.

What?

My memory suddenly opened up wide. I could hear Mr G.G.'s voice saying, We might as well turn back, and the silence behind the transparent Studebaker where Johnny was lying on his back beside me, holding on to a little axe underneath the loo door, and the Monster pointed at us and said something, and I went all hot and cold, cos he must have seen us, but then Mr G.G. shrugged his shoulders and said, We might as well turn back.

Who's Mr G.G.?

I told them, and was thrilled to bits at the idea of them pulling him in and listening to his voice and asking what he'd been doing in the early hours of the thirteenth of September. Whatever he had been doing, he'd have a rough ride for a while, and that'd serve him right. Just cos Christopher Nordberg, also known as Bengt-Göran, had a little dream. That's the way it goes when the flak is flying!

The bobby didn't ask anything at all about the Monster. Perhaps he thought it was a general kind of dream monster. As the way to the Monster also led to Johnny, I decided that the Monster was a dragon, in case it occurred to the Robert to ask about him. But he didn't, in fact.

Once I'd got that little fragment of a dream out of the way, my memory closed the door again and I forgot all the rest: the context, explanations, the natural explanation of the strangest of scenes in dreams.

The constable was happy for the time being. Only now did he take my real name – in case we wanted to know any more – whereupon Dad and I left.

Who's the Monster? asked Dad.

A dragon, I answered.

We've left the police station now. Who's the Monster?

Some sort of relative of Johnny's.

Some sort of?

I don't really know. It's true, I don't know.

Do you know why you were dreaming about Mr G.G. of all people?

I guessed it was because Johnny and I had been talking about him. Dad was happy with that explanation. I hesitated for a bit about whether or not to say that Mr G.G. was a family friend at Johnny's place. But I didn't say anything.

No matter how silly it might seem when you say it, but that constable prepared the way for the cop today. I'm certain I wouldn't have told the cop even a hundredth of what I have done if I hadn't been softened up to see that people like that weren't just uniforms and batons, but that you could actually talk to them.

Never talk to a cop! That's what you said, Johnny. But that was then. That was before your next and last lightning visit.

We were playing gratey on Repslagargatan. The chance of the ball bouncing right down to Södergatan added a bit of extra spice to the game.

Repslagargatan? says the cop. It's six years since it was called that.

One of these days, I'll explain why we, the front line troops representing adults and kids in the parish of Maria Magdalena, insist on calling the eastern end of Södergatan Repslagargatan. Another time, another time, can't muck about now!

Johnny came. He wandered backwards and forwards and didn't stand still for a millisecond, his eyes jumping around all over the place. Even George, who normally doesn't see a thing, noticed he was on edge.

He must want something special. I went over and asked how things were. Johnny said quickly and softly: We're supposed to go to the hut again. But . . .

238

At that very moment, it was my turn to play against Sten.

What! yelled Johnny after me. Don't you want to!

I concentrated on the ball, but when we'd finished Sten beat me easy. I went back over to Johnny and asked what it was all about, in fact.

There was obviously something up, cos Johnny checked sixteen directions in one glance, and his eyes were just one dazzling green flash. Then he came up close to me, very close to me, and muttered, Hell, Chris! Sorry! F-f-forgive all of me. N-n-no matter what I do. Promise.

I promise!

Specially as I realized straightaway he was quoting me. That always means something special. But what, this time?

Hand out to shake on it.

Instead, I got a bunch of fives out of nowhere. Johnny's greatest hit, right on the jaw, and I crumpled. Not because of that, but because of another blow at the same time, which I didn't feel at all except that it floored me. Oddly enough, none of this hurt me, though the sound of the punch echoed all round Repslagargatan, the lads said later, as if my skull had cracked open. Then he put the boot in, an enormous kick just where it hurt. But it was a gigantic fake, as big a fake as the sound of a splitting gut. God knows how Johnny did it.

I just had time to wonder if the men in white coats should be sent for, when the lads came racing up to rescue me. By then Johnny was up on his bicycle, yelling horrible things about me and all the rest, and racing away like mad.

Everybody was amazed to find I was still alive when I sat up without a scratch, shaking my head to clear the confusion.

Felt worse than that, I said, and could hear the buzz as my reputation soared.

Cor, what did you do to make him as mad as that?

Nothing I could dream up would do, so I said that's

something between Johnny and me.

You can say that again, blimey, cos this was over the top and nobody expected to see Johnny again after this.

Sometimes, you get flashes of insight. I realized Johnny had checked in all directions and been very precise when he floored me, and he'd prepared me for it, and he needed my help. All I had to do was to head the ball into the net, so I flaked out on the pavement and said to the lads that I can't make it after all, I've been clobbered, you'll have to carry me home.

And carry me home they did, stout friends that they were. The solemn procession marched across the South Side Grammar yard and up Kvarngatan and as far as my pit. Mum nearly had a fit when eight blokes marched through the doorway carrying her one and only, specially as they were as silent as the deep midwinter, as I'd requested. When they'd gone, still silent as the grave, I jumped out of bed and asked her if she was daft enough to believe anything. She went through the roof.

That night I sat for ages, wondering and wondering whether I ought to say something. Cos it was then, when you floored me, Johnny, when you floored me the way you did, that's when it was that everything changed, and I realized that this was more than I could handle. You do understand, don't you, that I just have to tell everything! You will forgive me, won't you, for not going blank and shaking my head when the cop appeared: Nope, never seen that bicycle before.

Never talk to a cop, you said.

Hell, Johnny, if only I knew! Am I letting you down or helping you? Johnny?

Anyway, at long last I got down to it, and sat with a big piece of paper to write down all the truths and lies surrounding Johnny.

That will have explained quite a bit, says the cop.

That did explain quite a bit. And when I'd finished contemplating the clarified picture that emerged from my miniature writing on that big A3 sheet, I got up and gathered all my card index boxes except my secret one, and went downstairs with them and slung them in the dustbin.

You did WHAT! Dad was completely shattered. When he'd recovered, he raced downstairs and retrieved the card index system from the dustbin. But I didn't want to know. He could do what he liked with it. I've no idea what happened. Maybe it'll turn up again in the autumn of my life and I'll recognize it with a tender smile, but just now I was in bed contemplating my misspent life.

A life filled with rubbish, pointless facts, data about everything you could think of.

A pretty boring way to live, that was the first thing you said, Johnny. Now, all of a sudden, I understood what you meant, and agreed with you. A pretty boring way to live, cos life is replaced by data, figures, facts on cards. Then you turned up, Johnny, and turned everything upside down, cos I never got any data from you, no facts to collect. If only I'd learnt how to really live, like everybody else, the art of listening and seeing, I'd have caught on to who you really were much earlier.

Useless, absolutely useless, that's what I reckon I was.

And when that feeling started to ebb, it was replaced with panic. What was I going to do about what I thought I'd discovered! I lay there on my bed, hearing all over again what you said: We're supposed to go to the hut again. But . . . , and I listened to your tone of voice, and the way you yelled, Don't you want to!, and I tried to understand what you shouted when you raced off afterwards, but I couldn't hear; the punch that wasn't a punch, and the kicks that weren't really kicks sent me a message and I couldn't hear anything else. All I could see was the other hut, the one that was burnt down with the help of paraffin, and could see you when, only half a day earlier, you condemned it almost without looking at it: It's not meant to last.

It was time for Chris to do something.

Time to go to Dad and say, Dad, I think Johnny is a pawn in a game he can't cope with, and this is what has happened . . .

But I didn't go to Dad, cos I was frightened he would go through his usual routine and tap me on the forehead and ask if I was feeling all right, and what an imagination you've got, Chris, will you never grow up? And I couldn't face it. Just now he was trying to get over the shock of the card index business. Incommunicado.

And I didn't go to Mum, even though she'd have believed me and said that truth can be stranger than fiction. I reckoned that as usual she'd have passed the buck to Dad, and so I would be back to square one. Plus that when Dad started to go on about when was I going to grow up, Mum would remind him of how old I was, and then all *that* business would be off again. Just now, Mum was pretty mad with me because of the joke about the stretcher-bearers. Incommunicado.

And I didn't go to the police station and ask to talk to my Flaten constabule, cos it just never occurred to me. If it had occurred to me, the very thought of his Bengt-Göran guffaw would have been enough to put me off.

And so I didn't go nowhere, and didn't say nothing.

A pity, that, said the cop, jangling Johnny's bracelet.

My charm's letting me down: it's not glowing and it doesn't hurt my hand at all. I'm listening, waiting for the Signal. I don't hear any signal. I can't reach Johnny.

This is where the bicycle was standing, says the cop, pointing. The chalk mark.

The cop guarding the door nods and lets us in.

I check what it says over the door. It's a habit of mine. The Bjurholm habit. The same old illegible sign. It's still there, anyway.

His Adidas had been flung into the repair shop. Chalk rings.

In the room behind the curtain: his Tangerinos. Duly marked.

I peer into that room. So this is where Johnny lived. In principle. It looked more like a monster's den than anything else. A cupboard with its own entrance: a shutter, a blocked-up window or something of the sort leading out to the main entrance. A dishevelled bed. A

242

chair. A chemical loo in the corner. Where was there room for Johnny in a hole like this?

And the bracelet?

The cop points outside. Next to the bicycle. The little cross. Had been lying on the saddle, perhaps.

You went past here, Johnny. Without your Tangerinos, without your Adidas. Your bicycle was outside the door. You put the bracelet on the saddle, no, you throw it in that direction: Fly to Chris!

The Monster drags you out, in a hell of a rush, the workshop unlocked, your shoes on the way out, your trousers still in your poky little room, even your bicycle unlocked. Johnny! You can't have been prepared.

The cop takes over.

Mrs B., up there in number seventeen, sees two men drag a kid over Bjurholmsplan and fling it into a big green car. The kid, who's dressed only in a red shirt (crimson?), is kicking and struggling and obviously resisting. But doesn't make a sound. For that very reason, and because the people involved have been seen around here before and given the impression of being well-known to each other, for these reasons Mrs B. hesitates at first, but then decides to make a phone call.

She has trouble in getting through, though. She's not the only one to have seen the incident, or to have hesitated, and then made up her mind, and there are about ten other people managing to block the line for each other, before Mrs B. is the one who gets through in the end and calls out the police. Mrs B. has no idea where the green car is going to, nor does any other of the witnesses. Without much hope, the police check all the roads out of Stockholm.

He falls silent.

Ah hah, so that's what happened.

I wait for the Signal, but everything is so deathly silent.

But for Christ's sake, Johnny! Charms and great oaths of loyalty and all that stuff! In a business as serious as this! How childish we were!

Oh, Johnny, how childish I was! Just when I was beginning to catch on, had caught a little glimpse, smelt the whiff of your terror and the blackness that surrounded you, I screamed that I was dying. I let you down, Johnny, and then when I let your fear fool me, and let myself be lulled into calmness by your song about the glowing bracelets, then I let you down again.

Let's turn the clock back, Johnny! I'll keep my mouth shut, and you can come out with your Really Big Secret. I'll share it with you, no matter what it looks like. I'll keep it, Johnny. You share it with me. Share with me your horrific reality, all your terrifying, complicated Alternative World, that's wriggling its way silently through mine, my own world, where the sun shines down on me, simple, lucky Chris, who's been living his own protected life without the slightest idea about your Alternative World that's existed alongside my own, which you were hinting at, but didn't dare to hint at, which you've been into every day without forcing me to go with you, without showing me the slightest little bit of it, until then, there in the hut, when I messed up the chance of crossing over the threshhold into your Alternative World, the chance of getting through to you, just when you really needed me, when you'd stretched out your hand to me. Then, Johnny, that's when we must turn the clock back to. We'll take the Alternative where I hold my tongue and listen and get to know, and we're not swept away by the big black wave, since you can tell me everything now at last, so that now we'll be two, and then we'll work it out, Johnny, we'll work it out, cos once you've blabbed you can't come back here to Bjurholmsplan, but you'll have to go into hiding, come home with me, and you can have a home, Johnny, not just a bit of a smelly monster's den, and a name, Johnny, you can have an English mum and a Swedish dad and a French sister, and me as a brother, and regular pocket money without having to do little favours, and you can be free at last, like you want to be, and Dad will look after the business of talking to the cops, and the cops will sort out all that murky workshop business before all this happens that has now happened.

Come on Johnny! We'll have another go! We'll open the fifth dimension and jump off this horrible Alternative and take another one. Where everything will be all right!

Can we go to Flaten?

Wherever you like, says the cop.

It surprises me, but the cops have seen worse things I expect, that no so-called witness can give the make of the green car, which has after all been coming and going and standing parked in Bjurholmsplan, looking quite different from all the Volvos and Lloyds round about. But I've provided them with the make and number.

The police interrogators also asked the witnesses about the size and sex of the child, and whether he/she really had only a shirt on. The witnesses were all agreed that they were embarrassingly unsure. For Christ's sake: a kicking, struggling Johnny! They must have been able to see if he had his underpants on or not. But the police are unable to find that out. Strange gaps have occurred in the witnesses' memories. But I've provided them with the size and sex of the child now.

How long ago was all this?

The alarm was raised last Wednesday.

Saturday today. Three days!

The cop says there could easily have been another three days if he hadn't managed to hit the jackpot today, his lucky day, at the corner of Swedenborgsgatan and Maria Prästgårdsgata.

Cos nobody in Bjurholmsplan, or in the next block, or in the Söder district all round Bjurholmsplan, or in the whole of Stockholm, Sweden, the universe all round Bjurholmsplan, had the slightest idea about the workshop or the people coming and going there. And apart from Johnny's things there hadn't been anything to go on. There was just one thing the cop was following up: that those two men and that child who'd been seen could be connected with various other cases he'd been involved in.

What exactly does he mean? I wonder, of course, but that's nothing to do with me. The cop says nothing, just rummages in his briefcase. Changes tack:

Your summary, your bit of paper with all Johnny's facts and inventions . . . He takes a pad out of his briefcase. A real goldmine, I should think. Just think, if only you'd come to us with it even so.

But now I can answer him back on that one all right, cos that's a lot of rubbish, locking the stable door after the horse has bolted. Yes, just think if I'd gone to the cops with my bit of paper. Down in Folkungagatan. I've been there twice before, and seen the kind of people they have on the reception desk. Last time I had Dad with me, and I was more or less a wanted man, so that was OK. But three years ago I tried to get one of them to do something about my bicycle, which had been stolen. Dad thought reporting it was something I ought to be able to manage myself, and he sent me.

Christ, you wouldn't believe how interested the bloke was. He could barely rouse himself from his slumbers. I'd just love to see him looking through my columns of Johnny facts in small handwriting, trying to stop himself laughing, if he even bothered to do that. Cos here was a little master detective who'd been reading too many comics, and he's cooked up a thriller set just here, hohoho, in my area, hohoho, that I know inside out. Take your little essay, laddie, and go with it to the Olofsson Brothers printing works in Götgatan, and ask them to publish it for you all neat and tidy. You might even make a profit on it.

Hum, says the cop, and I can hear he thinks I'm partly right. He puts a piece of paper on my knee. Points to it.

I read it:

    11/12 Neumunster
    18/12 Hamburg
    29/12 Itzehoe
     4/1 Flensburg
    10/1 ?

     4/3 Regensburg
    15/3 Landshut
    22/3 Munich
     5/4 Augsburg

13/4 Nuremberg
19/4 ?

28/5 Stockholm
13/6 Jönköping
20/6 Gothenburg
 4/7 Oslo
18/7 Arvika
 8/8 Gävle
28/8 Stockholm
 5/9 ?

What's this?

Try a guess, says the cop.

I guess Circus AIR, and I know I've guessed right.

They're sometimes a very difficult lot to keep track of. But they keep turning up. They had to break off in Nuremberg, though they had planned to work their way up through Germany and over here. But there was trouble. With some of the artistes. What, and how, and then – we don't know about that. The Swedish tour started as planned.

The cop falls silent. He looks at me.

I look out of the window. Don't want to look him in the eye. That would force me to say something.

But I've said all I'm going to say now, Johnny.

Johnny! For Christ's sake!

We suddenly find ourselves at the front of a column of cop cars and black marias. I show them the path to the bunker. The light's fading. It's getting dusk. It'll soon be dark.

As we rattle along the woodland path, the copdriver lets two other cop cars pass. The radio's buzzing with secret conversations. Loads of constabules are keeping in touch.

Suddenly the cop car in front shows his red brake lights, and the copdriver slams his big hoof on the brake pedal. My cop puts his hand on my shoulder and forces me down a bit. I think you guessed right, he says. Sit still for a minute.

In front of us, they're creeping up very cautiously, very cautiously, towards a big green luxury liner, a certain Studebaker. When no machine gun starts shooting out of the back window, they go over it thoroughly. Take pictures from every angle.

Now police and dogs are spilling out on to the woodland path. Even so, it's deadly quiet. The dusk is thicker here near the bunker.

Chris Nordberg can lead the way for a bit now, says the cop softly to somebody. You'd better make sure he doesn't get hurt.

All of a sudden, I'm Mr President of the United States, surrounded by burly bodyguards. I haven't actually felt frightened so far, but all this business . . . It's too late to pull out now, of course – I was only joking, see, can we go home now – or to ask for explanations – not one more inch, gentlemen, until you have thrown light on the following points for me . . .

I keep on going up the hill. Towards the hut. Mainly by instinct. It was Johnny who led the way last time. I didn't pay too much attention to where he was going.

It gets lighter the higher we go. We're getting closer to heaven. It's not as dark as it was down there. *What time does the sun set, did the sun set, today? Do you know that it's light, quite light, long after sunset and long before sunrise? Do you know that the quite light period in the morning and in the evening as well, is longer up here in the north than it is down near the equator? Do you know why that is? Do you know why the full moon is low in the sky in summer but high in the winter, the exact opposite of the sun? Shall I tell you? You wanted to learn a bit about everything, and this is living knowledge I've found out about since we were here last. It was dark at night then around here, even though the moon was out. But it was low in the sky, it didn't clear the tops of the trees. It rose at three o'clock today, 14.58 to be precise. You don't need to learn that. That's dead knowledge, unnecessary detail, the kind of thing I collect cos I'm so used to it.*

248

We didn't see it then, at 14.58, the moon that is, cos we were too busy with the cop, but now it's up there, pale and almost full, and it'll help to light things up tonight.

Laddie, where do you think you're taking us to? I'm called back by a question in a low voice.

. Here somewhere. Somewhere around here. A hut. The hut of huts. Just over a mound, round about here. But it's a perfect position and you don't see it from any direction until you're right on top of it. There's a chain over the entrance, to strangle intruders with. A little hiding place in the corner, with a burnt-out flashlight, a little axe and a sheath knife. Meant, I think, for building the hut with. Now the hut's finished, there must be some other purpose.

Here!

Wham **But I have time to see** *the bodyguard* **through the hole** *turns me round* **where the door should have been** *and pushes me away* **something light** *and out of range* **where it should have been dark.** *and back* **Because there's no wall behind,** *along the line of cops* **the hut is partly torn down.** *marking the route we've taken* **What the light thing is** *though straightened out a bit* **I can only guess** *and down* **but the nightmare** *and up* **fills in,** *to the cop,* **adds to,** *my cop,* **joins together** *who sees that I've seen* **to make a picture** *and knows that I know* **from which I'll** *and that the rest of my life* **never be free.** *I'll see it, over and over again.*

The whole film is being run without sound, and with a hell of an awful bulb in the projector. Unreal silence is pounding against my eardrums in the dusky wood, nearly a night-time wood now. The only thing I can hear is myself, cos I've lost control altogether and am blubbering away nonstop and crying my eyes out, when did I start that? Why did I start that?

Just give it time! The cop is holding my right arm and left shoulder and pressing a little bit every time I start blubbering. It feels pretty good, soothing, that grip, but I can't put a stop to my turmoil, which is leaking out in the form of tears and sobs. What's happening? Can't we put the light on and take another story instead! I don't like this Alternative.

We should change it. Johnny! Where are you? Did I see rightly?

A bobby appears and gives some sort of a signal. Two ambulances have driven up.

The cop shepherds me into the back seat of the car and sits beside me. Shadows loom in the woods.

We set off down the bumpy track. It gets lighter as the woods lose their grip.

There'll be quite a lot in the papers. Tomorrow. Yes, tomorrow. The cop is talking quietly to me. Clearly: We've been having trouble in stopping leaks so far. Now there'll be no stopping them. It'll all come gushing out now. A load of rubbish. The same as it always is. When something like this happens.

Something like this?

But you knew Johnny, you don't need to bother about . . . Just don't read it. You know the truth.

I heard what he said. Exactly! Help me, somebody!

The cop is sitting there fanning himself with the photo from Circus AIR of Miss Juvenile on the tightrope in Hamburg, Landshut, Augsburg or wherever. Flap, flap with the photo – it's not exactly warm, for Chrissake, I'm freezing, I am – and at the same time he's squeezing my shoulder with his other hand and rummaging in his briefcase with his third hand and directing the copdriver to Nynäsvägen with his fourth hand: We'll take you home now.

Home! Pass the wheel to me, and the accelerator, I'll do the driving! Straight into the hillside over there. Thud, finis, silence.

But oh no. We're going home. Mum's on the sofa and Dad's in his chair, home is the place that'll always be there. Waiting for me. We're always here, Chris, and we're with you. Nothing can be changed, but you know we're here to help.

God, Chris, you're a lucky blighter!

Then he was gone.

Johnny, Johnny! Why did I never catch on!

Flaten disappears behind us in the darkness. Sinks and takes Johnny down with it. I know the truth? I, who knew Johnny?

I know the truth, I knew Johnny. Too late! I got to know Johnny too late.

Flaten is out of sight now. He's gone. Too young, too lovely, too far, far away. Does Flaten exist now? Does anything when we can't see it? And now, like the wrong answer to a question I haven't asked, snow starts falling, the first snow. Soon everything will be hidden.

Johnny! I was going to find out all about it one of these days. But not like this, eh! Not like this! Cos if you fall down a hole before you've got round to telling me . . .

In that case, it doesn't matter at all, said Johnny, lifting up his red head one centimetre from my shoulder and letting it slump down again. Repeated, in a whisper: Not at all, and from such close quarters the faint whisper cut a hole through my eardrum and etched a question mark on my cerebral cortex. Behind him were the four passages from the north. He'd had one chance in four to run away from me. He took one of the other three, and hesitated in front of the darkness in the gaping hole. Came back to me and promised to tell me all one of these days. Came back to me, cos just then life had some value, and maybe more important than running away was knowing how much what I said about Bjurholmsplan meant that I knew about him and the workshop and the life he hid so carefully away. But when he heard there was nothing, I'd seen and understood nothing, nothing I even suspected at all, then he calmed down, didn't need to run away, could promise to tell me everything one of these days.

What would have happened if I'd said a bit more, if I'd asked about the cobbler's that day?

Was I unsuitable company for you even then? Did they threaten to kill you if you played with me? Was I under threat as well even then? How could I be dangerous, me who didn't understand

251

anything, who just when you were going to tell me, got scared and yelled that I was dying. Yelled so much that you broke off and shut up.

Now you've fallen even so, far down into the gaping black hole with crumbling edges and no railings. You didn't get round to telling me anything, and it does matter. I have to piece everything together myself, and that's not the same thing. Cos it's too late now to help by understanding. Flaten has disappeared together with you in the snowing darkness under the moon, and no longer exists, cos I can't see it any more, and I was the bloodhound, and even though I couldn't read the scent, I showed the way to you, shortly before the darkness of night engulfed the hut, before the real hounds needed to come, before the snow came to shroud everything, but it was too late even so, cos you'd walked the tightrope over the abyss, without a safety net of course, you always do, cos if there's a safety net you lose concentration and get careless, and you knew you'd make it, or you wouldn't have started out, but you miscalculated, you didn't read the contract, last Wednesday they showed you the small print, and the worthy gents, who were your mates for a year a long time ago, the school year 54-55, will remember you with admiration, but not me, cos when you fall, I fall as well, I'll follow you as soon as tonight, I'll go there tonight, I'll climb over the rail, and close my eyes, cos I'm frightened, Johnny, I'm so frightened, close my eyes and fall, and we'll meet somewhere in the Alternative World, somewhere far, far away from all this, cos you are Johnny, my friend, and I'm so fond of you.

And even so I left you in tears, all alone there up against the wall. Forgive me, Johnny, I didn't understand at all, I got scared, can you forgive me, I got so scared and screamed that I was dying, when I should have been listening. And you should have had a chance to explain. And everything that was so secret and peculiar would have become obvious and self-evident, and I'd have believed you, whatever you said, at last I'd have believed you, Johnny, cos at last I've realized that everything is true, and it's true what Mum said, that nothing you can think up in your imagination is so odd that it can't happen somewhere or other in the world. But Mum knew quite a bit by then, didn't she? And had promised not to say anything? She kept her promise, Johnny. Her lips were sealed, and she said nothing about why you naturally couldn't come to dinner

252

on Whitsuntide Eve, or go to the circus, or the whole of that long,
hot summer. And she kept Sis quiet, even though she'd no doubt
have loved to tell me all she picked up when she heard Mum prise
it all out of you, Johnny. You ought to know that if she promised
to keep quiet, she did keep her promise, and she never came closer
to breaking that than when she agreed with me that my amazing
story was no stranger than what could happen in the real world.
That was the nearest she came to splitting, when she heard what
track I was on to.

Anything can happen in this world of ours. We don't need any
Alternative Worlds. It's incredible what childish rubbish I
believed, Johnny, instead of seeing and hearing. If only I'd seen
and heard, we'd have coped. But didn't you understand, Johnny,
that I was just a child. I was a child until an hour ago. I
c o u l d n ' t see and hear. I had to have everything spelt
out. Didn't see, didn't hear what Mum caught on to right away.
I was a child, and I didn't even realize there was anything to see.

Johnny, what am I going to say to Millie? He understands even
less than I do.

All your bottles of Tizer, Johnny. Who dare go anywhere near
them?

Johnny! For God's sake, Johnny. Forgive me and come back!

The cop apologizes to the copdriver and switches on the
light in the back seat.

Johnny! I won't tell him anything! I know the truth. I claimed
I knew you, J, as in John, as in Jewel, as in Jaguar, as in . . .

You can have this, Chris.

And the cop gives me a photo. A better picture,
clearer, of Miss Juvenile in close-up.

Can I keep it?

The photographer was certainly pleased with this
picture as well. The glittering little costume emphasizes
her body, which has not really developed into that of a
woman. The photographer was certainly pleased with
what he managed to highlight, and what he managed to
conceal. The costume makes her look almost naked.
White naked skin that has never seen the sun. With black
hair and a pale face like that, she could pass for Chinese

253

or Japanese. But Miss Juvenile is neither Chinese nor Japanese. She is a genius on a bicycle, on a tightrope, on a broken trapeze, and on any deadly combination of all these.

In the picture, she's smiling in close-up at the photographer, at me.

It's a marvellous, white smile. And there's half a tooth missing from that smile. At the top on the right. From where I am.